RIVERS OF DAMASCUS
AND OTHER STORIES

RIVERS
OF DAMASCUS
And Other Stories

By
DONN BYRNE

*

THE CENTURY CO.

New York   *London*

FOREWORD

In publishing these stories by Donn Byrne there is nothing I can say to add or detract from their merit. Certainly there is nothing I can say, as he would have, who always had the right word for everything. . . . In the Dedication to *Changeling* he writes: "I would as little think of sending a story friendless into the world as I would of sending a child, a horse or dog. . . ." But when a man starts hurriedly on the longest road of all, his child and his horse and dog have to look to others. . . . Maybe they'll find kindliness, maybe they won't. . . . So it is with his work. Somehow I feel these stories will find friends and a welcome and so I send them forth.

DOROTHEA DONN-BYRNE.

Coolmain Castle,
Kilbrittain.
Winter, 1931.

CONTENTS

RIVERS OF DAMASCUS

I

RIVERS OF DAMASCUS

"Sweeter to me are Albana and Parphar, rivers of Damascus, than all the waters of Israel."

Now if he had been a white man, with his little spare body, his powerful hands, his light legs and wizened face, you might have taken him for what he was, a jockey. But as he was colored, you would hardly think of that. One is apt to forget the black man's light, strong legs, his beautiful hands for a horse's mouth, his strange, caressing way with animals. Besides, one's experience of jockeys is that they are invariably well-dressed in that exaggerated mode that passes for smartness on Broadway and Piccadilly. But this one was dressed in a French suit, baggy trousers with gussets, waisted coat, and shoes that turned up at the toe like a Turk's slippers. His favorite seat was on the Promenade des Anglais at Nice, where he sat on a public wooden bench and sunned himself like a cat because there was nothing else for him to do. His name—none remember it now —was Les Armstrong.

Now a negro in Nice is not something to look and wonder at and perhaps shoot, if you have a spare cartridge, as he would be in Ireland. From Martinique, from Madagascar, from Algeria they come and are welcomed as free men and brothers. They dress like the smarter sort of Frenchman, and often are "princes in their own country." But this poor chap, sitting on the smartest promenade in the world, dressed in a suit of cheap French reach-me-downs, was Virginian American, and proud of it. To him a khan of India or a bey of Algiers was a nigger. He was an American. He did not proclaim it in an arrogant manner, for there was no arrogance in him. As he sat there on the Promenade des Anglais reading his Continental edition of an American paper, picking possible winners at Auteuil, and wondering which of the surreptitious French bookmakers he could trust with his ten or twenty francs, there was about him the dignity all small gentle people have. A Moor of Tunis in white burnous, with prayer carpets for sale, approached him. There was a quiet superiority in the little jockey's: "Nix, guy, nix!" that put him, who was a sheik in his own country, as all Riviera Moors are, into his proper plane of color.

And yet if he had not been so loyally American, as indeed it would have been to his advantage not to be, one could hardly have blamed him. For it was only two afternoons ago that paying his fifty centimes, or half a nickel, he had gone into the Jetty Casino, on the off-chance of picking up a little on *petits chevaux*. The throbbing drum and the moaning bassoon of the band playing the blues had drawn him in curiosity to the dancing-floor. There they circled slowly around, English peer and demi-mondaine, American millionaire and shady countess, professional gambler and his female lure, Egyptian prince and fair, post-war Englishwoman, little Provençal shopkeepers who love to dance. And honeymooners from Scotland, or Birmingham perhaps, who are thrilled to the core at being one with the mad, bad life of France; and who will bore their grandchildren with descriptions of how wild grandpa and granny were when young. The little jockey looked on with pathetic face, for he loved dancing. A slim Creole instructress from Martinique, whom he had spoken to once, took pity on him.

"*Voulez-vous . . . ?*"

"Why, dog-gone, I'd just love to. You sure are one decent girl!"

They had made a half circle when the band stopped. It would go on again in a second or two if the applause warranted. High above the clapping of hands, a woman's voice rang out abruptly.

"Look here, I'm not going on if this thing's allowed."

The little jockey turned around. A hard-faced brittle woman was pointing at him. Les Armstrong didn't know her, but he knew her type. He had often seen it flash from limousine to baccarat rooms in furs and diamonds. He flushed and turned to the little instructress.

"You *excusez* me, mademoiselle. One moment."

He went toward the hard-faced woman, making up a little speech as he went: "Ma'am, if you want me to, I won't dance on this floor again. But, if you don't mind, I'll dance this dance, because this little professional girl asked me to. Ma'am, I'm sorry, I'm real sorry."

But he never got a word of it out, for the woman's escort, a burly man of six feet two, caught him a vicious crack with the right fist on the side of the head. It was a fat man's punch, untimed, all elbow; but it was heavy. It caught the little one-hundred-and-fifteen-pounder on neck and ear and smashed him to the floor as if he had been picked up and hurled. It stunned him. Attendants, detectives, what not, rushed over. In all the commotion Armstrong could hear the fat man's voice say:

"I'm an American, sir! and we don't stand for these guys dancing on the same floor as white women."

The little jockey knew that, American or not, if he had been a French negro, by now the fat man would have been led off by police to be placed in jail, unbailed. The interpreter was bawling in his ear.

"You wish make no complaint? No, you no wish make complaint. No, he make no complaint."

"No," said Armstrong quietly, "I don't want to make no complaint."

He tottered up and away, leaving the little instructress, her blazing eyes filled with tears, her body crisp as a tiger's, without a word of farewell. Somebody pushed his hat into his hand. He slunk past the loud boule table, and out into the mellow sunset.

"I ain't ever going into that joint never any more."

He walked along the promenade blindly.

"I had no right to dance on that floor nohow. . . ."

"Dog-gone, what could I do, when that little girl asked me. . . ."

"Them black Frenchmen dance. Nobody says a word. . . ."

The worst of it was he had recognized the big man who struck him. He had seen him at the Longchamps races, and later outside Monte Carlo. A year before when the English hunter, Devon Pride, had won a big race with himself up, the fat man had pushed through the crowd when Armstrong was on his way to the scales with his saddle

over his arm. "Attaboy!" he had shouted. "Attaboy! You showed them Frenchies what an American boy can do!"

"He ain't no American. . . ."

"Ain't I heard that guy outside the Café de
Paris knocking America to a bunch of Englishmen
and saying he was so sick of it he couldn't live
there any more? Yes, boy, I did."

He stood and looked at the flaming Esterel.
There were tears in his eyes. His heart was more
hurt than his ear and neck were.

"He ain't no American. . . . No American
would hit a little guy like me. . . ."

The truth of the matter was that he was ill—
more ill than even he knew. At times his face would
take on a brownish gray color and his knees trem-
ble for no reason. But this would pass, and he
would feel all right again.

Years of sweating down to keep his weight down
had taken the vitality out of him; and homesick-
ness, that thing that gnaws like a rat, had eaten his
heart. Because he had never accustomed himself to
read anything but newspapers, and because that
dingy little room of his in Old Nice was so lonely,
his nights would be passed in bars a little more
sordid and less artificial than those of Paris.

Hither would come, when the tables of the Casino closed, women in diamonds and men in evening clothes for a cocktail or a dance or a look at

the underworld. Once when some of them were present he keeled over.

He came to in a second or so. A burly man with the red face of a butcher, and wearing a white carnation in his dinner jacket, was holding his wrist. Little Armstrong didn't know it, but the beefy citizen was Sir Michael O'Callaghan, the Dublin surgeon known to all Ireland as "Big Mike."

He had come south "to cut the tripes out of some Grand Jook begob!" but the colored jockey was getting for nothing the thought and sympathy that had cost the Romanoff half an emerald mine.

"Boy, you're sick," he roared.

"Yes, sir. I knows."

"Do you? What's wrong with you?"

"No, sir. I don't."

"Why don't you go home?"

"Yes, sir. Why?"

"What do you do? Follow the races?"

"Yes, sir. I follows the races now. I was a good jockey once. Some folks as knew," he added quietly, "said there was none better."

Big Mike thought an instant. Only those who knew him intimately, knew how deeply religious he was, would have caught the meaning of his next remark.

"Well, boy, there's a good time coming soon."

He dug his hand into his pocket where his bac-

carat winnings were; pulled out a thousand-franc
note. The little jockey shook his head.

"I don't want to hurt your feelings, no, sir, but
I ain't got as far as that yet. It sure was good
of you—"

"Well, you'll have a drink on me," said Big
Mike. "Garsong," he shouted in his abominable
French, "apportez un poo brandy quicko!" He
patted the colored boy on the shoulder and left
him. There was nothing else to do.

"If that big man had been home folks now,"
the jockey would talk to himself afterwards on his
seat on the promenade, "I sure could have taken
his money. I couldn't let no stranger say an American boy had taken his money. No, sir. Dog-gone,
that guy sure was a white man."

He had been born outside Norfolk, Virginia,
and his early days had been happy. His father he
remembered as a cheery, fat, small man, always
laughing; his mother had been a raw-boned Louis-
iana woman. But his father died when he was
eleven, and the mother removed to New Orleans.
There his mother went bad, taking to drink and a
saturnine Jamaican who saw to it that she kept him
in the state to which Jamaicans of the better sort
are accustomed. The Jamaican, who bore the name
of Horatio Wilson Jones, beat little Les on every
possible occasion. Hence his dislike of New Orleans and his love for Virginia where he had been

happy as a child. The only refuge was the race-track, where he made himself useful, running errands for grooms and handlers. One day, as a joke, he was given a leg-up at exercise on a five-year-old selling plater. He went around the track as if he had been cradled in pigskin.

Now anybody can acquire a good seat on a horse, even—I have it on competent authority—a Knight of the British Empire; but hands are indubitably the gift of God. And hands little Les had. So in the course of a few years he was taken on as apprentice, and later on rose to the dignity of having a black plate with his name on it in white letters—Les Armstrong. Within a couple of years he had won two or three sound races. And then he began "pulling the hat trick," which means winning three races in one day. He did it two or three times a season, so his future was assured.

He went North to New York for the summer season at Empire and Jamaica and Tuxedo, where for various reasons he didn't do so well. There is a great deal more in racing than meets the eye. And wizened white jockeys cannot be blamed, if you look at the matter from the human standpoint, because they are not enthusiastic about a colored jockey winning. In my own most sporting country, in a large field, I should be tremendously surprised to see an English jockey win a race, no matter how good his mount is. But that is for psychologists.

An owner gave him the chance to come to Paris for the season, to ride there and at the seaside courses, at Deauville. Armstrong had heard of the great Paris races, of the fine horses, and the flower of European society, the beautiful midinettes, the royalty on the lawn. "Dog-gone, I'll go," he laughed. "I sure wants to see this Paris."

He found out very soon that little interest was attached to the horses. They were an adjunct to the betting-machines. For flat racing, few out of the multitude cared. Hurdles and steeplechases were the popular idea of what the racing should be, the jumps being thrown in to make the gambling a little more thrilling, as deuces are made wild in a poker game. Of how a horse was bred few cared. To whom the horse belonged mattered a lot. And owners' instructions were often very puzzling. One had the impression of them meeting the night before the race, in the Casino. "This poor Gaston," the Alphonses would say, "this poor Gaston, my old, has not won a race at the meeting. Impossible! But I, who speak to you! His pleasure here will be spoiled, utterly spoiled. Also his legitimate will say: 'I told you so! Why didn't you stick to politics?' Gaston must win to-morrow. No! No! Gaston, we insist!" All this may be untrue, but one got the impression. Also, Gaston won.

With the four-year-olds and five-year-olds over the hurdles Armstrong was singularly successful. He seemed to know to an ounce what a horse could do. Warily, waiting for the exact second, he would nurse his mount along, that touch of the nervous muscular hands telling the horse that he knew what he was doing, until the most nervous fractious ill-treated racer knew that it was in the hands of a comrade and a master. Owners might rave, bettors tear their beards and weep, as French bettors will, but until his moment arrived, Les never moved, and then, a touch of the little finger on the reins, a tightening of the knees, and his husky friendly: "Horse, let's go!" and he would sweep along to take his easy win or certain place, as the mount was worth. The sight of the fluttering silk, the black face and black hands pounding up from behind came to be a recognized feature of certain race-courses. *"Le noir, il gagne, il gagne encore,"* they would shout on the lawn, "the black wins, wins again." It was as though he were the color on a roulette wheel. And at steeplechasing, too, he lifted three or four of the big plumes, and a host of minor ones. For some reason or other the horses took to the colored American jockey. They liked his hand, they liked his confidence, they knew he was a master in his craft.

Then Armstrong's luck turned.

He was riding, for a French owner, a big brown

gelding called Mistral, a son of Chimney Sweep, a fine fencer and a horse with a great heart; and coming to the last hurdle, he felt that little give in the stride that told him his mount had gone lame.

"Dog-gone!" he said. "This baby's gone and hurt himself."

His eyes shifted, pivoted in his still head, to the mounts beside him. He noticed the falter, the half-stride lost at the hurdle. From the lawn in front the crowds were shouting "Mistral! Mistral!" A big English gray beside him began to stretch. He leaned over and showed Mistral the whip. The big dun never quickened his stride.

"Dog-gone," Armstrong said, "he ain't got nothing no more."

The shouts came louder. *"Tuez-le! Tuez-le!* Kill him! Kill him!" And some voice was calling in English: "Beat him up, Les! Beat him up!" Armstrong slackened his reins.

"Another race another day, boy," he said to the big chaser.

He was half-way across the lawn when the owner accosted him, a huge, burly man with a huge curling, black beard like that of an Assyrian king, oiled and perfumed. His black eyes were like snakes' eyes, alive with venom.

"Vat you do?" he shouted. "Vat you do?"

"I pulled up your horse, monsoo, because he'd gone lame."

"Vy you pull up, ha? Vy you pull up?"

"I said: because your horse had gone lame."

"Couldn't you get a place, ha? No? Yes, you get a place?" He leaned over half smothering the little jockey with his exquisite beard. People began to gather, chattering.

"I guess I could have, if I'd killed that horse, but I ain't going to kill no horse for no owner, no, sir."

The Frenchman's fingers contracted, like the claws of a hawk. They suddenly descended on Armstrong's shoulder, ripping the silk jacket from his back, leaving him a ridiculous figure in a sleeveless gray woolen shirt, with black arms like brittle sticks, among the concourse of chic women and men dressed in gray cutaways and black stocks with diamonds in them. The owner waved the torn jacket in the air.

"*Ainsi aux caguins!*" he bellowed. "Thus treat rascals." He might have been the chief executioner of an antique commonwealth holding up a bleeding head. "Thus perish traitors!" It was all ridiculous!

"I don't care," Armstrong said. "I ain't going to kill no horse for no man. A win is only a win," he said, "but a horse, well, a horse is a horse."

It was ridiculous, but—

Cæsar's wife must be above suspicion, but what must Cæsar's jockey be? The cold attitude of that righteousness is terrifying. To pull a horse, to slacken up, all this is right if the owner says it is. But, to be under the suspicion of not obeying the owner's orders is the chief sin of the racing world, the penalty for which is the chief penalty of the racing world—no mounts.

He may be all right and he may not, say owners; he's a nice fellow, he's a good rider, but this is a hard enough game as it is, without taking extra chances—

All the mounts he got now were rank outsiders with which he was expected to do miracles, but miracles are not done on race-courses unless the stage has been carefully set beforehand. The vanishing favorite of a race-course must be as carefully prepared as the Vanishing Lady in vaudeville. The other mounts he got were horses conditioning up, who hadn't a chance in the race, but were out for exercise. Added to this, his luck had definitely turned. Riderless mounts seemed to like getting in his way in preference to other jockeys'. And three times he took a toss trying to jam through at fences, where, had he had a decent horse, he would have waited his time. Little by little his name disappeared. That thing the French denote as luck, and which we more sensible folk call the phenomenon of the law of average, had left him. And when that thing leaves a man definitely, he is in a bad way.

There is something about French money, too,

that lacks power. It hasn't the efficient look of a five dollar bill, nor the crisp solidity of a pound. It has a consumptive, appealing look that makes you extremely generous with it, so you part with it saying: after all, it's only francs. It is only when they are gone that one considers that those flimsy notes might not have been so anemic after all. Also, if there is one person who is more foolish about money than a prize-fighter, it is a jockey, for the fighter has usually sense enough not to bet on fights.

So after a while of barren racing and money given into that most heartless of all human contraptions, the totalizator, Armstrong felt himself poor.

"Dog-gone," he said, "I must ride me a winner."

He went South to Pau. The local papers greeted the Parisian jockey with a column of eulogy. But after he had been down the field three consecutive days, the papers were silent, if the public weren't.

"Dog-gone," he puzzled, "I must have passed a funeral, or a cross-eyed woman, or something."

At Marseilles it was the same story. No winners and plunging on the pari mutuel, until he discovered with a shock that he was down to his last thousand-franc note. A thousand francs is roughly fifty dollars; but fifty is a good masculine sum with which much can be done. A thousand francs— well, all you can do with it is spend it.

He had, as all men have, one song he was fond
of singing. It was the only song a white man had
written for negroes that the negroes love: "Carry
me back to old Virginny." That was the song he
whistled or sang as he tested girths and leather:

"Carry me back to old Virginny,
   There's where the cotton and the corn and taters grow.
   There's where the birds warble sweet in the springtime,
   There's where this darky's heart am long'd to go."

There never had been any one to work for,
barring owners for whom one rode, and his only
experience of cornfields was to see them as he
passed in trains, but he would sing the little song
as though the words translated a life of personal
experience:

   "There's where I labored so hard for old massa
   Day after day in the fields of yellow corn —"

But this he understood—

   "No place on earth do I love more sincerely
   Than old Virginny, the place where I was born."

Night would steal over Marseilles, the last rays
of the sun bless Notre Dame de la Garde; along
the ancient Prado the lights would come up one by
one, the Cannebrière blaze suddenly, and he would

feel that he was in a strange city, stranger than any he had known. Here people were interested in ships, not in horses.

He moved along the quays of the Vieux Port, and like an answer from Heaven to a breathed prayer he saw on the counter of a freighter the name *Elisha Hopkins,* Baltimore.

"Dog-gone," he said, "Baltimore, Maryland."

If it had occurred six weeks before, when he had money in his pocket, and no sense that his luck was black out, he would have gone direct to the master and bargained for a passage home, or made friends with the doctor, as the ship's cook is familiarly called, who was probably one of his own race. But bad luck brings timidity.

"I'll just sneak aboard and lay low, and when the boat's off, I'll come out and tell the stewards I'm an American boy out of luck, and everything will be all right. Yes, boy!"

He did manage to slip up the gang-plank, and work into a life-boat under the tarpaulin. It had been raining, and the boat, for all its cover, was half filled with glutinous water, in which he knelt shivering. But the hawk-eyed mate noticed something amiss, and had the cover off.

"Come out o' that," he directed. He was a florid Scandinavian type. Armstrong came out.

"Stowaway, hey?"

"Boss, I'm an American—"

"That's what they all are."

"I'm trying to get back home," he said. "I'm sure sick of this France."

"You'll be sicker before you're through, my lad." He motioned up two policemen from the pier. Armstrong trembled.

"You ain't going to turn me over to the cops, boss," he pleaded.

"You didn't think I was going to give you flowers, did you?"

"Boss, you wouldn't do that to an American."

"I done it to fifty, kid. You're the fifty-first." The mate was cruel. He was one of those men in whom cruelty is a vice, as drugs and drink are in other men.

"I guess," Armstrong gave in, "I'm out of luck."

"Look-a-here," the mate gave him a baffled wicked glance that made him shiver. "You're in luck. That's what you are. What I does to stow-aways, when I finds them aboard at sea, though I says it myself, it's a shame. They don't exactly die, but they ain't any good after. You believe it, nigger. You're in luck."

So the police took him, speaking words to him he couldn't understand, and the judge, in a language he couldn't understand, gave him a month. They kept him sewing mail-bags and coats for Moroccan soldiers, while he never spoke. Warders

with beards and warders with fine mustaches saw
to it he worked: *"Allez-houp!"* they would call, as
to a broken-down cab-horse. Occasionally his little
song would come to his lips in a quavering
nostalgia.

"There's where the birds warble sweet in the springtime,
There's where this darky's heart am long'd to go."

But *"Silence, le noir!"* they would shout, and he
would bend over his sewing again, his eyes blinded.

They fed him on fish, which he could hardly eat,
so nauseating did he find it. They gave him a
cough, which can be cured, and a broken heart,
which cannot. And on the thirtieth day they took
him out and gave him his own clothes again. They
led him to the door of the jail, where he stood
blinking for an instant in the sunlight. They pushed
him along. *"En route!"* they called, "off with you
now," and they added, out of the kindness of their
hearts, *"Au revoir!"*

On leaving Marseilles he walked eastward
toward Italy, not for the reason he needed car-
fare, but for this: that he feared that every one
on the railroad carriage would know he had been
in jail. For each of us, white, black or yellow, has
his degradation point. It may be drink or drugs,
or nobbling a horse, or cheating at cards. With the

little jockey it was having been in jail. It put him
in his own mind on the level with those of his race
who used razors in brawls, of the traveling negro
hoboes who are accused of brutal crimes. His
thought went back to the laughing father in Norfolk, whom he remembered so dimly, so affectionately.

"I'm glad the old man croaked," he said. "It
sure would have hurt him bad, to know his boy
was a bum."

"Yes, boy, that's all you is," tears came into his
eyes. "You is a bum, a plain bum."

He trudged along the long road to Nice, a
withered black speck of broken humanity, by the
Mediterranean, bluest of all oceans, cat-like, in-
different. It which had seen Tyre and Sidon, the
crowning cities, go; Greece crumble; Rome pass—
not one breath, or chime of sympathy came from
that harsh Latin sea. Atlantic, our mother, would
have breathed comfort. And the sullen supercilious
Alps, they had seen so many pass by. The greatest
Cæsar, gallant Eugene of Savoy, Napoleon. What
did they care for the black speck on the road?
Some ancient hoary mountain may have blinked in
its sleep, remembering how centuries ago the black
folk were Lords of the Isles of Lerius and the
scourge of the littoral, and thought: Have these
bronze supple men gone too? Have they come to
this? Everything passes, everything grows tired,

everything breaks. Only we, born of ice and fire abide—we and the stars.

He had an impression that in Nice his troubles would cease. There was a city with Americans; Nice was a city with races—some of the biggest stakes in France were run for there. It would be a month or more before the races began, but he would lie up and get well—get rid of this cough, dog-gone!—and luck must change. There were two desires in his heart—to get back to Virginia, and to ride a great horse to victory before he went, for when he went back, he knew, it would be going from fair to fair with the trotters and pacers. He would never swing a leg over pigskin any more.

Armstrong found Nice a pleasant town. Here and there were bars behind which were men who had been in America, French waiters who had picked up a good deal of the American language and a certain aptitude in mixing cocktails, and returning to France had been raised to the episcopal rank of bartender. Though few of these had been further south than New York, yet it set the blood warm in his veins to talk about Empire racetrack, and Butler's horses, and Jamaica. And they had heard of Ral Parr's great string in Kentucky, and Man of War, whose immense stride was a miracle. To these ex-missionaries, now bishops, of the catering world, he would discourse on the temperament of the horse.

"There is something about a horse, dog-gone, look-a-here. If a horse is a mean horse, he's just naturally mean. If a man is mean, it may be his relatives, it may be his wife, it may be he ain't a well man. But a horse ain't got no relatives, ain't got no wife, and if a horse is sick, you call the vet. Then if it's proven to you that a horse is born mean, then you got to get around that some way. Look-a-here, a man may be yellow, and you never find that out in all your life. But if a horse is yellow, you find it out the first time you're in the home stretch and the favorite's creeping up on you. You says: Horse, here's where you pay for your oats, and if he lies down and dies, boy, you know he's a dog. A horse ain't no actor. Me, I knows horses, but I don't get men."

And then he would say, in a queer tone of voice, very different from his enthusiastic tone of before:

"Horses remember you!"

One day a piece of luck came his way. A fifty to one shot rolled home at Marseilles, on which he had ten francs. So he could still go around his accustomed haunts.

At all these places he was welcome, because at two o'clock in the morning he gave an air of disreputability to the place that was worth money. Most of the night bars were intensely respectable, the proprietor insisted on it, and his wife more so, for little Jean-Baptiste, or Pierre-Marie, when he grew a marshal like Petain, or a premier like Poincaré, mustn't be ashamed of his origin. So the pretty ladies were dragooned like a girls' school. If they wished to be rough, let them go outside. But they drew customers, and Armstrong's shiny black face made the bar look like a hell-hole out of some hack-writer's novel. *Ex-Africa semper aliguid novi.* Africa always provides a novelty.

They were very decent to him, by and large. The pretty ladies never bothered him, for they had wisdom enough to see he was a clean little cuss, and they liked him for it. Also they understood in a vague way that a man who is interested in horses is interested in little else. They bothered about his cough. And were vituperative on the subject. Why did he allow himself to be made a fool of? *Tiens, tiens!* It was a shame. Ah, those rascals!

And often they would ask him to sing his little song, and he would give it in his fair tenor, always preserving the rhythm but sometimes leaving out the body of the music to emphasize the words.

"No place on earth do I love more sincerely
Than old Virginny, the place where I was born.
Carry me back to old Virginny
There's where the cotton and the corn and taters grow.
There's where the birds warble sweet in the Springtime,
There's where this darky's heart am long'd to go.

Carry me back to old Virginny
There let me live till I wither and decay.
Long by the old Dismal Swamp have I wandered
There's where this darky's life will pass away—"

And sometimes there his voice would take on a
quaver, or sink into a whisper, and he would say:
"I ain't feeling much like singing to-night, folks,
if you don't mind." And the barkeeper would nod,
for he too in America had had his moments of
nostaliga, and the pretty ladies would look sad,
and not speak, but apply themselves to their grena-
dines or bocks, drinking daintily as birds.

Whenever one thinks of France in a far country
as for instance, in America or Ireland, one thinks
of roulette wheels, and it comes as a distinct blow
to know that roulette is not allowed. Roulette is
gambling. *Petits chevaux* are allowed. But that is
not gambling, that is piracy. Baccarat is allowed.
But that is not gambling; that is just over the hills
to the poorhouse. If you want the Royal and Ancient Game of Roulette you have to leave France
and go to Monte Carlo.

He had looked forward to seeing this roulette,
to seeing the strained faces of the players around
the baize, to see the wheel a blaze of color, and
hear the whir of the ball, the hoarse cry of the
croupier: *"Riens ne va plus!* No more bets!" or

the announcement of the result: "*Quatorze gagne, rouge pair et manque!* Fourteen wins, red evens and below the line." The click of chips, the rustle of bank-notes, all the strain of the hot, crowded rooms, heavy with stale air, all this he wanted to see, for there are three things we all wish to know about in this life: Love, Death and Monte Carlo.

At the desk they refused him entry. An official who spoke English much better than he did, punched him all around the ring in machine-gun French. He kept smiling that insincere, chilly smile which tells you there is nothing doing.

"I guess there's worse'n me comes in' here, boss," Armstrong said. "I guess when all's said and done, I'm the honestest of the bunch."

His objurgation moved them not. Three men had cursed them that week, one as he jumped to death from the upper Corniche Road; one as he shot himself in a back room at Mentone, and one as he went overboard from a small row boat he had hired into the black Mediterranean. All three had called God to witness their end, and yet no heaven had opened, nor had the Casino been consumed like the cities of the plain.

He was wandering into the sunshine, where the palms sighed and the pigeons drummed, and going toward the Café de Paris, where he wondered would they refuse to serve him, when a large hand descended on his shoulder.

"Ain't you Les Armstrong, the jock?"

"Yeh. I'm Armstrong."

"I thought I was right," a hearty, insincere voice roared. "Boy, I got something for you. Come right here."

Armstrong studied the red-faced, hearty-voiced man. He had once been an American, he was one no longer, which was one up to the Western Republic. For his voice was loud; his feet were not in his own house.

"Come right along, boy," Armstrong was encouraged. "I got something you'll love."

"Is it, is it a mount?"

"Yeh, it's a nice big horse for you to ride."

"I sure likes a nice horse," he said. "Is it a good horse?"

"Ain't no better."

"Is it a square ride?"

"Do I look like a guy," the ex-American demanded hotly, "who would want to pull some dirty trick? I ask you, do I?"

If he had asked you or me, who are six footers, and handy with the mitts, we should have answered: You sure do! and awaited the result with interest. But if you are a small underfed jockey, out of luck, you don't have much *joie de cœur* in matching wallops. So Armstrong gave the soft answer that turneth away wrath.

"I ain't meant nothing, boss. Dog-gone, you

know. In this horse business a jock has got to be careful."

"Kid, you're all right. You're the guy we want. Come right with me."

He brought him over to the striped awnings of the Café de Paris. A huge dark fat man was sitting before a glass of Perrier. He was not jollily fat, as many fat men are, but fat in a sinister way, like some adipose evil thing in the depths of the sea. He had small black eyes that seldom moved, but have the keen edge of knives. He was scrubbed to the perfection of cleanliness, his spatulate, grubby hands were beautifully manicured. On one hand shone a great diamond. The other held a cigar. He never moved. His eyes just shifted slightly.

"Well, Chief," his scout called, "I got the guy we want."

The Chief slowly pivoted his eyes, as a searchlight is pivoted, on the little jockey. He moved them away again.

"Yeh, Chief," the ex-American told him, "this is the kid. You can sit down, Armstrong," he condescended.

The little jockey was not very comfortable, for out of this immense fat man there exhaled an atmosphere of evil. It was not very hard to place him. You will see him, or one of the eleven or twelve like him, at various Casinos during the season, at Biarritz, at Deauville, at Hamburg, at Cannes. They are the ones who are called the professional gamblers. Whence they come God knows. They speak English and French well, almost perfectly if that were possible, but French or English or American they are not. This swarthy one will be an Egyptian, perhaps; and this one a Greek, perhaps. They always win.

They win for this reason—that gambling to them is a business, and they have toward money an attitude that is neither yours nor mine. When you or I bet a hundred pounds or a thousand dollars on a fine horse, we bet it because we like the horse. We know of no better horse in the race. We have confidence in the jockey. The course suits both of them. And when we lose, we have lost money. We have lost something that cost us work and effort. A little share of power is gone.

But to these men money is not money but a commodity, as fish is to a fishmonger. There are so many counters on a table. They are not money. They are counters. What they spend outside is money. What they lose or win at the tables is a commodity. They exchange the commodity for money to spend, or invest money in the commodity. But of risking big sums they are not afraid, as we would be, and as they know we are. Also they have developed a sense of luck. When their luck is going bad, they will leave the table where they are risking tens of thousands, and go to a small table where you risk ten francs. This is known as "running the bad luck out." They are not alone. They have ancient vile old women who play for them at smaller tables. They have young girls, beautiful, perfectly groomed young girls to sit beside and encourage losers, suckers, that expressive term, whose vanity will not let them be quitters before the bright sympathetic eyes of the young girl. If you will ask me, I believe they are virtuous, these girls, to use that sweet old-time word, but they have sold their souls to the devil. The Tribunal of Heaven, I make free to believe, prefers their sisters of the street. Such is the gambler.

"Baron Ganzoni here," the scout explained, "has a horse for the Grand Prix de la Ville de Nice, and he wants you to ride. He'll walk it."

"I don't know," said Armstrong, "any Baron Ganzoni racing. And about walking that course, I heard of four that'll do it."

"Well, this horse is by Spearmint out of Moyra's Pride. His name is Kilkenny Boy."

"But that horse," Armstrong said aghast, "that horse belongs to a English dook."

"It did, kid, it did," the scout soothed him. The gambler leaned forward on the table. When he moved the slightest bit he breathed heavily, like some horrible animal coming at you in the dark of a hideous dream. "He don't no more. Listen, this horse is the goods."

"I know he's the goods," the jockey answered. "I don't see yet how he's your Chief's."

"Well, I'll tell you, kid. This English dook has no money, see, and he figures out he's had so much bad luck there's some good coming. So he sails into Monte for the baccarat with what dough he can collect, and right away he runs into the Chief.

"Well, you know baccarat. It makes an aëroplane look slow. In a while there's only the dook and the Chief in the game, and this dook's luck is certainly gone flooey. If it was raining, and the dook in the middle of the street, boy, if luck was rain, this guy would be bone dry. And before he knows anything he has nothing. He ain't the sort of guy to pull bum checks or rough stuff like that. He gets up.

" 'What? No more?' says the Chief. And he smiles dirty. Boy, the Chief's smile would make a rabbit furious.

" 'I'm cleaned out,' says the Duke, 'but I've got a horse at Marseilles that ought to win the Grand Prix at Nice. That's worth a hundred and twenty-five thousand francs in stakes. He won at Marseilles easily and he got a very poor ride. I don't even know how good he is, and weight won't stop him!' The Chief looks at me and I tips my mitt that what the dook says is O.K.

" 'Supposing?' says the dook, 'I match his luck against yours. Between himself and stakes and bets he's worth three thousand pounds. If you care to, put that up in a bank and I'll go you. You take the horse or I take your money.'

"The Chief looks at me, and I nods, it's O.K. The Chief puts up a quarter of a million francs on the table.

" 'Bank of a quarter million francs,' says the croupier.

" '*Banco!*' says the dook.

"So the Chief deals him two cards, and takes two. You know this game. The nearest to nine wins. You can draw a card if the other guy hasn't a eight or a nine.

" 'I'll have a card,' says the dook.

"The Chief turns up his cards and they's two picture cards, worth nothing. Boy, I nearly fainted. I'm standing behind the dook, and I sees he's got an ace and a two spot, making three, and the Chief chucks him a five.

" 'I've got *huit,*' says the dook. The money was won.

"The Chief pulls a card from the box, and looks at it for a moment before putting it down.

" '*Noof!*' says he. 'Nine!'

"And that's how we gets the horse!

"Now here's where we get a raw deal. We brings the horse from Marseilles and tries to get a trainer, but this dook, see, he may be short of jack but he's got a lot of friends. And all the trainers say: Sorry, but we ain't got no stalls. And all the jocks down here, Mitchell and Atkinson and Head, and the French guys and the Eyetalians, they all got mounts for the race. Kind o' cold and distant, just because the baron, see, he ain't in with the racing gang. Wouldn't that get your goat? So then I remembers you. And I says: Bo, what are you worrying about? Here's a guy will look back and laugh at 'em.

"What do you say, kid? What do you say?"

If he had not been so out of luck, he, too would have said: Sorry, but I got a mount for this race. But nobility, and contempt for sharp practice are perquisites of the reasonably rich. It is easy to be noble with a sound balance at your bankers. But try it on two-bits.

"Well," he thought, "the horse and me is on the square anyhow." And aloud he said: "I'll go it."

The ex-American pulled a wallet out of his pocket.

"Well," he said, "just to show you what I think of you, I'll pay you the winning jockey's fee now." And he handed him two hundred francs. "That's how I do things, see? And there'll be the same on for you with this pari mutuel, see?

"Now, look-a-here, kid, no cracks about this,

see? If the gang thinks we can't get a regular jock, boy, they'll leave this horse alone on the machines. They'll hardly put a cent up. And guy, we'll just take their shoes off. So put it away in your dome, and forget it till the day of the race. We'll show these dooks and dooks' friends they can't be cold and haughty with us, see?"

Well, that was legitimate. That didn't come into the infernal region of pulling or doping a horse. That was withholding stable information. There was nothing wrong about that.

Ganzoni, the gambler, spoke for the first time in the interview. His heavy glucose voice rumbled out:

"Are you in good shape to ride this race?"

Armstrong's heart sank for a moment. Had they noticed he was ill? Were they going to take this mount from him? Had the man's infernal eye plumbed through clothes and flesh and bone to the stricken organs beneath? Those horrible coughing fits which shook him until he was covered with sweat, and had to lean against something for support—did they know of those? It was only that morning when he was tying a shoe lace he had fallen on his face, and lain there for an hour, unconscious.

But sick and all as he was, he knew he had a good race in him still. He was certain of that as of—

"I'm all right, boss. You needn't worry."

Now you may laugh at the Var race-course as much as you like. You may say it isn't a race course, it's a motion-picture. You may say put an Irish hunter at those jumps and he will take them in his stride. Barring the Act of God or the King's enemies, a half-bred handy horse will walk it.

For the Act of God and the King's enemies seemed to have selected Nice race-course as their favorite winter resort. Here are hurdles a plow-horse will take. Here is an Irish bank that the hunter Pelican would skim over with the Meath hounds. Here is a stone wall a green five-year-old will take. Here is a water jump that is a great test of jumping, for a cow. It is all tremendously simple.

Yet lying hidden beside each fence are two small ghoul-like figures with a stretcher, small, wizened-faced men with cynical expressions and cigarettes, trolls, gnomes, the meaner sort of earth elementals, as a mystic might put it. And their stretchers are always in use. Of course every one laid on those stretchers, next day the papers will tell you, is in a fair way to recovery; but if you notice you don't see them racing again. The kind-hearted foreign customers might not come to the race-course again, if they heard a jockey was killed. So that in France jockeys never die.

For all that the jumps are low, they are narrow,

real estate in Nice being what real estate in New York is in a minor way. The fields are big, fifteen or twenty horses starting in a steeplechase. There you will not find the beautiful timing of the Irish meets, the nursing of the horses, the course craft, the burst in the home stretch. The horses in a big race are there to win. Four abreast and six behind they take the narrow jumps together. So that the Act of God and the King's enemies figure largely in the French racing equation.

Apart from racing, barring sweet Leopardstown— Leopardstown of the Irish heart, green turf and soft brooding hills!—there is no prettier spot on earth for a race-course. Beside you, you can hear the Mediterranean chime on the pebbly shore. Back of you, the little Var drowses downward from the Alpine gorges. Eastward the coast sweeps toward Monte Carlo in a bold reckless line. The red sails of the fisher folk show daintily on the peacock blue sea. The higher Alps are furred with snow. It will be crimson for a minute when the sun drops westward back of the Esterel. The gray sleeping towns of Roman days daydreams, like an old sheep-dog by the fire, in the bluish hills. And somewhence chimes a sweet old bell in a monastery calling the Fathers to lauds. . . .

The second race was over. The beautiful six-year-old mare, Carina, had carried off the La

Turbie hurdle race from a field of sound starters.
At the totalizators people were swarming to have
their bets paid. On the lawns mannequins, with
faces made up as in some exotic play about Arabia,
pass to and fro in clothes that represent more
value than their bodies and souls. Here passes an
Indian rajah, dressed in European clothes, with
a brown sealskin waistcoat and a huge watch-chain,
looking very much like a retired saloon-keeper,
but for his dark skin. He is entitled to a salute of
twenty-one guns from His Majesty's government,
as they will call it; but the meanest Frenchman
here jostles him as if he were just "George." Here
are two Egyptian princes, dressed in flaming oriental costume, that seem tawdry somehow, in bad
taste in this setting. Here is an Irish marquess,
dressed like a farmer, leaning on an ash plant and
wishing that "he was in Dublin this minute, so!"
Here is an ex-King of a European state, looking
very much like a cad. Beside him is a great Second
Avenue safe-blower, "resting," looking one's ideal
of an Italian prince. Through and over and past
them swarm the common or garden people. French
folk, vivacious, excited, chattering, like small birds
in a tree; English people, striding like male and
female Juggernauts, happily unconscious of the
comments of the trodden French; Americans, notable by the huge frames of the men, and outwardly tolerant of and inwardly a little awed by

this color and glory. Near by in the field a band
plays a quick fox-trot.

A fat and not scrupulously clean man climbed
a ladder by the starting board, and began clicking
runners and jockeys up for the big race. Number
One went, Velvet, Mark Baldwin's fast chaser,
with Poivier up. So went Carbusy; so went Sainte
Nitouche, "Little Puritan" it would be in English,
by Quaker out of Moralité; Viouret of the gray,
and great strain of Roi Hérode; Helicopter, that
excellent fencer; so went Parakeet, who never
looked much in a race, but was always in the running; so went Hans, who was to run in the Grand
National in England, Daniele riding him—

Number Ten went up, Kilkenny Boy. There was
a pause until the jockey's name was shown,'L.
Armstrong' painted roughly in black letters on a
piece of white planking. There was no glint of
recognition in eyes that would have been charmed
by it six months before. "Armstrong. *Connais
pas!*" "Never heard of him!" A man went by selling the *"premier jaune!"*—the yellow slip that
gives probable pari mutuel results. They turned
from the board to rush on him. . . .

In the jockey's room Armstrong was received
with coldness, while he worked into boots and
breeches, and pulled on the flaming crimson silk
jacket and cap that Ganzoni had chosen for his
colors. Only Fred Rankin, the English jockey rid-

ing Viouret, an old enemy, came up and shook hands.

"I'm glad to see you up again," he said, "but I hate to see you on this job."

"I hate it myself, Fred, but dog-gone, you know how it is, when you're out o' luck, boy, you got to take what you can get."

"I got the winner, myself," Rankin said. "I wish it was another race, and you had it."

"They tell me this horse is good."

"He's good for home— Listen, darky," Rankin's voice was sincere, "you're not looking well, why don't you go home to that place you're always singing about?"

"Old Virginny. Believe me, Fred, when I gets me a good winner, you won't see my heels for dust. Oh, boy, and how!"

"Well, good luck, darky!"

"Good luck, Fred."

They went down to the scales, Armstrong carrying his heavily weighted saddle. Outside the band had broken into the great hunting song:

> "D'ye ken John Peel, with his coat so gay,
> D'ye ken John Peel, when he's far away,
> D'ye ken John Peel, at the break of the day,
> With his hounds and his horn in the morning?
> Yes, I ken John Peel, and Ruby, too—"

Armstrong walked swiftly to the paddock. A French stable boy whipped the cloth from the big chestnut and took the saddle. The jockey took the snaffle and looked at the horse. His heart swelled.

"Dog-gone, boy," he said, "you'se a horse."

His eyes roved along the sweet line of body; the hind quarters, powerful as artillery; the legs delicate as a flower's; the pretty feet. The head was so small, so lovely. The nose could go in a cup. The eyes were a gentleman's eyes. They looked with wonder at the dark face above the crimson racing jacket. But the Irish chaser felt the masterly, knowing hands, and sensed everything was right. The jockey smiled with a dazzling show of white teeth.

"Boy," he said, "you'se a champeen horse. That's what you is, a champeen horse."

A burst of happiness came to him, and with it a flow of false strength. He tested girths and stirrups and sang as he tested them; not with any nostalgia now, but with happiness.

"Carry me back to old Virginny
There's where the cotton and the corn and taters grow.
There's where the birds warble sweet in the springtime,
There's where this darky's heart am long'd to go—"

The horse, knowing with the mystic sense animals have, that the merry heart is the good heart, turned and nuzzled him.

"Quit your kidding, horse," Armstrong rebuffed him with mock severity. "This ain't no picnic. This is a race."

"No place on earth do I love more sincerely
Than old Virginny, the place where I was born."

He took the reins and slid his left foot into the iron. The stable boy caught his right knee and swung him into the saddle.

Ganzoni lumbered up.

"I know nothing about horses—"

"Yeh," Armstrong agreed.

"But it looks a good horse."

"What do you say, kid, what do you say?" the ex-American boomed heartily.

"I says: Anything that beats this horse wins; and I says: I ain't seen anything like this horse."

"He's at tens," the scout whispered hoarsely. "And the Chief's put on some dough for you. There's some jack coming to you, kid, if you comes in first."

"It's finding money," Armstrong grinned.

He followed the other horses through the gate into the course. A thrill he had never known, when he was popular and lucky, ran through him as he passed the stand and lawn swarming with people. The buzz of comment, the white faces, the flash of field glasses, it was all a throbbing, swarming mass of excitement. He loosed the chestnut for a dash down the field. The big horse broke into his beautiful stretching canter. The wind whipped into Armstrong's silk jacket like a pleasantly cold shower. They skimmed a hurdle like a swallow.

"Dog-gone, boy," Armstrong grinned, "you're it." He pulled the horse in and returned to where the others were waiting. Velvet, the big black horse that Poiver was riding, vicious and eager; Sainte Nitouche, quiet as a mouse. Viouret, quiet and watchful, with Rankin up. Immense Hans, with his Italian rider, stupid, relying on his great stride to carry him home. The silken jackets were a strange mad jumble of color in the Midi sunshine. Green and crimson, brown, blue with white spots, purple, orange—they shifted and mixed as the horses moved. A man in a slouch hat raised a white flag half a furlong away. Horses pranced, turned, curveted. Riders cursed in English, French, Italian. Of a sudden, like a figure in a country dance, they turned their backs on the starter, and cantered downfield; and then, as if answering a command of some invisible master of ceremonies, they each turned again and came forward gently in a line that was at first a little ragged, gradually grew even as the horses stretched out. Their hoofs thumped like drums on the sunburnt turf. They swept on, like a squadron on parade.

Then with an abrupt movement, the starter whipped the fluttering white flag to his feet. The crowd roared. On the lawn a bell rang madly. The crowd roared again. In a dozen languages they called the world-old cry.

"They're off!"

For an instant on the left hand side of the riders the stand appeared, an ant-hill of swarming folk, a flash of a thousand field-glasses. And then it whipped out of sight like something seen from an aëroplane. The first hurdle showed; its white rails, its stiff, bristling bush. The horses took it leisurely, carefully. Back of them, the crowd cried:

"They're over."

They swept along the right hand course, fighting for position now. Américaine, the sweet little mare, galloped along, first of the field. Behind came Savvice, the huge Italian jumper. Parakeet and Hans raced together. Viouret lay easily on the rails. Back of the field Armstrong held his mount. The Irish chaser was fighting for his head, not understanding why this rush of mounts should take precedence of him. He was not yet the cunning old racer that appreciates a yard here, an effort saved there. He was still the wild free hunter that loved horn and hounds.

But "Dog-gone, boy," Armstrong was soothing

him, "take it easy. This ain't no waltz. This is work." And, "Easy baby, easy, I'll say when." And the big horse eased down, galloping sweetly, confidently. They took the second hurdle. Ahead the course forked to left and right. They swung to the right hand side, Américaine still led. Entente, an outsider, swirled along, in a mad rush. None paid any attention to him. The battle was not on yet. They swept toward the first water jump, a hedge with a treacherous dike on the far side. The little mare skimmed it. The outsider faltered, took it clumsily, came down. He rolled over on his jockey. The jockey lay still. Carbusy's iron caught him on the head, where he lay. A woman near the rails screamed like a rabbit caught by a stoat. The field swept on.

But for the slow thunder of the hoofs all was silence. The jockeys were still as clay figures set on moving platforms. Their eyes never left the ground ahead of them. Their eyes were half-closed, wary as eagles'. Their hands were still. Their peaked wizened faces showed under the silk caps like creations of some artist with a morbid twist in his mind. They galloped on. Behind them the mountains rose, before them the sea chimed. About them, hemming them on all sides, were dark rings of people, on the rails, on the tops of motor-cars, in trees. They paid no heed. They might have been riding between land and stars.

Big Hans, ugly-headed, splay-footed, with his clumsy, deceptive, dangerous stride came creeping up on the favorite. Rankin's voice came from the side of his mouth.

"If you cross me, you Wop, I'll cut your face off with the whip." But his eyes never moved. His hands never moved. They took the hurdle easily. The little American mare fell behind. Now the race began to quicken. Velvet and Viouret, Hans and Parakeet began duelling for position. The biggest of the hurdles rose before them. The leaders took it carefully. Armstrong heard the crash and thump behind him as more of the field came down.

Suddenly Parakeet began to slow up. They passed him. *"Estropié,"* his rider called. "He's gone lame."

They huddled the left hand side now, going toward the big bank with the hedge. As they went for it, each called on his horse. "Hip!" Rankin shouted, and brought his hand down sharply on his horse's ribs. "Ey-ah," shrilled the Italian jockey, and Hans rose like an aëroplane. The Frenchman sent Velvet over, with a vicious dig of the heel. Armstrong gathered Kilkenny Boy gently. The big horse slowed a little, then suddenly drove forward. He gathered his hind feet prettily in mid air. They were over.

Now, the field had broken into three parts. Ahead were Hans and Viouret, with the big black,

Velvet, sparring for mastery. Behind them a few
lengths Armstrong lay, quietly biding his time.
Back of him four lengths were the rest of the field.
They scrambled over the earthen ditch. They
swung toward the dike. They took it easily, Velvet
and Viouret gaining a little at each jump on Hans,
but Hans regaining it each time with his powerful
deceptive stride. At the stone wall Viouret faltered
and almost fell, regained, went ahead. The Irish
jumper cleared without laying an iron on it. They
swept toward the grand stand to take the water
jump. Big Hans rushed forward. They could see
Daniele try to steady him. The horse seemed to
bolt forward through the air. There was a crash as
he came on his knees. And for an instant, Daniele
appeared in the air, shot out of his irons as from a
catapult. He turned over in mid-air and came down
on his head. There was a long moan of horror
from the grand stand. Daniele, he was done!

From the corner of his eye Armstrong could
see the Italian where he lay, limp on his back, his
hands outstretched as on a cross, a froth of blood
on his mouth and nostrils. Behind thundered the
field. Ahead, riderless, big Hans loped. Velvet
and Viouret galloped on behind the other on the
rails, each awaiting the moment for the other to
crack. They swept around to the right again to
cross the line of hurdles the second time. They
quickened a little. Armstrong let Kilkenny Boy

out a little. He mustn't make the leaders suspicious, but he mustn't let them get too far away. The wind had been right behind him coming down the field, bellying his silk jacket out in front, and now as he turned the wind, the jacket whipped close to his body, and he had a feeling it was raining. He looked down. His jacket was wet with perspiration. His hands were wet. The reins where his hands held were wet.

"Dog-gone," he said, "that Italian guy, he must have made me sick."

He knew he was trembling in the saddle. His arms had no strength in them. He was afraid for an instant that the horse might feel there was something wrong.

"It's all right, boy," he said. "It's all right. Just a little weak, that's all."

They skimmed the hedge. He pulled himself together with a great effort as they came for the double fence, some inner reserve of strength giving his fingers the touch to steady the chaser, time him and send him over flying. They swept around again toward the ditch and hedge. Very hazily the leaders appeared to him, as though they were hazy horses in a hazy dream. Everything seemed furry. The landscape had an ethereal look, as though at any moment it might dissolve into nothingness. And queerly enough, the sea made a loud chiming in his ears, high above the thunder of the hoofs and the shouting. For a fraction of an instant this would endure, then would come super-clear lucidity. Ahead of them was the last jump, the bank and hedge, and the stretch home. Viouret was slightly ahead of the black horse, Velvet. He saw Velvet's jockey loose his right hand. The whip would be going soon. Rankin's head moved slightly, ever so slightly, to the left. He sat down to ride Viouret home.

"Boy," Armstrong whispered, "now we go."

With the old cunning, the old craft, he swung out to the left. His knees gripped a little closer. He went down on the chestnut's neck as they thundered to the jump.

"Over, boy!" he called. And they were over like a rocket.

But the last effort seemed to have taken all out of him. He was empty, it seemed, empty of vitality, of everything. He could hear crack-crack-crack-crack of a whip before him, beside him, now behind him. He had passed Velvet. Now he was racing beside the favorite, now he passed him. Ahead of him loomed the black mass of the grand stand, the circle on top of the winning-post. A great roar came to his ears, and curiously enough, above that the chime of the sea.

He heard the swish of Rankin's whip, the crack of it. The favorite crept up, crept, crept . . .

"Horse," he called in agony, "I'm done. You

must win yourself." His fingers caught the mane to avoid falling off.

The big chestnut felt the favorite come along, come up to his forehand, come up to his neck. With an immense burst of fighting speed, he hurled himself forward, the stand, the favorite, the winning-post were passed in four gigantic strides. Armstrong faintly heard the roar of the crowd as he won, clearly heard the insistent chiming of the sea, of a sea.

With the wisdom all good horses have, the chestnut slowed up, cantered, walked. He stood for an instant to give the little jockey a chance to sit up. He turned toward the paddock. A stable boy ran up and led him into the weighing enclosure. Canzoni's scout met him with a frown.

"You cut that a bit fine," he criticized.

"Did I?" Armstrong said dully.

"Yeh," he said. "The Chief's sore. You might have lost us our dough. He says you rode a bum race, and he ain't going to come through with no bonus for a bum race."

"No?" He turned to the stable boy. "Give us a hand down," he said. He tottered on his feet when he was on the ground. He managed to get the saddle off. He turned to the horse for a moment.

"Boy," he said—he probably didn't know what he was saying—"boy, I'll see you again."

He walked toward the chair, and sat down in it

mechanically, his saddle in his lap. He tipped the scale down.

"All right," said the weightsman.

But Armstrong didn't hear.

"Get up."

But he didn't move.

"He's fainted," Rankin, who was waiting his turn, suggested. "That darky's sick."

They carried him off and laid him on a couch.

"He's cold and stiff," somebody remarked.

"He's dead."

Ganzoni bustled forward, roused out of his lethargy.

"But I win my race," he called excitedly. "Don't I win my race?"

"Yes, you win your race," the officials told him. "But what about your jockey?"

"Him! He's nothing to me," Ganzoni lifted his shoulders. "Besides I paid him in advance. But there's no objection?"

"What objection could there be?" they assured him. "He weighed in."

The gong rang. Everything was all right. The totalizator could pay. New jockeys appeared. New horses were brought out. The day merged into the short Mediterranean twilight. The moon that had just been a vague shape in the east became an immense silver penny while as yet the sun had not

gone down. A little mistral sprang up, and the
Mediterranean, sleek as a cat, turned like a cat,
and struck back in small vicious snarling gray
waves. The mountains became forbidding. The
band, because there were so many Americans at
Nice that year, played a medley of American
songs, giving to them that faint twist of unbelief
and cynicism with which French bands will always
treat songs of sentiment.

"Carry me back to old Virginny," it played,
  There's where the cotton and the corn and taters grow.
  There's where the birds warble sweet in the springtime,
  There's where this darky's heart am long'd to go."

And two small ghouls, smoking cigarettes, removed the last of the jockey to an unseen place,
where he would be kept until dark. Thence they
would remove him to the house of the friendless
dead. And lest his name should be forgotten, they
had chucked on his chest the piece of plank from
the starters' board with "L. Armstrong" on it in
hasty, uncouth letters.

"No place on earth do I love more sincerely,"
the band seemed to sneer. "Than old Virginny, the
place where I was born."

But the band might have saved its irony. He
had ridden and won a great race. Also, he was in
Virginny now.

II

FOSTERAGE

I

SOME are born generals, to paraphrase the old
Master Mason, as Hannibal, Julius Cæsar,
Napoleon Bonaparte; some become generals, as
my uncle Gillamore; and some have generalship
thrust upon them, as Pedhar Grady.

When the word "general officer" is snapped out
at you, as one of these Freud merchants would
snap it out, there immediately comes into your
mind the picture of a genial gentleman nearing
sixty, whose uniform is wonderful and whose boots
have a varnish putting Michael Angelo to shame;
who wears a mustache, curling in white dignity, for
a general officer must not be confounded with an
actor; who "horrumphs" like some genial sea-
animal; who reads the novels of Jane Austen and
of Thackeray, and of Benjamin Disraeli, and
whose mask of geniality and crass stupidity pre-
sumably conceals a mind like a chess master's—
God knows, it must conceal something. There is
the typical Anglo-Saxon general officer of brigade

or division or staff. But Pedhar Grady was not Anglo-Saxon. He was of the Gael.

What you would have taken Pedhar Grady for, had you met him on the road, is a mystery. But as a general officer or as a soldier of any rank indeed you would not have placed him. A smallish young man, not much over thirty, with a mass of black hair and with kindly gray eyes, with the body of an agricultural laborer and a student's stoop, the only decoration he wore was a small badge announcing that he had the pledge for life against alcoholic stimulants. In Ireland, however, this is an order that ranks with any decoration for valor. His clothes were an Irish tweed and woolen socks that a duke might envy, and his shirt a fine Ulster linen that a duchess would have liked. However, this is not to be accounted to General Grady for good taste, for the dress was a matter of pure political ideals, being of Irish manufacture, and in cut it was exclusive, its excellence being offset by the fact that the shirt-maker would have been a good sailmaker, and the tailor had once been great in College Green, before he "took to the dhrink." He had been "on the dhrink" now for a matter of twenty years, and the General's suit had been cut in an attack of the minor horrors.

To be general of a division that has but a skeleton existence and owes allegiance to a commonweal that may live "*de jure*" but certainly has no "*de facto*" state may sound ridiculous, but the truth is that the skeleton division and the ghostly state and the general officer gave a great deal of trouble to each at various times, and to all at one time of three large and imposing races, to the Constabulary of the Dominion of Ulster, to the Army of the Irish Free State, and the land and sea forces of His Majesty. The peers and commons of England thought they had settled everything to every one's satisfaction: to their own for they had got rid of a troublesome problem; to Ulster's, for it had given that headstrong province its own way; to Southern Ireland, to whom it had given a beautiful new Free State. But General Pedhar Grady and a round dozen of his kind seemed to put sand in the new beautiful works. General Grady had been brought up from childhood on the pabulum that Ireland is the greatest country in the world, and that Gaelic civilization was a state approximating to the seventh heaven. At twenty-one a fierce-eyed Irish-American, who looked exactly as Jeremiah the prophet must have looked, swore Pedhar Grady into allegiance "to the Republic of Ireland now virtually established." From Captain—there are no privates in the Republican army, it being a skeleton force, privates, non-coms and subalterns to be furnished by Providence on demand—Pedhar Grady had risen to be general officer. Some time before he had been told by the competent authority at Dublin that the force was to be disbanded, the Free State being the Republic he had fought for, but General Pedhar Grady, surveying the new order, found that it did not resemble the vision of the Irish-American Jeremiah, and decided that he and his force should carry on. He had an interesting but abortive field engagement with His Majesty's forces on the border, and after that a series of meetings with Ulster Constabulary, serious, dour-looking men, and Free State soldiery, good street fighters. Sometimes flying from Ulstermen, he found refuge with the Irish Dominion soldiers, and sometimes routed by the Free State, the Ulstermen embraced him as a brother, and once, on the run from both parties, a brigade commander of English regulars had hid him for a week-end. "Plucky beggar!" the big Yorkshireman had told his friends. "And besides, in his district there has been none of this assassination business." The Yorkshire officer had been very decent, addressing him as "general" all the time.

Then for a while came a sort of unacknowledged truce. The Ulstermen sat quietly on their side of the fence. The Free Staters had a beautiful new Colonel in the district with a beautiful whippet tank, and a third-hand aëroplane, while Grady's division kept quietly in the hills, only coming down occasionally to raid a bank or attack the town jail. Though the new dominion troops occupied South

Cooley, yet it was only by the grace of Pedhar
Grady that they were allowed to live.

In a country of strange nooks and crannies
South Cooley is perhaps the strangest. In the
streets of Beldalk, its capital, each invading force
Ireland has ever known has fought bitterly, from
Phenician to Communist. And each has left
corpses, and camp followers, probably female,
there. So that in Beldalk town you will meet men
and women with Arab faces, with Danish hair,
with heavy Norman jaws, with the lilting speech
of the Scottish Highlander, with broad Lanca-
shire accents. Also there is a small colony in that
town which speaks the Welsh tongue. The reason
for this is, that every force traveling through Ireland from North to South or South to North must
pass through that town. South of it lie the fertile
plains of Leinster, north of it are the natural de-
fenses of the Ulster clans, great mountains and
rugged passes, and eastward is the mournful Irish
sea.

For all that this town and barony have been a
sort of cockpit for Irish wars, yet in the district
there were only two notably military families, the
Gradys, of whom General Pedhar was now head,
and which family had never been on a winning side,
and the Grants of Abbeygrant who had never been
on a losing one. The head of the Grants was Sir
Norman MacLeod Grant, who was as different

from Pedhar Grady as the families were different.

The first written records of the Gradys date from Shane O'Neill's rebellion against Elizabeth. Thenceforward Gradys, especially the Gradys of Cooley Beg, are to be noted in every rebellion. They fought against Cromwell. They fought with King James. They fought in France. They fought with Emmet. They fought in '98. They fought in '48. They fought in '67. They fought in 1916. And now Pedhar was a general of rebel forces. Some historians claim that the Gradys discovered fighting. But this is wrong. Fighting was invented by Julius Cæsar who wrote a book on it.

The Grants, in that strange and rainy country which lies north of England, and is called Scotland by the Scottish, and divers unpleasant names by other people, had a great reputation for fighting, but for fighting with extreme canniness. They had a distinct gift for leaving a losing side in good time and joining up with a winning one. They had come to Ireland with Edward de Bruce, great Robert's brother, and when he, King of Ireland, died, and his forces went back to their native Alpin, the Grants had remained behind and become undoubtedly Irish. They took part in the Ulster plantations, siding with the Stuarts, but when King James showed a losing streak, as at Londonderry, they joined with Dutch William and made great havoc at the Boyne. They also listened to common sense

as stated by Castlereagh. At times they were called
the King's Grants by the Irish, at other times the
rebel Grants by the English. But no matter what
they were called they throve. They had Abbeygrant, which is one of the pleasantest estates in the
world. They owned also part of the fisheries of
Lough Neagh. They had grazing lands in Meath.
They had quarries in Connemara. They had also
the most famous ghost in the marches of Ulster,
that mountainy borderland where ghosts are a con-
gested community.

To have a family ghost in Ireland gives you
more rank than the records of the Ulster King-at-
Arms will afford you. For after all, the records of
heralds are a human fallible thing. Ghosts are intensely respectable, and seem to have a horror of
the bar sinister. So that many a family, outwardly
most virtuous, are discovered to have a little failing by the disappearance of the family ghost, or
its cropping up in the line of a younger son. There
is a belief that the banshee follows all Irish families, a woman wailing, a white-robed distraught
figure. As a matter of fact the banshee is a plebeian
sort of ghost. It is, if I may be pardoned one more
vulgarity, the Ford car of ghostdom. The family
possessing a banshee look from the ground of a
commoner to a marquess toward that Irish family
whose horror is "It." No other name has ever been
found to fit that dread apparition in the Meath

Castle. There is such a thing as spoiling mellow sunshine and soft starlight by attempting to describe that dreadful thing, so that, if it please your worships, we will leave "It" alone. There are the Gormanstown foxes, the myriad of whom cover the lawn of Gormanstown when one of the Irish Prestons die. There is the Shining Child of Clanranall. There is the Grant's Piper.

Of all the ghosts of which I have an academic knowledge, the Grant's Piper seems to me to be the most beautiful and the least inhuman. These Grants, for all their canniness in policy, are noted for shining valor. Once the decision taken, none fight more gallantly than they. In South Africa, in India, in the West Indies, Grants with powdered, blackened faces and broken swords have faced the last assault with a grin and a surly fighting look, until, in the salt atmosphere of powder and blood, their knees have given under them and their broken heads fallen on their left shoulder. And that night in Abbeygrant the piper has played.

What the origin of this manifestation is none can say for sure. It is usually explained that in the Williamite war, the Grant of Abbeygrant and his party were ambushed in the passes of Gullionmore by a party of Irish rapparees. For hours they fought under the shelter of cairns and stone ditches until not a fighting man was left. None at Abbeygrant knew of the encounter. But late that

moonlit night, down the purple slopes of Gullionmore, past the old ruined abbey whence the
house took its name, where once the Franciscans
of Strict Observance sang matins and laud and
complin; past the oak wood chiming with bluebells
and golden with primroses, up the green sward of
Abbeygrant, the last survivors marched home, the
clan piper and the drummer boy. And the arches
of the old cloisters rang to the wailing dirge that
we have given a name and put words to in latter
days, but has been the wailing keen of the Highlander at all times and in all places. They walked
very unsteadily and had to stop at times so weak
were they, but the lament rang true and wild in the
Ultonian night:

> "I've seen the smiling of fortune beguiling,
> I've tasted her pleasures and felt her decay;
> Sweet was her blessing, and kind her caressing,
> But now they are fled, they are fled far away."

The piper's face was broken by a charge of
slugs, and was a crimson mask, and the drummer
boy dragged a broken knee and foot, but his small
brave hands tapped out the march:

> "I've seen the Forest adorned the foremost,
> Wi' flowers of the fairest, baith pleasant and gay";

The chiming of the bluebells ceased, and the
rustling of the oak-trees. The primroses hid their

gay heads, and a veil of cloud came across the
golden Ulster moon:

"Sae bonny was their blooming, their scent the air perfum-
    ing,
But now they are withered, and a' wede away."

Whatever the origin was, this is fact according
to the Grants and according to the country people,
they had appeared whenever a Grant had died
honorably. They had appeared, so family records
went, when Alastair Grant had fallen at Water-
loo. The first news of his end was the wailing of
the pipes and the tap of the drum.

"I've seen the morning, with gold the hills adorning,
  And loud tempests storming before parting day."

And when Jenico Grant had died in the Indian
Mutiny, cutting swathes of negroes down, and de-
manding room for a Grant to die, they had rung
out on that fateful Calcutta night.

"O fickle fortune, why this cruel sporting?
  O why thus perplex us poor persons of a day?"

But for Uniache Grant, who had joined the
Argentines against Whitelock, for him no piper
played when he died. Nor did the piper and the
drummer walk for Archie Grant who died with

Cronje's Boers. The bayonets of an Irish regiment did for him, and left him, unhonored and unpiped, to a renegade's grave in a foreign land.

Wherever a Grant was fighting for his country or for the right, the women-folk of the Grants had always an ear ready for the ghostly piper coming down the slopes of Gullionmore, the wild grave notes of the dirge, the deep background of the drone, the tapping of the limping drummer boy:

"Thy frown canna fear me, thy smile canna cheer me,
Since the Flowers of the Forest are a' wede away."

They listened for it with terror, but they listened with great hearted pride, for did it not token that a Grant had gone as a gallant Irish gentleman should:

"The Flowers of the Forest are a' wede away,
A' wede away!"

II

They called Norman Grant "lucky Grant," because while he was in his early thirties he had achieved everything worth having, seemingly, on this mundane plane. His grandfather, Sir Piers, had died in his eighty-fifth year, full of peace and dignities, and left young Norman title and lands.

Norman's father had been that Archibald who had fallen under Cronje and who was not mentioned in the family. If Norman's father had been a renegade and traitor, giving aid and comfort to the King's enemies, Norman bade fair to make up for the last generation's deficiencies in loyalty, for in three years at the German War, he had become a battalion commander, achieved a Military Cross and a Distinguished Service Order. His baronetage was an Irish creation of 1622, so that he needed no titles or honors to implement it. A couple of nice wounds invalided him out, so that in 1918 he was attached to a military mission, given a red band on his cap and sent to America. In 1919 he returned with his wife, Pernella Prideaux, of Kentucky, whom he had met at Churchill Downs, which is the Mecca of every good Irishman who goes to America, for there you see the Kentucky Derby. When news came back to Ireland that Grant had married an American heiress, there were not a few heartburnings and a good many sneers. For since the German War to quote a negro chantey, "a good man's hard to find." Such is the personal end. Every Irishman wedding abroad is a loss to an Irishwoman. Also, American wives take part in Irish politics, and mostly unwise and being well-off, the damage they do is deep and various. So much for politics. There is an esthetic objection, it being held that every American heiress speaks nasally and has a "pop" in the background who has made his "pile" in "canned goods." Such is the abysmal ignorance of the Irish she-aborigine of the upper classes!

But Pernella Grant herself was an answer to all their objections. The Irishwomen sportingly said that the better opponent won. The new bride of the Grants was not a beautiful woman, such as are seen on the cinema. Nor was her figure startling in perfection. She had a sweet-lined, healthy body, and a lovely friendly face. Her hair was black, and dressed in an old fashion. A great knob of it at the back of her head. Her eyes were large and gray. Her mouth was no small mouth, but such perfect teeth had seldom been seen in the damp Irish land. She had a soft Southern intonation. In fine, her presence was more felt than admired. She was not a fine woman, which is Irish for a female of Phidian presence. But she was so lovable that everyone took her to their hearts. One could imagine her singing "Carry me back to Ol' Virginny," or "My ol' Kentucky home," with dignity, which is not an easy thing to do.

Her social standing was vouched for immediately by the fact that her father had a big stud farm in Kentucky. Right away she was received with enthusiasm. When it came to a question of politics, when she said her husband's politics were her politics, all was settled. For the present

Grant's record in the German War vouched for his feelings in the matter.

If Pernella Grant had not potent beauty, her husband, Norman Grant, was nearly as handsome a man as Ireland has ever produced. He was a nice handleable size and a decent weight. His features were beautifully cut, nose and mouth as in old sculptures of Apollo, and he had the Irish brown eyes, deep and clear like some rare jewel. His hair was of a red that is more often seen in women than in men, and it rippled back from his forehead in waves. His voice was clear and deep, with no tricks to it. Had he elected a theatrical career he would undoubtedly have become a matinée idol, as the phrase is. With all his military glory, and standing in Ireland, with his wealth, his wife, his good looks, yet there was something unsatisfied about the man. He was no women's darling, but at the same time, he was not a favorite with men. There was no sense of fellowship about him. One always wondered what he was up to, what he wanted with you, what he wanted out of you. Everybody admired him, had nothing to say against him, but didn't care for him at all. This, in Ireland, is queer.

Queerer still was this, that in Ulster, where new folk are not welcomed by peer or peasant, Pernella Grant became at once a universal favorite. It was not that she was a merry girl, for she was a low-voiced, grave-spoken woman. It was not that she made friends with men, for any one could see that she considered Norman Grant the mirror of manliness, and the vessel of masculine beauty. But one felt coming from her such friendliness and beauty of heart that put dour Ulster to shame. If one were in trouble one could tell that girl, you would say. It was a very queer thought that Ulster had existed for thousands of years without her in it, so much at home did she seem, so much a part of purple mountain and purling stream, and sad dignified rowan-tree and sweet wild hyacinth. A countryman talking to a Dubliner in a Beldalk drinking house enlarged on her virtues.

"What is she like so?" asked the Dubliner.

"Bedad, misther, if you were to ask me what color eyes was at her, or what shape o' shoulder I couldn't tell you. But to give you an idea of what sort of woman is in it, I'll tell you this. I'd rather be looking at this woman nor at Peter Maher the time he was leathering hell out of the champion of the world. Begod, and God forgive me! but I'd liefer be in her company nor at the Derby race and an Irish horse winnin' it. By the Yerra Jasus, if even yourself, and you've got a murderous, pocket-pickin', horse-nobbelin', towny look about you, had a twist of your wrist in her skirt and her dying, the next place you'd find yourself would be at your ease in the green fields of Heaven."

"She's a Phaynix, so!" said the Dubliner sarcastically.

"She's the Phaynix, and the paycock, and the cushie dove."

Maelmorra MacQuaid, the great Erse poet, resident of Gullionmore, ninety years of age, and beyond the vanities of the world, descended from his Olympus to write about her, a tribute he had accorded "not to the Queen, herself, no! nor to Anne Parnell." Out of his great courtesy he wrote in English, "because the Irish tongue was not at her." The result was quaint.

"I make this protestation," the poem began, "that in the
     Celtic Nation,
  In any social Station, her Equal does not stand.
  And if the beauteous Venus, were to leave us out of,
     meanness,
  Her absence would not pain us—we have Pernella Lady
     Grant!"

A bit warped, my masters, a bit out of kilter, but had Catullus to sing of soft-speaking, soft-smiling Lalage in the King's blinking English, would he have put up a better fight? An open question, gentlemen, very open.

It seemed to Pernella a miracle how much at home she was in this now sweet, now harsh, eternally moody country. She was never tired of the wonder of the heather, the heather that seen from

afar is a great mountain's purple cloak, and near is
the sweetest, bravest flower that blows. The mountains like Gullionmore and Little Cooley were
aloof, mysterious, dignified, and at times had veils
of cloud above them, as though some strange rite
of gods was being celebrated on their peaks, too
great for men to see. In the golden sunset their
slopes were like some goddess's shoulder, a sweet,
gracious line. The trees of Ulster were close to
her—the ancient oak-trees with their leaves the
dark green of ivy, the friendly ash and the proud
austere mountain ash; the hazel-trees heavy with
fruit. And here and there in Ulster were streams
by the edge of which the iris flaunted, and where
were swans. And when primrose and bluebell fled,
the golden buttercup and soft wild rose came to
take their places. Even the rain was kindly. It
swept down in fleecy mists from the mountains
washing the hedgerows and painting the green
trees. At evening tide the sun lingered on Killevy
Lake, a golden lake amid purple mountains, and
the trout leaped in the clear evening air, and the
moon rose in a clear sharp sickle, or in golden
majesty, or there was just the friendly dusk in a
blue cloak, in a soft voluminous blue Irish cloak.

Everything in Abbeygrant was kin to her. The
granite walls of the old mansion, the red brick of
the garden. The heavy furniture of an earlier day;
the immensity of silver; the open fires of peat and

bogwood; the candles in the silver sticks; the old monastery without its Celtic cross; its little graves in the woods where were buried the kindly brown brotherhood; the cloisters where now grew the bluebell and the tall grass. She could close her eyes and hear the monks sing complin. Out of ancient days for her rang the small ancient bell.

But chiefest of all things she loved in Abbeygrant was the tradition of the piper and the small limping drummer. Other Grant women had loved them, loved them because they had piped their beloved to their last rest, loved them because they conferred a potent of nobility which no King of Arms can confer, Lyon Garter or Ulster, a distinction that the wealth of neither Zaharoff nor Rockefeller could buy, but Pernella loved them for themselves. Their duty, their loyalty, she thought wonderful. She could see the mountainy battle where the Grants fell, the leaping, murder-out rapparees, their pikes gleaming, their eyes gleaming, the high Irish battle-scream coming from their throats, and the company of Grants kneeling shoulder to shoulder, firing their muskets, a white cloud of smoke through which flashed small red tongues of fire, the crash of the old explosion, above it the tap of the drum and the wild skirling of the pipes, until last of all their company the piper and his little boy went down.

She could see them coming up the greensward

of Abbeygrant in the moonlight, the blood-blinded
piper and the lamed boy. She could hear the wild
lament ring out among the cloisters:

"I've seen the smiling of fortune beguiling,
  I've tasted her pleasures, and felt her decay;
  Sweet was her blessing, and kind her caressing,
  But now they are fled, they are fled far away."

While the fighting men slept, after the battle
whose brunt they had borne so gloriously, yet the
piper and the boy still carried on their ancient
loyalty. When to the green commons of the Gaelic
Heaven, where there is hurling and story telling
and dancing and drinking at the close of day, there
came the news of the great death of a Grant, the
piper remembered his ancient office. And with an
"up, laddie!" to the drummer, he would tuck the
bag under his arm, and on his shoulder spread out
the ribboned reeds, and, fingering his chanter,
while the boy hung around his neck the antique
drum—ah, Pernella understood their loyalty so
well!—they marched out of the world of shadows
into the soft Ulster night, and the country folk
and the folk of Abbeygrant were told that once
more a hero had gone to his heritage:

"I've seen the Forest adorned the foremost,
  Wi' flowers of the fairest, baith pleasant and gay;

Sae bonny was their blooming, their scent the air perfum-
   ing,
But now they are withered, and a' wede away."

III

When one looks at this England of some years
ago one is inclined to feel a little sorry for it. Irish
poets stalked like Hamlets through Trafalgar
Square, their high Celtic wailing drowning the
sweet linnet-like notes of the English bards; Irish
soldiers grabbing off marshals' batons and Knight
Commanderships of the Monkey and the Goat, as
the Most Distinguished Order of St. Michael and
St. George is known among the irreverent; Irish
statesmen stating in loud tones—nothing particular, just stating. They had demanded Irish freedom so long and so fiercely that they ended by believing they wanted it themselves. Nothing in
history is quite as heartrending as the return of
Irish exiles to their free land. And England sat
back quietly and breathed. It was like getting rid
of a brilliant turbulent guest out of your house.

In Ireland before the German War, the exploi-
tation of England was the main career. You got
elected to Parliament; you became an under-
secretary of this, that or the other office; if you
were a soldier you governed a dominion, cape
colony, or what not. You started an odds-on favor-

ite for His Majesty's Most Honourable Privy
Council. But now things were altered. You had
your own army; your own parliament. The trouble
was that for a brilliant, warlike and statecrafty
nation, there was not enough army, parliament
and offices to go around. So naturally the obvious
thing was to start others. You had a government
de facto. There had to be a government *de jure*.
There was also an added starter, a government *in
futuro*. These were all three starters in the Irish
stakes, the Dominion, Republican, and Soviet
governments, the Dominion State favorite, nicely
weighted, and lying on the rails, the Republican
nag not too far behind and content to fight to a
finish, and the Soviet entry just out for exercise
and experience—as yet.

Now the success of a revolution is a delicate
thing to bring about. You may have your revolution, bring down your Government, and yet the
revolution be a failure. A revolt is always born in
the gutter though it be conceived in castles. When
it is over, you must get sponsors for it, dress it up
to catch the eye of the world. It is not sufficient to
put at its head "Mr. Jones" the pale student-like
genius who carried it to fruition. The public will
only ask who the blazes is Mr. Jones? And new
States haven't got time to explain anything. So you
go get Lord Brokeranhell, whom all the world
knows. If Lord Brokeranhell will do a little fight-

ing so much the better. So Lord Brokeranhell and his pals take over the revolution, and Mr. Jones gets the air and learns the inevitable lesson that revolution is a mocker, and comes to the sad conclusion that His Majesty the King is a nicer sort of person than Lord Brokeranhell. There is always a Lord Brokeranhell or a Sir Henry Bust around the corner looking for a good racing "job," or a deal in boot-legging, or a nice itinerant revolution. Sometimes, however, the revolutionists get hold of a man who besides being impeccable in family is also sound in finance, and has a keen brain and foresighted ambition. These men use the revolution instead of the revolution using them.

When Sir Norman MacLeod Grant, baronet, of Abbeygrant, found that the natural course of his ambitions was damned, to wit, England, he turned to see what could be done with Ireland. He was shrewd enough to see that even Ulster in the long run offered no further scope than, say, Bermuda. Southern Ireland had immense possibilities. In the event of modern science forging ahead, Ireland was naturally the aviation port of Europe for the New World. Already shrewd birds were calculating on buying ground for hangars in Galway City. In the event of Europe going red, Ireland was one jaw of the nut-cracker that would nip John Bull. Progress and prosper with a New Ireland, or stay in the rut of centuries, living the life of a landed proprietor on the border, which was going out of fashion. How long landed proprietors were to exist even in a legally governed country was a problem. And even if they were to exist was it a career for a young ambitious man. "Lucky Grant" decided it was not.

He was not the first to secede from ancient loyalty. Others of higher rank than he had decided that glory and prosperity in a new born Ireland were better than glory and exile in England. People tire so soon of exiles. He was acclaimed into the new order with open arms. He felt he knew enough of Ireland to see that the country would not be satisfied with a less measure than complete independence. Besides he was one of the few of his order in the Republican ranks. The plums and honors would be for him in the long run. He did not go as far as going out on the hills. He gave the forces aid and comfort and the propaganda of his name.

Pernella was glad. Her knowledge of politics was a superficial one. In America she had always thought of Ireland, Greece and Italy as being the three most romantic units of the old world. Greeks and Italians were not kin to her, but Irish were. There is nothing so intoxicating as a cause and on the face of it, there was no cause like the Irish. Place a gaunt intellectual Irishman beside a ruddy stocky Englander, and the ordinary man

will wonder that the Irish were ever the subject
race, for the outsider will not see the wisdom and
sense of fair play beneath the beefy English ex-
terior, and he will not recognize the fanaticism
and morbidness in the Irish eyes. An outsider is a
terrible thing!

As they met her and talked to her, these
prophets of the new Erin, Pernella felt as if she
were in an atmosphere of pure cold water and
great gallantry. The projects of this revolt to
medievalism entranced her. It was the vision of a
Rosetti. In the new nation, every one would be
noble. They would wear the ancient Gaelic costume, the kilt for men, and Grecian robe for
women. Everybody would take the pledge against
intoxicants. They would speak Erse, that was
moribund or dead, but could be revived. There
was considerable discussion as to whether smoking
would be allowed, but it being discovered that
tobacco could be grown in Ireland, smoking was
graciously conceded. But modern dancing was se-
verely frowned upon. Its lewd embracing was to
be supplemented by four hand reels, which were
graceful and energetic. Horses were to run races,
but there was to be no book-making. Improving
works were to be read on Celtic civilization. A
land of saints and scholars, went the battle-cry.
Such was the intellectual republic.

When you christen any insanity ideals, it goes

down with women. They are so hard-headed in ordinary affairs that they become unbalanced in imaginary hypothesis. To Pernella Grant this land of monks and harpists, both male and female, was not only wonderful but possible. She became heart and soul engrossed in the movement. She met this one. She met that one. She met Pedhar Grady.

The young republican general liked her. None could help liking—loving—Pernella. He felt a little sorry for her enthusiasm, for he knew perfectly well himself that the dream of the Gaelic state was a bit far off from what the reality would be. So did her husband. In every step you rise in the degrees of revolution, you discard some of the ideals of the entered apprentice stage, until probably at the top you recognize that the government you are founding will just be a little worse than the government you propose to destroy, and what the people gain in one large reform they lose in a hundred comforts. The only persons better off, after the turmoil and assassinations, are you and your pals, because if you are wise, foreseeing people, you have cinched jobs. General Grady knew this. So did Norman Grant.

But Pernella was living in a strange dream, and Pedhar Grady had a great respect for dreams. He had no intention that she should be disturbed. He had no particular liking for her husband. He knew

the type too well. When you have been a guerilla
warrior for seven years, been in gaol, been on
hunger strike, been chased by military, policemen,
shadowed by informers, there is very little of human nature you don't know. He knew that this
new admiration of Grants' for his father, the
Commandant Archie Grant who had fallen with
Cronje, was insincere. He knew that Grant was
only in the movement for what he could get out
of it. He also knew that Grant was in deep, deeper
than Grant himself knew. He scented disaster in
the future. One gets to scenting things, as an animal scents them, when for seven years you have
been a hunted man.

He was often up at Abbeygrant for dinner, for
Norman Grant was keen on being good friends
with the divisional officer. Sometimes a young
Catholic priest in black clothes and Roman collar
would walk in, or a nurse in blue cloak and hood
would drive up, and each of these would be Pedhar Grady. Quietly men would post themselves
around Abbeygrant armed with rifles to protect
their chief. And within Pedhar would go through
dinner, telling in a matter of fact way incidents in
his campaigns; of how he had escaped from Dart-
mouth prison dressed in the clothes of the warder
he had bound and gagged, of his capture of the
Auxiliaries' ammunition wagon in Drogheda, of
his attempted raid on Dublin Castle, and how he

had swam the Liffey on Christmas night. And
Pernella would play after dinner, and sing the
rebel song of the Shan Van Vocht, the Poor Old
Woman that has been the rallying song of Irish
revolutionists for centuries.

"Oh, Boney's on the shore,"

(went the United Irishman Version)

> Says the Shan Van Vocht;
> Oh, Boney's on the shore,
>   Says the Shan Van Vocht;
> Oh, Boney's on the shore.
> You can hear his cannon roar.
> We'll be freemen once more,
>   Says the Shan Van Vocht.

> Oh, Boney's on the strand,
>   Says the Shan Van Vocht.
> Oh, Boney's on the strand,
>   Says the Shan Van Vocht.
> Oh, Boney's on the strand;
> With a sword in either hand;
> He's a royal rebel man;
>   Says the Shan Van Vocht."

And as he listened to the soft contralto, saw her
sincere face, her sweet sincere face, Pedhar Grady
decided that if tragedy were to descend on this
house, he would do his utmost to protect and
shield her.

But he didn't get the opportunity. It happened, as in revolutions all things happen, much too quickly. Grant had listened to the Dominion man, while up to the neck in opposition plans. The Dominion men sprung a new one. The colonies and England are hanging by a thread, they said, and if we stick by this dominion government, now throwing our weight with the other commonwealths, now with the mother country, we, Ireland, will undoubtedly govern the Empire. It sounded good. It was downright practical politics, and Grant preferred it to vague visions and the prospect of further fighting.

"Are you with us?" he was asked.

"I am," said Grant, "under certain conditions."

His conditions came a bit high, but at last they were acceded. He was returning home to Cooley to announce his change of heart when, at the stop at Drogheda, three men came into the railway carriage.

"Colonel Grant?" Yes, he was Colonel Grant.

"Th' officer wants to see you."

"What officer?"

"I think you know." And they came closer to him.

"I'm afraid I can't go," Grant told them.

"Then we must arrest you, so!"

"By what authority!"

They showed him their authority. They were

three large automatic pistols of the type known as "Peter the Painter."

"All right, then. Bring me to your officer."

They took him by car to a small cottage on the banks of the Boyne, and brought him into the presence of Th' Officer. There was nothing idealistic in Th' Officer. Th' Officer was a squat, high-jawed man in the middle forties. He looked up at Grant. There was an oil lamp burning on a red table-cloth. There was a pile of papers kept in place by a heavy Colt .45 revolver.

"Are you Sir Norman Grant?"

"I am," said Grant.

Outside the Boyne rolled gently to the Irish Sea. The moon shone goldenly on the Irish plains. The chestnut-trees rustled in the Irish wind. The kine slept in the fields. Not even an owl hooted. It was like some ill-staged play. There was nothing convincing about the whole performance. Even the names were fictional. Nothing was real but the hard gray eyes of Th' Officer.

"You took an oath of allegiance to the Republic of Brobdingnag on April the seventh. On April tenth you received the appointment of staff-colonel on the Brobdingnagian forces."

"Why, yes," said Grant.

"Since you have been in communication with delegates of the Kingdom of Lilliput. You have accepted a nomination for the Lilliputian senate."

Grant said nothing.

"Have you anything to say why sentence of death should not be executed on you?"

Grant was lurching forward to knock over the lamp and grab the Colt when the men who had arrested him gripped and locked his arms. Then he knew it was all up.

"I don't suppose," Grant said, "that there's any possibility of your giving me a gun and letting me have a go at the four of you."

"Not a chance!" said Th' Officer.

"No? Still and all, you might thank me for the compliment," Grant sneered.

"Take him outside," ordered Th' Officer.

And two days later he was discovered by a couple of children on Boyne banks. He was not the first Grant of Abbeygrant who had met his death there. An elder one had fallen assisting Dutch William in a battle that shall be remembered until the end of time. The elder Grant had been surrounded by men who had fallen by his hand in line of battle. But here a couple of horses grazed and the bees were loud, and the swirl of the pike was seen in the river. In him, as was known when the word was told that Sir Norman MacLeod Grant, baronet, of Abbeygrant had been done to death by conspirators, in him were three Peter the Painter bullets, and on his chest written on grocer's brown paper and attached by

a safety pin, was his epitaph. "Convicted
Traitor," it said, and underneath the end of him
was explained, "executed," and all was signed by
the meaningless but terrifying phrase "By Order."

But before the world knew of Norman Grant's
end, Pernella knew.

IV

If Pedhar Grady had had his way about the
matter, Grant would never have been killed.
Though he would have been loath to lose Pernella Grant from the land she loved, and that
loved her, yet you can't condone treason. Treason,
it would seem, is a great deal more to be feared in
a factitious than in an actual state. Grady would
have been content with burning Abbeygrant to the
ground and chasing its owner to England, where
he could do no harm. For talk of his wrongs as
much as he liked, the English would have just
said: "It's just as well you got away with your life,
old son. What abominable swipes those people
are!" and let it go at that. Grady had daring,
brains, patience, but he would never get a field
marshal's baton in guerilla warfare, he had no
frightfulness.

He had no regrets for Grant, but for Pernella
he was immensely sorry. He knew she worshiped
her husband. He knew of Grant's death within a

couple of hours of its happening. A courier going
north on a motor-cycle stopped at divisional headquarters and jerked an eloquent thumb toward
Abbeygrant.

"He's gone," said the courier, resting by his
motor-cycle.

"D'ye tell me so?" said Pedhar. "When?"

"Around nine o'clock."

"Where?"

"At Dro 'da."

" 'Tis a pity!"

"He was no loss!"

" 'Tis not o' him I'm thinking, but o' her."

"Thrue for you, General. She's the heart o'
corn. Well, good-by, General!"

"Good-by, Captain."

Grady thought quietly for ten minutes. Then he
sent for a man of his, an old soldier of Highland
Light Infantry, who had been pipe-major. The
Scot had been born in County Down, and the German War being over, and no other on the horizon,
had joined the Irish guerilla forces. He was a
burly man.

"Finnegan, have you got your pipes with you?"

"I have, General."

"Have you got a tune called the Fowers of the
Forest?"

"Though I says it myself, General, there's none
plays it better."

"Have you a drummer boy?"

"There's wee Para Gorvey."

"I want yez to go down to Abbeygrant, and give the tune. The foxy one is after getting plugged, and no loss, but the division is under great compliment to Lady Grant, and it would hearten her up, maybe, if she'd hear the tune."

"I'd pipe through the seven streets of Hell for Lady Grant," said the pipe-major.

"D'you think yez can act ghosts?" asks Grady.

"If after being chased by bloody Specials and Free State troops for two years and a month," said the pipe-major, "I'm not the dead spit of a ghost—"

"Off wid yez then!"

The general officer did not see Pernella Grant for a month afterwards. He met her one day when he was walking with his adjutant from Greenore, dressed as cattle dealers. She was riding along the seashore on a black cob. Grady raised his battered hat. She looked at him coldly a moment and then she reined in.

"I wonder, Pedhar Grady," she said, "that you don't crawl into the ditches with shame when you see me coming." There was a great flush that was more than a flush of anger. But there was fire in her eyes.

"Well, now, Lady Grant—" He was bothered.

"You came up to Sir Norman's house," she ac-

cused him. "You ate at his table. Your men shel-
tered around Abbeygrant when they were being
chased like rats. He gave you his name to help
your cause. And because he was kind to you, you
waylay and assassinate him. And you accuse him
of treachery. Pedhar Grady, Sir Norman Grant
did not know what treachery meant!"

Grady said nothing, but Bronnigan, the adjutant, was hot-headed. He had no intention of letting these accusations pass.

"Oh, begob, ma'am, Lady Grant," he said, "I
don't know—"

"Oh, you don't," said Pernella coldly. "Well,
I do. There are witnesses who never lie. The
Grant piper has never played for a traitor or a
coward. And the night of Sir Norman's murder,"
she looked straight at Grady, "with my own eyes
I saw him. With my own ears I heard the Flowers
of the Forest skirl through the moonlight."

And gathering up curb and snaffle she rode
away.

V

To Abbeygrant now came the strange unearthly
beauty that comes on all things Irish before they
die. Never had the old house such a grave sweet
outline. The ruined walls of the monastery gave a
sense that but yesterday Father Prior and Brother
Almoner had gone about their gentle offices. The

shoulders of Little Cooley and of Gullionmore
rose splendid and purple, like great potentates, in
the golden Ulster summer. The skylark all but
burst his throat with song and the hives of Abbeygrant hummed like organs, so great was the music
of the bees.

Though Abbeygrant was no longer Pernella's
—it had passed to a tea-planter in Ceylon, a third
cousin who had never known Ireland, and never
would, he said—yet she stayed on. She had a mystic idea that she must stay and guard it. Often, by
herself, she wept quietly that there was no little
son of her body to whom would pass on the ancient Ulster trust. All about her people were leaving. Here an old man would come with an old
world courtliness to say good-by. An old lady
would leave for Bath, in England, where she could
think of God in peace. The laboring men would
stick their spades in the ground and go. The
grooms would pause curry-combing the horses,
and suddenly think: "Amn't I the world's fool to
be staying in this God-forsaken land?" And the
next heard from him would be an Australian or
Canadian letter sending money for his women
folks to follow him. A sense of impermanence
hung over the country-side.

And though Pernella visioned staying there for
year after year, yet she was to go soon. There is
wonder in loving Ireland. There is tragedy in be-

ing loved by it. The kiss of gods is always a mortal
wound, and the lovers of Ireland die on the gal-
lows, in the dungeon, or of that ailing which we
simply call a wasting away. The gentle rain that
gives so much color at sunset, the soft mists that
endue with emerald beauty the wide Irish fields
have a subtle poison, and he or she who gets it in
their systems is marked for death. On them at
first comes beauty, the beauty that goes with the
waving heather, with the slim bogflower. A little
coughing, and when the handkerchief comes away
one notices one is wounded.

She was such friends with every one now, with
the grim Specials, the jubilant Dominion men,
with the harassed Rebels, that all noticed it.
Every one in Ireland avoids saying exactly what
it is, or even to seem to notice it, but all were wish-
ful for her to go away—the South of France or to
Switzerland, where "she would pick up in a little
while." Soon Pernella herself knew, but she would
not go. To see Abbeygrant closed, as she had seen
so many other houses closed; the gardens wild;
the bees untended in wintertime, when frost and
starvation would kill them—oh, no! she would
not go.

All about her now was a tremendous atmosphere of love. Near Abbeygrant was no fighting.
All parties seemed to agree to make that sacred
ground. Also between Specials and Staters and

Rebels there existed a silent conspiracy to tell her everything was all right; the country was grand; in a little while everything would be settled down. " 'Tis how," said a Free State Colonel coming in after a forty-eight hour battle in the mountains, " 'tis how I am getting sick of this peaceful English life!"

In a little while she could not ride any longer, and in a smaller while, it seemed she could not walk, but there was always some one to be with her. And when at last she had to give in, and have nurses, her visitors would always talk of the grand times she and they would have at the next Dublin horse show, "yourself in the saddle, and the country like a lamb itself, or a shlip of a pig knows no devilment, or a pussy cat and her playin'."

Not only did the county people themselves wish to show kindness. But all that was Ulster and Irish did. So fine a summer none remembered. The flowers lingered, loath to go. The corn and wheat she could see ripening from her window, rippling in the wind, vital, fair, like the tresses of some Scandinavian queen of romance. The bees hung about the creeper on the walls, singing their soft, never-monotonous song. The swallows darted about in the twilight. When there was no moon there was the multitude of stars. And one day at the full of the September moon, the west wind came.

"The summer is over," sensed Pernella.

There came upon her the desire to see Gullionmore in the sunset and she asked her nurse to raise her so she could see it. There it lay proud and purple in the soft golden light. There was the shoulder of it, sweet and gentle and strong. By some queer illusion she felt she could put her hand on its shoulder.

"It's so near," she said aloud.

" 'Tis four miles away, m'lady."

" 'Tis not four feet," whispered Pernella.

And suddenly she was very limp in the nurse's hands . . .

VI

So splendid the night, what with the last full moon of summer, that Pedhar Grady could not understand that any one could be dead this night of glory. And then after a little thought he could. A stormy, a raining night would be so difficult for a gentle new soul to find its way about. . . . He was sitting in the private room of Molly Shea's "Stook of Barley," the little drinking-house a furlong and a half down the road from the gates of Abbeygrant. Before him stood the pipe-major and the drummer boy.

"I've never heard," said Pedhar Grady, "that the Grant piper—if ever there was such a thing, which I don't believe—played for a Lady Grant.

But if ever a Grant deserved piping, 'twas herself."

"You spoke true, General," said the pipe-major.

"Well, off wit' yez, then," said Pedhar Grady.

He sat there in private state after they had gone, wondering to himself about the eternal mystery. A man or woman would be one minute full of strength or grace, their brain working, their voice speaking softly, warm with friendship, and the next minute they would be a wax image, dumb as a fish, unresponsive to all friendly in the world. Where had it gone? It was a subject that was beginning to interest him a lot, for he had that indefinable feeling of luck about to go away. Any of these days his number might go up. 'Twas a mystery, so. He looked at his dog, the red Irish setter with the beautiful brown eyes. If he were to take out his automatic and bang into the dog, in a second it would be a broken lump. And where would that intelligence and affection have gone? 'Twas queer and queer. Inconsequentially it came into his mind that he oughtn't to have the dog at all. Some day they'd track him through the dog.

"I ought to· get rid of ye," he said, "but sure I haven't the heart to let ye go."

The dog looked up at him and moaned a little.

"What's on ye, anyhow?" said Pedhar Grady. Through the window through which the moon-

light came, came the roll of a muffled drum. It was
as though it were right under the sill. An instant
later came the shrill dirge of pipe-music, the high
clear grace notes against the hum of the drone:

> "I've seen the smiling of fortune beguiling,
> I've tasted her pleasures, and felt her decay;
> Sweet was her blessing, and kind her caressing,
> But now they are fled, they are fled far away."

"Bedad," said Pedhar Grady, "I never heard
better piping. I didn't know he had it in him."
The dog sniffed around, whining in panic. "Will
you hold your whist," he called. "Sure, you've no
ear for music." But the dog would not be still.

> "I've seen the Forest adorned the foremost,
> Wi' flowers of the fairest, baith pleasant and gay."

Grady thought of the heavy pipe-major, and
could see him in his imagination. Once the reeds
were stretched across his shoulder, the lumbering
figure became martial and full of fire and dignity,
the arrogant strutting walk, the high head of him.
And little Para Gorvey, freckle-faced, snub-nosed.
He remembered how at fourteen, in the Bally-
voyle, the child had handled a rifle bigger than
himself with the coolness of an old guardsman. He
was only a child, but a lion in the streets, little
Para Gorvey.

"I've seen the morning, with gold the hills adorning,
And loud tempests storming before parting day."

The pipes shrilled. The dog cried. And suddenly the door opened and the pipe-major entered.

"What the devil—" said Pedhar Grady.

" 'Tis how some one else was there before us, General," said the pipe-major. " 'Tis not ourselves alone had the idea. I was no sooner there, me and the wee fello', than we saw another piper and a drummer."

"Would it be the Specials or the Staters?" Grady wondered.

"I don't know," said the pipe-major, "because I got out as soon as I saw them, for I didn't want there to be any trouble, General, and herself there in her last sleep."

"I wish it had been us," said Pedhar Grady, "for 'tis many's the kind thing she did for us, both before and after—the accident."

"O fickle fortune, why this cruel sporting?
O why thus perplex us poor persons of a day?"

"I'll say this," said the pipe-major, "that I've never heard better piping, abroad or at home. I've never heard more souple fingers tickle a chanter. She's getting a grand skirl, the poor lady. I'd give money," said the pipe-major, "to hear that fellow play the Desperate Battle. I would so."

Little Para Gorvey walked into the sitting-room, lugging his drum.

" 'Tis a pity, Para Beg," said Pedhar Grady, "but some one was before us, it seems. Whether Staters or Specials, I don't know. Did you see their faces?"

"They had no faces," said Para Gorvey.

The drumming and the piping went on. The dog cowered in a corner. Grady kept looking at the child's white face.

"Thy frown canna fear me, thy smile canna cheer me,
Since the Flowers of the Forest are a' wede away."

The pipe-major rose and touched the bell.

"If you don't mind, General," he apologized, "I'll have a sup o' whisky. I know it's contrary to discipline. And myself, I'm an abstemious man. But to-night there's a chill in my bones," said the pipe-major.

III

THE COLLEEN RUE

I

THE wizened, swarthy stool-pigeon turned, flitting like a ghost, from Sixth Avenue into Fifty-seventh Street. The big Irish detective followed, lounging lazily at the side door to Marie's, the great dress-designer. The stool-pigeon stopped to light a cigarette. The cigarette dropped from his fingers. He bent to the ground. O'Connell passed him lazily.

"They're upstairs," Guinea Joe whispered huskily, out of the side of his mouth. "There's three of them."

"All right—beat it!"

"You ain't going up alone?" Guinea Joe never looked up. He fumbled at his boot-lace. "They're bad guys. You ain't going up alone?"

"Beat it!" O'Connell's tone was decisive. The stool-pigeon stepped into Fifth Avenue like a ferret, disappeared. Inside the door, the young detective kicked his shoes off, and, noiselessly as a cat, for all his wrestler's bulk, he stepped up the stairs. He listened for an instant outside the store-room door.

"We'll make about eight bundles out of them and pile them in the car. It's a pipe."

"Ninety dresses, and each one of them worth five hundred bucks, and they'll get twice as much in South America for them. Listen, fellows: There's nothing to it—"

"Cut it out," came an imperative voice, "and get to work! The cops is fixed, but you never can tell what will turn up."

O'Connell pushed the door open and loosened up his gun. Inside, three electric torches punched through the dark like miniature search-lights. Three shadows moved about like mummers in the setting for a Dunsany play. On the floor, frocks that cost thousands of dollars lay piled like so many rags. O'Connell stepped into the room.

"You'd better come along with me," he said quietly; "the captain will be glad to see you."

The men whipped around like terrified rats.

The three torches converged to a white blazing point on O'Connell's black hair, his ruddy, Greek-featured face, his gray eyes—now dangerous slits.

"I'm O'Connell," he said quietly. "Come on," he snapped; "throw those gats into that pile of skirts or I'll bore you! Come on, Julius; I know you all. Get busy."

Julius, the "Fighting Yid," the most dangerous burglar in New York, walked over to the detective. He held his hands away from his sides.

"Listen, now, Mr. O'Connell," he pleaded, with singsong Galician intonation: "I know it—you got us. But be reasonable."

"What do you mean 'reasonable'?" O'Connell asked, ugly.

"If I go now to trial, I get it maybe a long stretch in, now, up river. Maybe, now, a hundred dollars—"

"Come on!" O'Connell was snarling like a teased dog.

"Three hundred."

There was no answer. The Fighting Yid took his handkerchief from his pocket and wiped his streaming forehead. In the background, his helpers stood tense, like quivering horse-flesh.

"Five hundred, by God! Five hundred!" he broke in hysterically.

"I'll see that five hundred," O'Connell drawled, as though in a poker game. With quivering, uncontrolled fingers, like the fingers of a drug-fiend, Julius took a roll from his pocket and counted five hundred out in fifties, twenties, and tens. Perspiration fell from the burglar's forehead on the saffron bills as great drops of autumn rain fall on leaves. O'Connell snapped it from his hand and pocketed it, his eyes never leaving the gang.

"Outside!" he barked at them. Without a word, the three piled through the door past him, slipped down the stairs carefully, and out in the street.

For a long time he stood at the door there, and the high blue arc-lights of Fifth Avenue, shooting their rays into the room, fell on his face, and showed it up gray and lined and set like a death-mask, and brought out vaguely the shamed, troubled look in his eyes, such as shows in the eyes of fallen women, only much more shameful.

II

In any Irish saloon in New York, on Third Avenue, for instance, from the Bowery to the Bronx; at Celtic Park, of a Sunday; at Jim O'Brien's, at Arverne; anywhere the Irish fore-gather, you can make yourself at home by dis-cussing three subjects. One is home rule. One is the possibility of finding an Irish-born heavy-weight champion of the world, such as they thought Peter Maher might be, or Tom Sharkey, or Jim Coffey, or Roscommon. The third is Jer O'Connell. The last is the most popular; the first two are abstract theses, but the subject of O'Con-nell is warm with humanity and romance.

"I mind him in Fermanagh, I do, begor," they will tell you, "and he was as good a wrestler then as

he is now. I mind him in Liverpool, the time
he was beaten by the Austrian, and he put up a
fight that broke the champion's heart. He lost, to
be sure—he lost. What could you expect? One
hundred and eighty-five pounds against two hundred and thirty, and Jer O'Connell only a slip of
a lad. Aye, but he fought two hours before he
went down."

"A great pity now," a canny Northerner will
put in, "that he doesn't go in for it as a profession."

"Sure—he loves the game; that's what it is,"
another will say. "And the money doesn't mean
anything to him. Tell me now: Can you see Jer
O'Connell traveling around from city to city, fak-
ing matches, the way the Poles do be doing and the
Turks and Greeks? Tell me now: Can you see
him doing that?"

"I cannot," will come the answer. "He's too
straight, Jer is."

"It was in Fermanagh, too, he first knew the
wife?"

"In Fermanagh, it was."

He is thirty-two now, Detective O'Connell is,
with the shoulders of Herakles and the waist of
Apollo, two hundred pounds of steel and whalebone, only twenty pounds heavier, and practically
the same man as he was twelve years ago in his
home in Lisnaskea.

Martin O'Connell is dead now, and his wife, Moyra, and Jer's sister, little Sheila, is alone in the big homestead on the hill—a pretty girl, as pretty in her way as Di De Bourke herself. A great place it must have been then, with old Martin, the ruddy farmer, attending to the work in the fields, and his wife, Moyra, pottering about the dairy, and little Sheila, winsome as a pixy, going hither and thither in the old-time garden, while Jer, son of the house, went from fair to fair, trading in cattle, or appeared at the wrestling-tournaments, meeting lively Cornishmen at collar-and-elbow, and heavy Russians pushing like draught-horses in the clumsy Graeco-Roman style, and deft, agile Spaniards and Greeks sparring for catch-as-catch-can holds— and coming home, in the main victorious, with an Irish song on his lips and a smile in his eye.

"In four years," wrote old Watson in the *Mirror of Life,* "O'Connell will be champion of the world if he persists. If he persists—for he has not the professional but the amateur temperament."

In Fermanagh they will tell you that Jer O'Connell left for New York because he was a roaming Irishman, irresponsible, happy-go-lucky. But little Sheila knows better, and I know better, and so does O'Connell's wife, who was Diana De Bourke.

I wonder how many men made serious love to Diana De Bourke in that one season of hers in London and in the two in Dublin town. A round hundred, I should fancy. There was none could resist her. A fine figure of a woman, you said instinctively, as she came into a room, giving tribute to that glorious presence. And then you looked from her noble, mobile proportions to the glorious head and face, and you drew in your breath so quickly that it seemed like a sob.

Balanced on those white shoulders, as delicately as a juggler balances an ivory ball on a wand, was a head that would drive men mad. A dim, regular face, like a strange white flower; magnificent hair, tawny red, like autumn apples —hair, one knew, that, if unbound, would come to her knees; eyes, now gray, now green, like the shallower parts of the sea, and chiseled lips that had the indescribable red of dove's feet.

They all loved her. They all told her so. They all asked her to marry them. In London there were John Crane, the young Oxford poet, who wrote her ballads, rondels, and *chants royaux;* Bassett Barett, the under-secretary of the Foreign Office; Carcassanne, the painter.

"You are in love," she told them, "with your idea of what love is, with me as a figure in the foreground." And she sent them off.

"Thank God!" they said later. "She is the

most beautiful woman since Helen of Troy. But
where her heart ought to be there is nothing but
a lump of ice."

To the older men in Dublin and in London,
such as Mendel, the banker, and Sir John Digby,
the polo-player, and Captain Hutchinson, of the
Inniskillens, and a host of others, she was very
frank.

"I cannot marry you," she told them, "because,
simply, I do not care for you as a wife should."

"But in time," they protested.

"No!" she said firmly. "I'm sorry; no!"

And they went away, one by one, some of them
smiling and losing gallantly, as a gentleman
should, and some of them paying her the compliment of drinking at great length and very expan-
sively, and some of them, very humanly, damning
her to hell. But they went away.

III

She must have been very glad to get back to
Lisnaskea, and, after these mental pawings, to
roam around with her father's tenant's son, young
Jer O'Connell, her childhood's friend with the
laughing eyes and singing mouth. They were
great comrades, those two, seemingly. On his
wrestling matches she would wager her dress-
allowance, and sometimes win, and less often not.

And when he would be at home, she met him continually and walked about with him through the flowering Maytime hawthorn-trees, when the primroses came out and the cuckoo called ridiculously from a quarter-mile away, and in November frost, when the black roads were inlaid with silver and the rabbits and the hares streaked up and down.

Together they would stroll around Lough Erne, he with his hunting terriers behind him, on the off-chance of an otter; herself, as always, silent. A lilt would come from his lips, and she would turn and find him looking at her with that half-roguish, half-impertinent, wholly innocent smile to which outlanders have applied the hideous and vulgar term of "blarney." She would recognize the tune and put her hands to her hair, smiling.

"Oh, the *'Colleen Rue'*—the 'Red-haired Girl,' " she would laugh. And laughing, too, he would begin the old street-ballad, with its swinging rhythm and intricate internal rimes:

"Are you Aurora, or the beauteous Flora, Euterpasia, or
    Venus bright?
  Or Helen fair, beyond compare, that Paris stole from the
    Grecian's sight?
  O fairest creature, you have enslaved me, I'm intoxicated
    by Cupid's clue,

Whose golden notes and infatuation deranged my ideas,
  O Colleen Rue!"

Her own eyes would twinkle mischievously,
and, half under her breath, she would sing ·back
to him:

"Sir, I am surprised and dissatisfied at your tantalizing
  insolence.
  I am not so stupid, or enslaved by Cupid, as to be duped
    by your eloquence.
  Therefore, desist from your solicitations. I am engaged—
    I declare it's true—
  To a lad I love beyond all earthly treasures, and he'll soon
    be embracing his *Colleen Rue."*

Then came a time when the song did not come
spontaneously to O'Connell. It was hard to smile
with the eyes. Something within was being re-
pressed, hidden.

It was about autumn-time, when the yearly emigration to America was at its highest, and the
men who had not gone to America were in England cutting the harvest, that O'Connell decided
to bundle and go. He spoke to old Martin, his
father.

"I'm off to make my fortune," he said.

Old Martin was furious, as he might well be.
Moyra, Jer's mother, was troubled. She won-

dered what had come over her son. But little Sheila wept to herself, for she knew.

"Why don't you ask her, Jer?" she murmured.

"As well ask the kingfisher on the stream to mate with the curlew of the bog," he said bitterly. Then he laughed. "I'll be bringing home a Yankee wife one of these days."

"You never will," his sister reproved.

So to New York came Jer O'Connell, young, laughing—in his sportsman's way, careless of all things, ready for anything. In due time his money gave out, as money will do, and it became necessary for him to do something for a livelihood. He might have become a great professional wrestler, but the naked commercialism of the American mat disgusted him. When he wrestled, he fought for supremacy—a clean, sporting fight, lose or win. But to travel from town to town giving crooked exhibitions to a prearranged decision— that revolted against every instinct in him. He turned away with a wry face.

"Why don't you join the police force?" a friend asked him.

"Begor—that's an idea!"

In due time, through the efforts of various officials of the Irish Counties' Association, and by means of his splendid frame and honest eye, Jer O'Connell was clothed in the blue-and-gold of the

New York officer, and on lonely nights he patrolled Broadway from Fourteenth Street southward, a deserted district, with but little to do. And, in the meantime, he came into prominence in athletics, wrestling at benefits here and there, and appearing occasionally in the bouts staged at neighboring vaudeville houses, where he nearly always won. His fellow policemen were proud of him.

"We've got Martin Sheridan, the discus-thrower," they boasted. "We've got Matt Mc-Grath. And now we've got Jer O'Connell, the wrestler. Is it any wonder they call us 'New York's Finest'?"

They discussed, as all New York discussed, his bout with Aberg, the Graeco-Roman, when O'Connell lost only after two hours' fight. They told one another with glee of the perspiration pouring from the face of Stanislau Bendyk, the giant Pole, when O'Connell slammed home the full-nelson hold and punished the European champion for twenty minutes until the Pole tapped the floor in signal of defeat. And they spoke of his bout with Cyclone Kelly, and of the night that they saw the shoulders of Hans Schreyer, the burly Saxon, nailed to the mat.

They regarded him more or less as an ornament to the police force, to be exhibited on athletic occasions, not as a trustworthy guardian of public property, until the night when, single-handed, he captured the Chick Torre gang on St. Mark's Place.

They had robbed a Harlem bank in broad daylight, had Chick and his helpers, jumping from a taxicab and shooting the cashier. For three weeks, the city and country had been combed for them. Hope was given up. They were said to be in Mexico, playing the races at Tia Juana, or on some cattle-boat out at sea.

He was on his way across to the Bowery from Broadway, humming a little song to himself, when he saw a figure come warily out of a saloon, sniff round like a rat, scurry along the walls as an intimidated dog might, disappear like a ghost in an apartment-house hallway.

"Begor, there's a man will stand watching," O'Connell decided.

Regardless of the law of entering premises without a warrant, acting on intuition alone, O'Connell was after him like a flash. Like a flash he was up the apartment-house stairs. He got his foot in the door of the top rear flat as it was closing.

"Who's there?" came a husky whisper.

"Just a friend who dropped in for a chat." He pushed the door open.

There were four men in the room, he noticed in the infinitesimal space of time before the light went out—three swarthy, undersized men—Italians, or possibly Jews—and a burly Scandinavian. Then there was darkness and spitting guns.

"Well, I don't know rightly myself," O'Connell will tell you, if you ask him to describe the fight at Number Seventy-three. But you gather that he jumped where one man was, with his right fist swinging clean for the solar plexus. The man fell like a pole-axed beeve. O'Connell dropped on his hands and knees, as the automatics thundered above him, feeling his way across the floor as he would feel it over a wrestling-mat. A touch of a trouser leg, and he had his arms about a man's middle. He swung the crook above his head in a rage that was all but berserker. He flung him away. There was the crash of glass as Chick's assistant went through the window, a scream as he hurtled through the air streetward.

"Wait; I get this big Polack." O'Connell heard the Swede mumble in the darkness. The blond giant rushed on him with arms swinging. They clinched. They went to the floor, fighting like mad wolves. In twenty seconds, O'Connell slipped home the dreaded head-lock. Under the terrible leverage of forearms and biceps, the Scandinavian's jaw crumbled like defective glass. There was the trample of feet on the stairs.

"I'm through, fellows," came the last man's voice. The lights flared up. A gun fell at O'Connell's feet. The swarthy Neapolitan walked over and held out his hands. O'Connell's handcuffs snapped home with a click.

The door was smashed open, and three police-men, alarmed by the shots and the broken body in the street, came pelting in. They looked around the bullet-hacked room. They looked at the two inert bodies. They looked at the prisoner. They looked at O'Connell.

"It's Chick Torre," they murmured in awe. "And the Wrestler's got him."

An exploit such as this could only end in prefer-ment, and preferment came to Jer O'Connell in the shape of being advanced to the grade of detec-tive, a thing for which he was as manifestly unfitted as a great Dane would be for running a course with a hare. But all about him the majority of the de-tectives were not the hawk-faced, keen-eyed crimi-nologists such as fiction of the cheaper sort is wont to portray. They were hard fighters, raised to sleuthdom by virtue of prowess—harsh, material men, with great knowledge of the world and iron jaws.

"How is it done?" O'Connell asked, in frank stupidity.

"We'll put you wise," said his fellow officers. "First, you got to get a stool-pigeon." And they explained to him that, as it was manifestly impos-sible for him to enter the saloons and resorts of criminals and by himself to extract the secrets of that closest of all guilds, it was necessary for him to employ a ferret to cozen information here and there, to pick up a trail as a bloodhound might, and lead to the capture. He must be assisted by one of the brotherhood. There was an adage about setting a thief.

"What do I give this stool-pigeon?"

"Give him?" they laughed. "You give him nothing. You just let him alone in his own line of work."

"Let him burgle—pick pockets?"

"Sure! You got to," was the hardened reply. "Every one does it."

It didn't seem quite right to O'Connell. Setting a thief to catch a thief was fine, but letting a thief thieve in order to catch other thieves— Still and all, that was evidently the only way to do. One had to. All the others did it.

IV

Five years passed, and Martin O'Connell, the bluff farmer, was dead, and his wife, Moyra, with him. The big farm on the hill was still there with little Sheila and a new-found husband in it. But Sheila, knowing her brother was trying to forget, wrote no news of the De Bourkes. So O'Connell did not know that the De Bourkes' mansion was haunted by poverty as by a gray ghost. He knew not that old Sir Roger, in his simplicity a little pinched, but not poor, had been hypnotized by golden literature which promised fortunes greater than those the Spanish captains brought from Aztec lands.

The old squire went to Belfast to investigate the promises held out to him, and there he fell in with vultures from Hull and Birmingham and Manchester, parasites of whom their own countrymen were ashamed. They rubbed their hands. "Here comes an Irish gentleman!" Their mouths watered. "Here comes an Irish gentleman!" There was in their eyes the hideous look of the stoat as he watches the proud and speckled trout. "Here comes an Irish gentleman! Let us treat him like a dog!"

And very like a yellow cur they treated him. Sir Roger could not understand it, as he would not believe evil of the least of men. In the end, it became patent to him. And the proud, dignified heart in him broke in two pieces. And he just died.

v

Through all the great opera-house, breaths were stilled as, under the flaring green lights above the white mat on the stage, the blond, giant Esthonian and the slim, pantherlike Celt sparred for a hold. A quick feint, a dodge, a moment of flying white bodies, and the Russian had O'Connell with an arm-lock and half-nelson.

Minow, one of the Big Five in wrestling, settled himself comfortably to punish the Celt, grinning his cruel half-snarl at the audience. The audience hooted back. There was no sportsmanship to Minow.

"Don't give in, Jer! Don't give in to him!" The admirers in the audience boomed like artillery. On the mat, the referee hovered around like an uneasy bird. Agony swept across O'Connell's face in flushes of white and red. At times, he would writhe like a snake. At times, he would twist double to an archer's bow and spring like a salmon. The Russian held him like a wild thing caught in a trap. The roar of the audience died suddenly. The crisis was too acute for sound.

In an instant, O'Connell sagged, became dead weight. For an infinitesimal fraction of a moment, he lay on his side, every muscle relaxed as though life had gone from him. Minow, for the same fraction, was puzzled. In that fraction, Minow lost. With the quick turn of a lizard, O'Connell had slipped from the hold, and was on his feet, dazed, staggering, completely beaten, but on his feet. The whistle blew the end of the period. The audience roared like the sea.

From her seat at the rear of the house, where she was with a girl companion, Di De Bourke rose and slipped through the lobby, her vague, flowery face set firmly. She went out to the street. The man at the stage-door did not stop her, so full of high purpose did she seem. She blundered up unknown stairs to the wings on the stage. She walked straight to where O'Connell sat among his handlers.

"I'll go ahead till he gets me, but I'm a done man," the wrestler was saying.

"For our sake, Jer, try, boy!" A burly policeman was near sobbing.

"I'm a done man."

"For the sake of old Ireland!" some fool urged.

"I'm a done man."

The referee raised his whistle to his lips. Diana stepped forward.

"For the sake of the *Colleen Rue!*" Her voice came clear like a bugle. "Beat him, boy; beat him!"

He looked up, as though he were a hunting horse touched by the whip, every nerve and muscle quivered. In a daze, he watched her.

"I'm dreaming," he muttered; "I'm dreaming." The referee's whistle cut into the air.

"You're not dreaming," came the voice clear again. "I'm here."

Minow can never explain to Esthonia what happened that night on Lexington Avenue. He remembers coming forward grimly to finish a beaten man. He remembers his left wrist being gripped instantaneously by ten steel fingers. He remembers a left shoulder pivoting into position under his own left armpit. He remembers spinning into space in the "flying-mare" throw. He remembers the dull crash of his head on the insufficiently padded mat, whalebone legs going about him in a breath-strangling scissors-hold. He remembers the roar of the audience, the referee slapping O'Connell's back.

"O'Connell wins," went the decision. "Time: one hour and forty-seven minutes. Hold: scissors and arm-lock."

He is no longer the pride of Esthonia, is Alex Minow. He cannot explain to his native province how he lost that match. He tells Esthonia there was magic used against him; there must have been, he expostulates. Esthonia laughs. And yet, in a way, the man is right.

VI

In due time they were married, and they went to live in a bijou apartment overlooking Central Park, such a place as a bachelor banker might have, or an artist of note; but a ridiculous place for a member of a police force. There was nothing too good for his wife, who had been Di De Bourke, O'Connell decided, and all his savings—a notable sum, when rewards were taken into account—went to the furnishing and maintenance of that home. And he spent the more on her because she had been a

governess in New York for six months and had
known comparative want. She—who was his queen!

"But you can't afford this money, lad," Di told
him.

"Leave it to me," O'Connell would grin.
"There's nothing too good for my *Colleen Rue*."

Passed a month, passed two months, while those
two hearts nestled together closer and warmer than
birds in a nest. Outside, the world moved by on
its daily affair, but to them, in that delicately purple
Celtic honeymoon, it seemed no more than a mirage
seen against an Afric sky. Time went by, measured
by no mechanism of clocks, or by rising moons, or
by the setting of suns. About his duties O'Connell
moved in a vague unreality, as though in some drug-
induced dream. And when he went home, he went
as swiftly as a bird cleaving through May twilight
to the blossoming bough where its mate and nest
are. And when he saw Di, both their lips would be
sealed and their hearts would speak in articulate,
intelligible beats; and from then till dawn, a windy
perfumed space would close about them, with shining stars.

And slowly from that trance and mystery they
awakened, as people inevitably do, and life took on
its proportions again—homely, cheerful, welcom-
ing. Outside, there was still traffic in the streets and
people; but a great radiance emanated from them.
And O'Connell and Di were happy, because they

had both glimpsed the Master Mason's pattern of existence, and saw the sweetness of it, and its broad harmony. And he was happy in his boisterous, bountiful way—bringing her presents and singing her songs.

"Was I Hector, that noble victor, who died a victim of
    Grecian skill,
  Or was I Paris, whose deeds were various, as an arbi-
    trator on Ida's hill?
I would roam through Asia, likewise Arabia, through
    Pennsylvania seeking you,
Through burning regions, like famed Vesuvius, for one
    embrace of the *Colleen Rue!*"

And she, happy in her own way—which was not demonstrative but very thorough—would smile that marvelous slow smile of hers. Her lids would drop slowly on the deep gray pools her eyes had become. She would kiss her finger-tips and touch him gently on the cheek.

"Dear heart! Dear lad!"

Perhaps it was because he had known nothing of women before, and perhaps it was on account of the difference of birth between them in Ireland, but, little by little, Di took on, in his mind's eye, a strange aspect. She was something to be loved, admired, adored—a being from another world, some pagan goddess who must be placated with gifts and burnt offerings. It always seemed to him unnatural that *she,* the *Colleen Rue,* should be married to *him;* as though it were some strange puzzle, he thought about it all the time he was on duty. All his love-making to her had been a passionate, poetic thing, far removed from the detail of life. He put her on a certain plane, and to her he gave all the trappings of it—comfort, happiness, luxury, adoration. He stood between her and material fact like a bulwark. She might have been an adorned mistress rather than a wife.

"Oh, heart, how can you love me so?" she would ask, with wonder in her eyes. And he would only affirm,

"I do."

And again time passed by, a year of it, it seemed to him now, and she was happier than ever. She knew next to nothing about his finances—he told her she mustn't worry herself about petty things like money. He was the man of the house. He would attend to that. He liked to see that glorious form of hers, splendid as her prototype and namesake's, clothed as well as any woman's in America. He liked to see that dim and flowerlike face peeping from a nest of furs. It was not because of a vanity that she was his wife, but because she was the *Colleen Rue.*

But in that year he was not so happy himself, for he saw the approach of the day when funds would be no longer in abundance, and the style of life he planned for Di would be unfeasible. That bijou apartment—how could he keep that up? In place of her tailored clothes, must she wear the ready confections of the common stores? Impossible, he said to himself. And what would she say if conditions like that arose? Would she be disappointed? Would she leave him? The mere imaginative figment gripped his heart with icy fingers.

"It mustn't be!" he swore to himself. "By God, it mustn't be!"

By now his name was in the papers regularly as a detective star. The information and cunning of his stool-pigeon, "Guinea Joe" Varesi, showed him trails that he followed blindly and unflinchingly alone when other men would have gone only in company with a squad. It was O'Connell who captured Ole Nansen, the dreaded yegg, after a hand-to-hand fight in a sail-loft on Water Street. It was O'Connell who escorted Ignatz Lefkowitz, the pickpocket, from Brooklyn to New York across on the Wall Street Ferry. When Lefkowitz jumped into the harbor in the darkness, O'Connell dived after him and swam around for fifteen minutes until he got his man and brought him ashore.

"He's got his nerve with him, that cop has!" the city admired.

It was to O'Connell, also, that Peter Robertes, the Western killer, surrendered in Hackensack—thus paying a great compliment, for Robertes knew that, with O'Connell, there would be no danger of a beating-up when manacled. And it was O'Connell who braved the pistols of the seven *Mafioti* in the Hester Street tenement, when headquarters were for getting a machine-gun.

"He never lets his man go," New York boasted.

Came the night when a certain dope fiend slipped up to O'Connell as he strolled down Seventh Avenue. From the side of its twisted mouth, the Thing spoke in a whisper.

"There's something doing down at the Central Coal Company's office."

"What's doing?" O'Connell demanded, in disgust.

"Just something doing." The addict leered and slipped away.

He waited not an instant to notify headquarters or to ask help, for the hunting feeling was on him, but went straightly south-eastward to the company's offices on Bleecker Street. Very quietly and efficiently he came up behind the lookout on the street, stunned him with a black-jack, manacled and tossed him into an areaway, to be picked up later. He slipped through an opened window and into the offices. The safe had been blown open and Guinea Joe and Barney Hammerstein, the "Yiddish Yegg," were cramming notes and bills into a satchel.

"So you've turned safe-cracker, Joe?" O'Connell

was amazed. "Come on; I got to take you in."

"You wouldn't do that, Mr. O'Connell!" The Italian went white. "After all I helped you, you wouldn't do that!"

"This is too big a job." O'Connell shook his head. "You had a right to stick to your own line. You got to come in."

But Joe knew he wouldn't be brought in. O'Connell was under too many obligations to him, and O'Connell was too good a sportsman to round on a pal, as the phrase is. O'Connell knew it, too.

"If ever again, Joe," he said sternly, and was very grimly mute as to the rest of the sentence. Joe knew he was saved.

"How about my side-kick?" Joe asked. The yegg edged forward, wetting his lips.

"He's got to come along," O'Connell answered, though he knew in his heart he could not honestly arrest the man, having let Joe go.

"I ask you, Mr. O'Connell!" The yegg went into hysterics. "Don't do it—I ask you! It was only a mistake. See, now—I show you. I got a little money. I ask you—be reasonable." He edged forward with a roll of bills.

O'Connell looked on hypnotized. All day he had been worrying as to the dying bank-account. When there were no more luxuries for his wife, what then? If he lived in ancient Macabre times, when Satan purchased souls for ringing golden counters, the enemy could have had his for five thousand dollars. Aye! One thousand, he had sworn to-day, on the street. The safe-blower held out the roll in quivering, nervous fingers.

"I got a mother, up in Simpson Street, Mr. O'Connell," went the singsong hysteria. "Look— I ask you. Just once. Here is twelve hundred dollars. I ask you—be reasonable." He thrust the roll into O'Connell's side pocket.

"Come on; beat it!" snapped Guinea Joe.

O'Connell stood uncertain, dazed. The pair moved off from his presence like phantasms. When he looked up, they were gone. He stood still for a dozen minutes, his face flushed, his head bowed. He walked outside and fired his revolver.

"I got tipped off to something here," he told the hurrying patrolmen. "But they got away on me." He looked to see if the manacled "lighthouse" was in the areaway. He, too, was gone. "They had to leave the stuff—"

Many men on the force took money in this or some other way, he knew, deny it as strongly as they might. There was nothing despicable in it. The thing was honored by tradition. A crook was a crook after all—stick him as much as the traffic would bear. The chances were that, if arrested, by the help of a good lawyer and a humanitarian jury, the man would go free. If you didn't stick him, somebody else would. It was "honest graft."

That hardly weighed with O'Connell, for he knew the thing was wrong. He could not have arrested Barney, anyhow, because of his own stool-pigeon. And he needed that money; he would have sold his immortal soul for that money, on account of his wife, Di.

The second occasion was less hard, and the third was easy. He took money without hesitancy now, on condition that the crooks took no loot with them. That was a salve to his conscience. He compromised only with men who were burglars and who robbed the rich. For murderers, for men wanted on account of shameful crimes, for the pick-pockets who robbed street-cart traffic, there was no mercy from him.

"It's honest graft," he tried to convince himself.

But something died in him. He had no longer pride in the presents he made the *Colleen Rue*. Strange lines grew about his mouth, and his eyes were sullen sometimes. He was always attentive to Di, for he loved her intensely, every minute, every day. It gave him joy to bring her to theaters, to Fifth Avenue restaurants for dinner, to spare nothing for her. Long ago she had given up asking if he could afford these things. She took it for granted he could.

"It's not every man has O'Connell's luck," some

of the police commented, "to marry a wife with a barrel of money."

"She must have brought him a quarter-million," went the shrewd estimate. "He spends more than the commissioner does. And she's worth spending it on. There's not a lady in the land can touch her for looks."

Time went on, and there was no diminution in his caring for the *Colleen Rue*. He still admired her. He still had joy of her. In him was the eternal reverence. But as he walked the pavements at night, no longer the old song sang in his soul and mind and veins, so that, somehow, listening, he could hear it:

"As I roved out one summer morning, speculating most
  curiously,
To my surprise I soon espied a charming fair one ap-
  proaching me.
I stood awhile in deep meditation, contemplating what
  I should do—"

But all he could hear about his head and his heart was the beating of the Furies' wings.

VII

He dropped his wrestler's bulk into an arm-chair in the little sitting-room furnished in white and gold. His jaw was set; the lines about his mouth had deepened into a bitter triangle; his eyes were heavy and shamed.

"If you play square—" he muttered to himself venomously.

Though only four in the afternoon, the place was dark already—a heavy January darkness. Outside, sleet was falling, neither rain nor snow but a dismal primeval drizzle, a setting for disaster.

O'Connell had returned two hours earlier than he had said he would, and Di was not at home and the servants were out. The unspoken charge of Decker at the Waldorf bar had sent him forth into the murkiness a broken man.

He had met the Western athletic promoter by appointment down-town to talk over representing America in an international wrestling tournament in London. Decker's cool, gray eye had taken him in from head to toe.

"I'd send you like a shot," he had told the detective, "if I were sure you'd be on the level."

"What do you mean?" O'Connell's face had flushed.

"What I said—if I were sure you'd.be on the level."

Two years ago, if Decker had said that to him, Decker would certainly have left the room a dead man. A chill struck into O'Connell's heart. Decker knew! And O'Connell had no right to resent the remark. He turned on his heel and walked out.

"If I were only on the square!"

All the way home, whither he had gone unseeingly as a wounded animal makes for its lair, it seemed to him that people were pointing him out. It was as though every one knew. He could meet no man's eyes.

As he sat there in the sitting-room, a great bitterness rose within him. So here he was who had been pride of his people! A grafting cop! A man whom sportsmen would not trust! He buried his face in his hands.

"I'm through," he said.

Well, there was one way out. They might call it the coward's way, but it was the only one. And people would never know. An accident while cleaning his revolver. He put his hand in his hip-pocket and pulled out the deadly blue weapon. Di would get his insurance—a big sum. That was all she cared for, he thought, perhaps with bitter injustice. From another pocket he drew forth a roll of bills. There were five hundred dollars there.

"From the loft burglars at Marie's," he laughed bitterly.

So intent had he been he never noticed that his wife had entered the room and was gazing with terrified, white face at the expression of his eyes and at the blue weapon held loosely in his fingers.

"What are you doing with that revolver?" She faced him quickly.

"Nothing," he answered smiling.

"You were going to kill yourself!" Her voice was panting. She dropped her muff and leaned across the table to him. Her voice had become very gentle. "Why, lad?"

He was silent, his head bowed. Her eye caught the roll of bills on the table.

"Is it on account of money?" she asked. An intuition flashed like wireless to her brain. There was a catch in her voice. "Jerry, is this—is this graft?" He was still silent. "Why, lad?" Her voice was as soft as though talking to a child.

He said nothing, but he looked up. His eyes went harshly about the white-and-gold apartment. They rested on the long marquise ring of diamonds and turquoise on her right forefinger, on the silver-fox furs she had thrown aside. He laughed. She never winced.

"Is this all?" she pointed to the money on the table.

"A drop in a bucket," he laughed again. "I've taken twenty times as much—ten thousand!"

He could no longer watch her eyes, there was so much pain in them, and he lowered his head. The dusk crept in more and more, and the little French clock on the grand piano ticked remorselessly. It seemed to him that each of those seconds was being told off on his nerves, so acute the jar was. The revolver slid from his fingers to the carpet.

"Because you loved me," she was beside him, bending over his bowed shoulders, "you gave me these things." He neither spoke nor bowed his head; but she felt in her heart the answer was, "Yes." She slipped into a chair beside him and drew his crisped fingers toward her. A minute passed slowly, its seconds seeming to go on in a stilted, tense processional. Against his rigidity he felt her seeking to flow all about him, as balm flows over a wound. Dusk rolled into the room in a strange, dark mist.

"And didn't I love you, my heart? Didn't I love you?" her voice was crooning to him. "And you never knew. Don't I love you now? Wouldn't I give my soul that you shouldn't be hurt?"

She caught both his hands in one of hers and tried to turn his face toward her, but his rigid muscles prevented that. She kept her arm about his neck.

"Listen," she whispered: "Do you know how I love you? Did you ever know how I loved you? Did you know I loved you in Ireland? Did you know, when we lost everything in Ireland, that I came here to be in the same continent you were on, although you should never know it? And when we were married, I seemed happy. But I was not happy at all."

It seemed to him that the arm round his neck and the hand in his hands were not material flesh but

intangible soul-substance, that she was not whisper-
ing in physical accents, but that her soul was pouring out some mystic message.

"I was not happy, heart, because you didn't need
me. All I could give you"—her voice caught for
an instant—"was myself, and that was not enough.
I wanted to help you. I wanted to give, give, give
all the time, for that is what love is." She gripped
his shoulder fiercely. "I've lain awake at nights,
man o'mine—oh, night after night when you were
out—fearing that some one would shoot you, and
I not there to catch the bullet in my own bosom.
I've waited and waited for you to get ill, so that I
could nurse you. I've wanted us to be poor, so that
my fingers could be scarred from working for you,
and I would rather have those scars than diamonds
out of Africa."

He had, he knew not how, come closer to her, and
from hand to hand there flowed a mysterious fluid
that seemed to merge them into one another until
they were one.

"And now my time has come." A subdued, tri-
umphant trill came from her lips. "That money
shall go back, every cent, not to those it was taken
from, but to the poor of the world. And everything
we have shall be sold. And we shall be poor. And
I will work, as I worked when I came here. And
you will put your gun in your pocket and your shield
beneath your coat, and go on your way stronger

than ever before." She put her arms about him triumphantly. "I'm glad," she said cryptically, "because I love you so."

The tenseness of years dropped from him like a cripple's support, and he felt broken, like a wounded man.

"I thought, when we were poor and you had not what you had in Dublin and London, you would turn on me," he confessed.

She drew back from him in a faint shiver, but a moment later her arms came about him again, infinitely tender.

"I thought," he breathed through the dusk, "that when you had heard I grafted, you would have put me aside as though I were an outcast, drawing your skirts from me."

She said no word, but her arms went about him in the darkness more closely than before, and she moved a little in front of him, as though to shield him from the world.

And somehow, too, he sensed there was a great pride in her heart.

"I loved you so, Di," he said; "I loved you so— and I never knew!"

He raised his head, looking over her shoulder, for he could not as yet bear to see her face.

Outside on the street, the great incandescent lights were turned on, and as their warm rays shot their way into the dark of the room, he felt that warmth and light were hunting the darkness from his heart.

"You see," the fearless detective was all but sobbing, "I never knew." He looked toward the windows, and he saw the sleet change in the beam from wet, cold, and disastrous drops into petals falling from a tree of gold; and it seemed to him that in his soul also the same miracle had happened.

IV

SEA CHANGE

FROM where he stood, leaning over the rail of the bridge, he could see, off to windward, along the horizon line, the great bank of cloud that resembled land. The lifting swell of the Caribbean had changed to a sharp, cross sea that shook the great freighter when she pitched with the sensation of a heavy blow on the bows. Westward the sun was setting in a red haze that suggested fire showing through smoke.

The whirring whine of the wireless had stopped, and the Marconi man made his way forward across the boat.

"What is it?" Captain Davids asked, not taking his eyes from the horizon. "Read it."

"Government hurricane warning, sir, Miami," the boy answered. "All ships make for port."

"Very well," the captain nodded.

He had known there was going to be weather, from the hazy cirrus clouds on the horizon, striped with purple and mauve; from the blood-red sunset of yesterday and the sunrise of to-day. The ugly sea running, too, that warned him; but that it was brewing for a hurricane—a hurricane of such dimensions as the Government aërogram signified—he hadn't suspected that.

"Take a look at the barometer," he told the third mate.

"Going down all the time, sir," was the report.

"Humph!" grunted Davids.

He looked down to the forward hatch where the first officer was standing, giving a cursory look at the lashings and battens of the tarpaulins. He saw his own wife down there laughing and being caught by the arm by the mate as the boat rolled to the sea. He heard that gurgling laugh of hers ring out as the roll changed to a short pitch and the mate had to catch her again.

From where he stood he could see the officer's smiling face and blond mustache, his eyes, big and violet-colored, such as an actress might have, and that lean, graceful figure of his. His appearance contrasted so sharply with that of old Tom Jennings, who had sailed with him as mate for thirteen years. This last time, when they had taken the *Canopus* out from New York, with her cargo of rails for Chili, old Tom had stood in the bows, grizzled, broad, hoarse-mouthed, cursing viciously at dock-walloper and deck-hand as they warped out from the pier. Forty-eight hours later old Tom was dead—his heart, which had threatened him for so long, had gone back on him at last, and they had buried him from the main-deck at sundown in a sail with some iron at his feet. And Davids himself had had to conduct the service, motioning when to lift the plank and whip away the flag.

At Havana he had taken on the new mate, who had been sent down by train to Florida to meet the ship, a young man, hardly over thirty-three, of the English Naval Reserve, but with a master's and extra master's certificates. He hadn't liked the look of the man.

"Do you think you'll be able to fit into the work, Mr. Bowater?" Davids had asked him kindly.

"Oh, I think so, sir," the mate had answered, but there was a smile to his eyes, a sort of challenging superiority, that made Davids dislike him immediately.

Grant, the huge Nova Scotian navigator, and Carlson, the Swedish third officer, disliked him, too. Davids could see that, beneath all their rigid ship's etiquette. The new mate had spoken sharply to Grant, warping out of Havana. Old Tom would never have done that. The dead mate knew Grant for an able sailor and a good officer; McKinney, the chief-engineer, that grim old Belfast man, had summed him up tersely.

"He's got the manner of an admiral and the looks of an actress, but if that's a sailor, give me the engine-room."

But one person on board liked him, if nobody

else did, and that was the captain's young wife. Within eight hours out of Havana, Minna Davids and he had become rapidly friends. They sat together when he wasn't on watch, and he told of the battleships in which he had trained for the Naval Reserve; of the great passenger ship in which he had been third officer, and of the friends he had made—people with names that awed her—and of the merry parties in his friends' homes in New York. Within thirty-six hours they were inseparable.

"The old man's a fool," McKinney, the chief, grumbled. "He's a fool in the first place for marrying her, and a fool in the second place for letting her run around with that sugar-coated mate."

He had been married only six months, and Davids himself was beginning to wonder in his mind whether he had been a fool or not. A man of his age—he was fifty-two now—had he any right to marry a woman of twenty-eight? True, he was as hale and hearty as any youngster of thirty-five, and one of the best and most reliable captains in the the merchant service, but didn't a young woman want a young man? He wasn't a handsome man, as other men may be handsome and distinguished at his age, and have a fascination for young women. He was sturdy and squat, though hard as iron. His face was obscured by a short black beard becoming more and more grizzled as years went on. His gray eyes were sleepy, and never seemed to animate except in times of danger. But Minna Ackstrom had taken him.

"She never said a word against it," he often thought. "But still, I don't believe she's satisfied."

She had never been satisfied in her life, had he only known it. She had come from a family that had been seafaring for generations, first in Scandinavia and later in America. It would have been impossible for her, with that blood in her veins, to marry any but a sailor. She had been too accustomed to luxury in old Captain Ackstrom's home, he who was the most respected salvage-master on the continent, to mate with any of the first officers, pursers or engineers with only a pittance who had asked for her hand. But when Davids came, a man with a fat interest in his line, and the savings of a lifetime, she had no objection. Davids had asked her father for his consent.

"She's a good little hooker, Captain," the salvage-master had said, "and if you can warp her out you can have her. She'll not be easy to handle in a seaway, though, I warn you."

And she wasn't. He could navigate, sail and steam by dead-reckoning or by observation across any sea, but he had never found the way of handling her. Not that she hadn't been a good wife to him, affectionate, obedient, kind, with a semblance of loving. But he didn't want that. He wanted to get somehow into the heart and soul of this dark-haired, gray-eyed, lithe and gay creature. He wanted a quality of singing love from her, a gaiety with him, a loss of that self-contained manner of hers. Would he ever get that? he wondered. She was so constrained with him, so happy with the mate down there. Should she have married him at all? Was not her logical husband something like the first officer—alert, young, handsome?

The first officer swung up to the bridge. The third handed over the watch. Eight bells sounded from the bridge, sharp and tinkling, and was repeated, dull and sonorous, from the bows. The air became moist and heavy, like a thick liquid. The sea dipped in irregular, ugly movement. The captain hurried to the mate.

"Mr. Bowater, I'm going to turn in for a few hours. Send a quartermaster for me the moment it begins to blow!"

"There's no need for disturbing you, sir," the first officer answered. "I can handle things."

"Mr. Bowater," and the captain's voice took on a little asperity, "you've been mainly on the South Atlantic run, haven't you?"

"That and from New York to the Plate, sir."

"Then, Mr. Bowater, you've never seen a Caribbean hurricane, or you wouldn't feel quite so sure of being able to handle things. Send the stand-by quartermaster, please."

He tumbled out of the chart-room at the call of the quartermaster, and as he caught the rail of the bridge a fine sheet of rain whipped into his face like a shower of pellets. Through the funnel guys and the wireless rigging the wind screamed fiercely. From the wheel-house six bells rang out, and very faintly from the bows came the answer and more faintly still the lookout's call: "The lights are burning bright, sir." The vessel lurched sickeningly.

He entered the pilot-house. At the wheel Janssen, the Danish quartermaster, held on stolidly. Bowater paced up and down, steadying himself to the pitch and roll.

"Nasty blow, sir," the mate ventured.

"It's not too bad," Davids answered. "We're just getting the verge of it." He turned to a quartermaster. "Get in the lookout," he ordered.

The navigator entered the wheel-house. As the door opened, a great burst of wind seemed to crash outside like the thunder of big guns. The door was nearly shattered with the crash as it closed.

"It's blowing like the Bull of Barney," the Second said. He looked apologetically toward the captain. "Pretty bad night, sir."

The mate still paced up and down. The deck swung over like a wall falling. The quartermaster clamped his knees into the wheel. The mate ended up at the wall with a thud. Slowly the ship righted herself, and they could hear distinctly above the dull reverberation of the wind the swash of the shipped water from the bows across the forward hatch.

The door was tugged at again. Some one was pushing ineffectually. It opened a few inches and then shut again. The navigator sprang forward and wrenched it open. Outside the night was like black liquid. The wind filled the room like a rush of water.

"Mrs. Davids!" he cried.

The captain caught her as she spun toward him, held her until she had steadied herself. He didn't seem pleased.

"I couldn't sleep," she explained. "It rolled so. I thought you mightn't mind."

"Afraid, eh?" he laughed.

"Not I," she told him boldly. "How do you expect a person's going to sleep with the ship doing a jig like this? Is it going to be bad?"

"Afraid so," he answered nonchalantly. "Government warns to make for port."

"Then it must be real," she answered, her face flushed with excitement. "I always wanted to see a bad storm."

He watched her for a moment, and his heart lifted with a great leap of pride to see how fearless she was. Yes, the sea was in her, and she was of it, body and blood. She had pleaded to be taken on this trip, claiming she had a nostalgia for the sea, but he had thought it was only avidity for a change. It was true, then. God bless her! he said to himself.

"Make for port! Make for port!" the mate was muttering to himself. His eyes seemed fixed with concentration, but his lips were loose and he had gone a little white.

Outside the sea was crashing at the vessel in a turbulence of frenzy. At times it sounded like far-off peals of thunder, and again like the crack of some mighty flail being lashed at its sides by a maddened god, and again it would strike short and viciously with the staccato sound of a battering-ram against a wall. The wind shrieked through the guys and roared past the davits and hooted deeply as it cut over the funnel's edge.

Eight bells chimed from the clock. The quarter-master changed at the wheel.

"My watch, Mr. Bowater," the navigator said. The mate nodded nervously.

Aft from the boat-deck, when the wind lulled for an instant, they could occasionally hear the bellow of the third officer:

"Lay on it! You slum-bred land-crabs! Rot you, get a gait on ye! Heave! Blast ye! Heave!"

The captain leaned against the wall and watched his wife in front of him hanging on to the wainscoting, and the mate beside him with his legs

braced to the pitch. She was looking at the mate
with puzzled, inquiring eyes, as though she felt
there was something wrong, that some bond had
broken between them. Davids kept his eye on both
of them. What had these two in common, he asked,
that she should look at him in that way? One did
not look that way at a perfect stranger, nor even
at an acquaintance of a few days' standing. Had
anything occurred between them? That was
hardly likely. Was it that she had begun to feel
an admiration for, an attraction to, this man,
which within a few days more, with the terrible
sudden quality of the sea, might verge into a wild
volcanic passion, as a typhoon develops out of a
very small cloud to windward? That was it, he
said, with sudden intuition. Yes, that was it!

There was a crash on the forward maindeck, a
sharply defined splintering sound that smote hard
on their eardrums through the thunder of the
storm.

"The emergency boat," Davids nodded. "It's
gone." The navigator was bending over the chart.

"What do you make it, Mr. Grant?" Davids
asked.

"Off Great Cayman Island, sir," the navigator
answered.

" 'Twas off there the *City of Devon* went
down," the Captain said. "Turned turtle in a hurricane, and never heard of again."

"Yes, sir," Grant nodded, "and the *Lurgan Lassie* and the *Patrick J. Shields*."

"And twenty others," Davids added. "The *Flying Beauty*, the *Queen of Hearts*, the old *Caribbean*, the *Simon Bolivar*—God knows how many! Talk about typhoons!"

He noticed again how little effect the danger had on his wife, and again he was proud. And looking at the mate he saw that, in spite of all efforts to control himself, the man was trembling.

"Mr. Bowater," Davids asked, "you made that examination this afternoon of the tarpaulin on both fore and aft hatches, didn't you?"

"Everything right, sir," the mate answered.

"I'd like to be sure of that," the captain mused. "Carrying rails, as we are, there's such a space that if water broke into the holds it would be serious."

"It's impossible, sir," Bowater broke in nervously. "With that sea washing over and the wind, it can't be done now. A man would be overboard. There'd be no chance."

"I'll look after it myself," the captain said. He slipped into his oilskins and caught up his electric torch. He smiled at the watch-officer's look of anxiety, and as he steadied the door to go out he noticed that his wife was regarding the motionless mate with a glance of poisonous contempt that made her eyes flash like daggers and distorted her mouth into a terrible smiling sneer.

At times it seemed to them that they were sliding down an inclined plane, so much did the boat dip in her pitch. They would sweep down until the quartermaster was bent forward over his wheel. Then there would come a buffet amidships and she would heel over like a bird turning on the wing. Outside the waves crashed and thundered in a sort of delirium, and the rain-laden gusts of wind made the canvas of the bridge crack like a gigantic whip. Her husband and Grant, officer of the watch, had slipped out of the pilot-house for a moment on the bridge. She could see them running down to port on the roll and then fighting their way back to starboard against the wind. Deftly the quartermaster handled the wheel, easing the ship to the pitch, minding only the storm and throwing only an occasional glance at the compass-card, with its mystic angles and triangles of black and white standing out dazzlingly under the lamp in the binnacle-hood.

She risked a quick glance at the mate, standing still and white against the wall. He hadn't moved for an hour, and then only to walk out on deck, as though he were going to turn in below. But the hurricane had appalled him and he had crept in again, as a dog might shrink into a house where he had been beaten, for shelter from the rain.

Through the open windows of the wheel-house she could hear her husband and the navigator shouting at each other in the lee of the canvas shield. The words seemed a vague question and answer howled by the wind itself.

"Think she'll make it, sir?"

". . . Worst I have seen in twenty years!" was all she could gather from her husband's rumbling tones.

As she looked at the mate again a great sense of spiritual disgust arose in her. So this was the man who had seized her fancy in one rapacious swoop, as a hawk might seize a sparrow! This was the man whose company and conversation had been so much to her! Once or twice his violet eyes had said that, given the occasion, he would be bold and kiss her and she, with her hot blood—she confessed it to herself—would have kissed back. She had been looking forward to hours on shore with him. With this renegade! With this coward shaking in wild terror at the gusty temper of the sea! Faugh!

The captain and the navigator came in. "How's her head?" the navigator asked sharply.

"Sou'-by-west, sir," the quartermaster answered.

The telephone rang sharply, a straining continuous jangle that had the quality of a scream for help. The navigator took down the receiver.

"Bridge," he announced. "Engine-room? Who's that, Gordon? . . . Yes! . . . Yes! . . . Go on . . . oh, the beasts!" He turned to the captain. "There's a hob broke loose in the engine-room, sir. Those Spanish firemen have gone crazy. They've knocked Irvine out and killed the second. Gordon's arm's broken and they've got the chief up against the tunnel and are trying to brain him with shovels. They want to put him in the furnace!"

The captain swung around with a bellow; he turned to the mate.

"Mr. Bowater, get the third officer and go below and fix up those firemen. Don't kill them; just knock sense into them."

The mate never moved. He shrank back against the wainscoting and his head waggled.

"Mr. Bowater!" Davids roared.

"I'm a deck officer," the mate complained petulantly. "I've nothing to do with the firemen."

The navigator looked up. "I'll go below, sir," he offered.

"You'll stay by your watch, Mr. Grant," Davids ordered harshly. "I'll go below myself."

He felt in his pockets. "Where's my revolver? It's all right! I'll get a spanner below." He started to the door.

Minna caught him by the arm quickly. He threw her roughly away.

"Keep quiet, woman!" he snapped, and with a bound he was out into the howling darkness. For an instant they could hear his megaphone shout, "Mr. Carlson!" and the third's reply, "Aye-aye, sir!" After that all was shut out in an outrageous thunder of wind and sea.

For a minute while they stood there—she, the mate and the navigator—it seemed that within a moment a violent tragic movement would break, as a cloud threatens to shoot lightning. Grant—huge, towering, tan-faced—appeared to swell until he had the proportions of a giant. His eyes shot fire at the mate, his great fists clenched and his heart heaved. In a moment he would have taken Bowater by the throat, but in that moment the clock struck seven bells.

The sound recalled him to himself. He was officer of the watch and second mate and it was not his place to brawl. He took one last savage glance at the chief officer and strode out to the bridge.

"I'll see you on shore," he muttered to himself as he went.

Minna's breath was coming hard as she, too, looked at Bowater. Some wild, primeval emotion awakened in her as she thought of that husband of hers—her man!—fighting those maddened devils with the fire-shovels in the greasy engine-room, with the floor rising and swaying like an eccentric pendulum, and the air hot with the sweat of the titanic machines. It was this man's place to go, and he had failed. Another had to do his work, to face his danger. A mad desire coursed through her to behave like a harridan, to assault him tooth and nail, to see his white face grow red from the smitings of her palm. Instead of that she kept quiet, white, erect, and her voice cut coldly at him like the lash of a whip:

"You stinking dog! You yellow cur!"

For a minute, it might have been, the unsteady pitch and roll that shook the plates of the liner as an agony would shake the vitals of a dying man, grew still and seemingly ceased. They might have been carried up into mid-air, and suspended, as Mahomet's coffin had been, on such an even keel did it appear they rode. She felt a tremor of fear at this sudden cessation of fury. She looked fearfully toward her husband. The captain stood with legs wide apart, his left arm hanging limp from the blow of a fireman's shovel. Across the right side of his head was a stain of mixed blood and hair. Along his left cheekbone was a jagged cut that had been bandaged hastily. A great awe for him came to her. He had come back from that hell-hole wounded and battered, but he had come back with victory.

The navigator's watch was over and he had gone below for deck work. The third officer, Carlson, the Swede, came in from the bridge. He glanced viciously at the mate, still white and mute in his corner.

"Look out!" he warned.

The wind began to whimper among the main-mast shrouds. It rose suddenly to a shrill whistle, then to a scream as of a locomotive, then to the dull reverberation of a fog-horn. It blasted into a pæan of frenzy. The sea struck the ship a monstrous blow.

"Ugh!" She stifled her shriek as she was torn from the floor and thrown terrifically against the wall. The chart-house swung like an oscillating lamp. She heard the mate break into a torrent of whimpers.

"Oh! Oh!" he choked. "Oh, heavens! Oh, heavens!"

She saw her husband above her, it seemed, clinging to nothing, as it were, with his one good arm. The helmsman ground passionately at the wheel. The Swedish officer of the watch stolidly counted off the angle of the roll:

"Thirty . . . thirty-two . . . thirty-three . . . thirty-seven . . . thirty-eight—no! she's coming back. Coming! Coming! Ough!" he finished with a grunt of relief. The helmsman gave a scared laugh. His face was white.

"Ease her when she pitches, and so long, my dear!" he sang beneath his voice.

"Luff her up," Davids ordered.

"Bring her up," the third officer repeated.

"Up it is, sir!" The quartermaster worked at the wheel in a frenzy. He cursed and swore beneath his breath as he heaved on the spokes.

"We'll have to get over a sea-anchor," Davids thought aloud, "and try to ride it out." He looked at the mate. Bowater had fallen to the floor and was whimpering there. "No good there," Davids shook his head. "I'll get the navigator. We can do it." He turned to go out. The third looked at him thunderstruck.

"My dear sir, you can't go forward in that storm with your broken arm. You can't, sir. I'll go. . . ."

"Mr. Carlson, you'll stay on watch, if you please."

Davids caught at the door-handle. Minna plucked his arm.

"John, if you don't come back!" she murmured. Her face was white and she gulped as she spoke. "John! John! I love you!" He looked at her a moment queerly. A little smile came into his eyes, and his mouth shut savagely.

"I'll come back!" he said.

His words sent a great thrill through her, and as she stood there, balancing to the uneasy motion, she was as near adoration as she had ever been in her life. It seemed to her that, through some great

elemental change, scales had dropped from her
eyes and her heart, and she saw this man, with
whom she had been mated, as he really was. Not
an old man, sleepy and lethargic, but a being
great enough to challenge and fight the unchained
powers of the universe, thunder and lightning and
hurricane, and the mammoth fury of the sea. She
had, before now, thought ship's etiquette a foolish thing, a moldy remnant of ancient days, and
she had laughed at the respect and attention the
officers gave her husband. They were humoring
an old man, she thought, and she had smiled in
her sleeve at the idea of these able young men
deferring to him. But now she knew why they did
it—because of his ability to handle ships and men,
to battle with the sea and outstrategy the wind.
A foster-son of Neptune and milk-brother to
Boreas!

The mate rose shaking from the floor. His face
was savage.

"He got us into this," he shouted, "he got us
into this! It's he that's drowning us! That old
fool!"

"Shut up!" the third officer warned. There was
a snarl in his voice, as of a dog.

"I won't shut up! I say it was his fault. Here
we are! Adrift! Adrift!"

The captain came in, wiping the salt water from
his face. The mate continued:

"You could have seen there was a storm coming in Havana. There was no need to put out! Endanger everybody's life for a load of freight! You're no sailor! D'you hear me, you?"

The captain walked toward him: "Keep quiet, Mr. Bowater, please!"

"Don't touch me!" the mate nearly screamed. "I know my rights! I'll protect myself!" He slipped his hand in his pocket and pulled his revolver. At the sight of the blue gleam the captain's uninjured right arm swished through the air like a flail. It curved like a hook for an instant, and the hand clenched. There was a sharp crack as fist struck chin. Bowater crumpled up and rolled over. The captain turned to the officer of the watch.

"Get the irons, Mr. Carlson," he said.

Westward, over the port bow, the landfall of Belize showed. They plowed painfully toward it through a long oily swell that swung like a great hammock. The captain was gazing ruefully at the twisted davits and bent bridge dodgers, at the wreckage of the boats and the place where the wireless house had been. The second passed.

"Oh, Mr. Grant," the captain called. "Will you go down and tell Mr. Bowater to get his gear ready? I'll be dropping him here. I'll not press the charge of mutiny. I'll just put him off the ship."

His wife crept up behind him. She leaned against him and suddenly broke down crying.

"Thank God!" she sobbed.

"That the storm's over? Is that the reason!"

"Yes," she whispered.

He smiled tenderly, pressing her close to him. He knew her real reason, and he was thanking God, too.

V

GRAFT

I

HE stood for a moment at the door of the restaurant before plunging into the eddy of Wall Street—a big, portly figure of a man, ruddy, well-shaven, sleek—and whiffed up a clean odor of the spring day with the same somewhat gluttonous expression that was characteristic of him when sitting before food or savoring the aroma of a cigarette. A taxi flashed round the corner with the thin, alert, aging face of some one looking out of the window, a face keen like the blade of a spear. Trainor nodded patronizingly, but with a warm, bland smile. The alert man threw him the curtest of nods.

"A smart man," Trainor paid tribute; "always on the job!"

He moved down Wall Street toward the Mint Building with a long, dignified gait, hat slightly back on his head, cigar jutting from between his lips with an upward tilt like the bowsprit of a clipper. People looked at him as he passed, for he was an imposing figure of a man, a man who would have been handsome and compelling had he taken care of himself. But his waistline was running to bulk, his face, that should have been sharp and clean-cut, was becoming gross, and his eye was too cold. At the first glimpse you might have liked him, so comfortable did he appear and so unrestrainedly fond of life. You might have taken him for one of those old-time merchants who drank old wines and patronized sport, and whose business, by some mysterious dispensation of Providence, prospered and grew. But after a minute's conversation with him you had the impression of a dank coldness in the air, the atmosphere of a moist cellar, instead of the hearty warmth to be expected from the imagined type. And you noticed three things in rapid succession: That the gray eye, the whitey-gray eye beneath the square brow, had a glint that was mean, that was selfish, that was untrustworthy; the mouth wide and tightly pressed, corners drawn back—a mouth that might whine like a punished dog's, or might snarl with the snarl of a frightened fox, or might sneer with the cold, vacuous, vicious sneer of a puny man; and the third point you would notice was that the chin, which should have been the king-pin in the external structure of his character, had been nullified by the growth of flesh about it, had become, as it were, a mere osseous projection that seemed to serve as a pet for a double chin.

As he moved down the little hill of Wall Street, through the mass of business men, chic stenographers, pert office-boys and weary telegraph messengers that made the street eddy like a treacherous stream, there were many who nodded to him and passed on. He seemed to have a myriad of acquaintances, but none friendly enough to stop and shake hands or to ask about his health or business.

A few of the men seemed contemptuous toward him, a few seemed furtive in their nodded greeting, as though he were a person not to be known, a few were frankly not desirous of seeing him. A pale, hawk-faced lawyer with a breezy Western client by his side nodded in response to Trainor's pleasant smile.

"Who is it?" the client asked.

"Oh, that?" the lawyer queried. A little yawn of distaste showed on his face. "That's John Trainor, the purchasing agent for the Azure Star Line."

"What's wrong with him?" the Westerner smiled. "You made a face like a kid taking medicine. What's up?"

"Well"—the lawyer spat the words in disgust —"if you want to know, that's the damnedest grafter, liar and thief in the city. He's not even a

big one. He's a cheap piker." He shook his head.
"And the queer part of it is that ten years ago he
used to be one of the decentest fellows in the
world."

"Grows on you like dope," the client nodded.

"You've got it," the lawyer turned to him.
"You've laid your finger on it. That man doesn't
know how deep in it he is. Some of these days he's
going to be caught with the goods, and then—
good night!"

It was not unknown to John Trainor, this dislike which the men of his world and their women-
folk entertained for him and seemed hardly able
to dissemble. He explained it to himself in a
variety of ways. These were envious of him, he
said, envious of the ability that had at thirty-five
made him one of the most important officials in
one of the largest steamship lines in the country.
He did not see through their veiled hostility and
distinguish contempt behind it, for it would have
been impossible for him to grasp that such a feeling could be entertained toward him. He considered himself, with his bland manner, with his
ever-ready smile, with his quick jokes, his lavish
lunches, to be one of the most popular men in the
downtown district. He had associates, he had
what he called friends, men of his own easy-going
type, who were accustomed to gather at lunches
and dinners and to dud the more staid and con-

servative members in their business grouches and kill-joys.

He turned into Broad Street where the current from Wall Street turned at right angles and widened, as a river widens on its way to the sea. Brokers hustled in and out of the Stock-Exchange like scurrying mice. Hoarsely the curb brokers raised their voices in insistent, raucous cries. They bubbled in their milled inclosure like water in a boiling pot. On the steps of the Mint a solitary office-boy sat and ate lunch with the dramatic air of a philosopher. A warm golden sunshine fell like a shower of fine rain. It divided the width of Broad Street and the narrowness of Nassau and Wall, and the peristyles of the Stock-Exchange and the soaring heights of sky-scrapers, into acute stretches of orange sunshine and gray shadow with the sharpness of a line drawing.

"It's a nice day," Trainor said to himself, and he nodded again patronizingly, as though he were commending the sun for shining and the sky for being wide and blue.

He looked about him before entering his office. One hundred yards away, near the dingy bulk of the Mint, a clergyman was raising his somber bulk on a box or some other eminence. Even at that distance Trainor could catch some detail of the strong, frank face, and he recognized it as that of the preacher whom brokers called affectionately the Bishop of Wall Street.

"What shall it profit—?" He heard words and pieces of sentences wafted toward him indistinctly like the intermittent sound of distant bugles. "What shall a man give in exchange for his soul?"

His mouth tensed back into that ugly, vacuous sneer of his—triangular wrinkles about the tense corners and upper lip lifted to suggest snarling teeth.

"Bah!" he said disgustedly. "That sort of thing gives me a pain!" And he strode in toward the waiting elevator.

II

For three years—that was thirteen years before—he had been purser on the flagship of the Azure Star. He had been an efficient man and a handsome man, if what every one says is true. He had been meticulously exact in the discharge of his duties and scrupulously honest, possibly because at that time it had never occurred to him to be anything else, and possibly also because there is little scope for dishonesty in the narrow compass of a purser's duties. His work had been to make out manifests of cargoes, to keep accounts of tickets, to interview merchants who were despatching freight. He was then the clean sapling of the tree that to-day had gone lost and rotten—a tall, clean-featured, clean-limbed man of twenty-five, whose skin the suns of Brazil and the Caribbean had bronzed to the color of a leather saddle. Even then his smile was ready, but it was sincere; his jokes were fluent, and he laughed at them himself, not as now, when they were only details in a business machinery, produced to have a psychological effect.

The black-mustached captain and the ruddy, clean-shaven Danish first officer and the paternal old doctor and the battered quartermasters would smile as they watched him banter with the passengers.

"A fine, clean, upstanding lad," they said; "the sort of man we want at sea."

But before their eyes, had they only known it, the timber of him was beginning to germinate the first seed of decay. It was pleasant for him to have passengers to talk to, to be looked up to by many of them, to flirt with their daughters, to hear the easy sea confidences of themselves. It was this probably that was the ruin of him. About him on every side he saw people of immense wealth—coffee nabobs going to and from Brazil, rubber planters who reckoned their millions by tens, great manufacturers from the States traveling to investigate the new Golconda of South America. With these people he ate, drank, slept, people to whom his day's salary was a tip for a head waiter. They told stories of the great hotels in New York; of dances at Sherry's and the Plaza. They smoked cigars and drank wines that were the apex of excellence. Their women-folk invited him to dinners and dances and teas when he came ashore. And out of it all there grew a great hatred in his soul for the red-inked manifest and the narrow stateroom and the routine of cargo and tickets. Once in Barbados he saw a Brazilian throw overboard a five-dollar gold piece to the boys who were diving about the bows of the ship.

"And I make less than that a day!" Trainor had muttered bitterly to himself. And it was not the idiotic lavishness of the deed that hurt him, nor the social injustice of it, but the fact that this man had money to burn while he, Trainor, had little more than none.

From such thoughts arose the desire for dishonesty. Now for the means. Among that stream of business men up and down, it was inevitable that there should be some shady soldiers of business fortune who considered their chicane to be smartness, and whose ideal of business was to get the better, by foul means if there were none fair, of their competitors and associates. Over the drinks in the smoking-room they told tales of lying, deceit and fraud that were, as the phrase goes, within the law, and therefore, to their minds, accepted business. He saw that nearer home too. On every line he saw the occasional grafting of chief stewards, the petty intrigues between office and bridge, the plundering of ships' stores, the bribes offered under the guise of presents.

"They all do it," he said to himself, "they all do it; and why—" And he was silently thoughtful.

There were two qualities that made for his success in business later and that stuck to him now, his reticence and his intuition as to the character of other men. To the tanned officers on the bridge and to the paternal physician he uttered no word of his thoughts. They went ahead, believing him to be clean and upstanding, as they expressed it. They continued praising him to old Elias Dyer, who owned the line and gave to it such few activities as he could spare from his model farm and red-haired Irish setters. He stroked his fine country gentleman's face with its fine white mustache like a deer's inverted antlers.

"If this is such a fine young man," he stormed in that bluff, explosive manner of his, "why haven't we got him in the office, damn it! Tell me that!"

Trainor was made assistant purchasing agent.

For six months or more Trainor had carried on his work in every way that the line expected of a

man with his reputation. He had little time to
devote to plans for the future, because in the first
flash of his new position he had married the
daughter of Captain Sanderson, that tall, cadaver-
ous old skipper who had beaten up and down every
sea from Canton to Callao, and to whose spirit
there was as little dishonesty or deception as there
was flesh to his bones. There is to every man a
great capacity for love, no matter whether he be
crooked or straight, which will last until the spirit
from which it emanates is completely covered and
calked and imprisoned by evil and sordid things.
Until then the crookedness had touched his spirit,
or soul, if you like—not in black splotches but as
a gray mist. It had not as yet begun to clog the
pores. In those days he loved Millicent Sanderson
with every atom of devotion of which he was
capable.

It was, queerly enough, his devotion to her that
brought him to his first bribe. Daniels, the hawk-
faced man in the taxi to whom he had nodded
earlier that day, had called one morning in an
effort to sell lubricating oil to the company. His
price had been two cents a unit higher than that
of the other bidder. Trainor was about to send
him away.

"Oh, by the way," Daniels had said, "you're
just married, aren't you? Congratulations!" He

dipped his hand into his pocket and brought out a plush case. "A little wedding present for the missis."

The little wedding present consisted of a gold bracelet set with minute pearls and stones—it might have been worth a few hundred dollars. Trainor looked at the man in wonder.

"I don't understand," he said.

"There's no need to understand," Daniels had laughed. "Can't a business firm be courteous to a business man's wife? Put it in your pocket and don't say another word." He smiled a little cynically when Trainor slipped it into his coat. "Now there are some things I want to tell you about oil."

This was not what he had expected. He was not quite certain that the gift was not legitimate, though he mentioned it to no one, and spoke but hazily of the donor when he presented it to his wife. The real thing came later when a salesman was trying for an order of paint.

"The reason we charge so much higher," said the salesman naïvely, a fat, jolly man who was hailed everywhere as a good mixer, "is, in the first place, because our stuff is so much better than any one else's, and secondly, because of the higher commission—yours and mine."

"My commission?" Trainor asked.

"Yes, sir. Our company allows me nine per cent

on the sale and it allows you three. Your commission is a perfectly legitimate thing, done to stimulate trade. Of course as it might be misunderstood it's confidential, just between you and me. It's strict business."

"I didn't know," Trainor hesitated. "I haven't been on shore long—"

"Naturally, naturally," the salesman nodded in appreciation, "you're not wise to everything. But we'll soon put you. Now how much of this chromo-oxide will you need?"

For weeks after this his heart would jump into his mouth at the sound of the door opening. In fancy he saw the gray-mustached owner striding through the opening and driving him out of the office, as the angel with the sword of flame drove Adam from his garden. Little drops of perspiration stood out on his forehead, and his flesh wrinkled as if with frostbite, and a cold chill struck him in the chest. But nothing ever happened. The incident was repeated. There was less terror this time. There was less waiting until the next offense.

And so it went on, and more so every time, during the long space of ten years. The amount he received—on the side, as he called it—doubled his salary and more. It allowed him many of the luxuries he had envied when he was a poor devil of a purser on board ship. He had long ceased to get any thrill of terror out of it. It had become a business transaction. He never spoke of it at home. But why should he? he asked. One doesn't talk of business to one's wife. The matter was done quietly and efficiently—the salesman took care of that. Currency passed from hand to hand. No cheques; no incriminating documents. Others in the office might suspect it, might even know it, but what were they going to do about it? They couldn't prove it. No one could discharge him except the owner, Elias Dyer. And heaven help any employee who made charges to the old shipping master without anything to substantiate them!

But what was wrong about it? he asked himself fiercely. Why shouldn't a man pick up a five-dollar bill if he saw it lying in the road? Why shouldn't he take an apple from a tree if there were no one to pluck it? Wouldn't he be a fool if he didn't? This was no longer the day of simpletons. And everybody did it. Whom did it harm? It took away from Elias Dyer the price of a new red setter or a Sealyham terrier or a Berkshire otter hound. Why should he, John Trainor, sweat in poverty to indulge the foolish whimseys of a doddering old idiot—with his farm and his dogs?

"I suppose I'm to starve," he said cynically, "while he acts the English squire? Not much!"

Yes, what was wrong about it? Nothing dishonest certainly. Why, if he wanted to be dishonest he could hold back cheques, falsify accounts, clear a hundred thousand and skip away to Morocco or Tangiers, where extradition is an amuseing thing and does not obtain. But he wouldn't do that, he said. That would be dishonest.

He thought of the sea officers with the clear, clean eyes and the frank expressions; the honest men about the wharves; the plodding clerks inside; the straight business men in the streets, who followed their rigid iron law of honesty and subjected themselves to the discipline of things, whose mouths were prim, whose smiles were not unctuous.

"A man's a fool," Trainor mused, "in sticking in one rabbit's rut of action or thinking. You've got to give and take. You've got to have latitude. You've got to know opportunity when it calls to you, and get what's coming. Otherwise, you're a damned fool."

III

Somehow when I think of Millicent Trainor, I think of her as I think of Helen of Troy—a great, noble, dignified figure of a woman, and pathetically lonely. Not that she was beautiful. Her most devoted admirer could hardly call her that. But such a fine, free light played from her face, and there was so much frankness and so much life in it that one, when seeing her, subconsciously thought of something natural and noble and free, as of some slow, majestic melody played on the strings of a harp. She was a tall woman, taller by an inch than her husband. Her forehead was too broad and high for anything like beauty. Her nose and chin were insignificant. They were such as a thousand women, well proportioned, well formed, had, but without anything to distinguish them. But her eyes were of a deep gray, grained like fine granite, with small, deep pupils and startling orange splashes in the iris. With the minute, thick, golden eyebrows and lashes they gave the impression of two strange barbaric jewels set by a master craftsman. And there was also her mouth, a small, darkly red mouth, with the lips running into excellent curves, not perfect, not the chiseled perfection of a stone goddess, but warm, expressive, mobile things that showed the flash of her teeth faintly, warm, healthy, strong teeth, not impossibly white. And as she moved about with her long, strong, clean-limbed action like a blood mare, one had the impression of a cool wind sweeping over heather, of Artemis sweeping through the twilight with the crescent moon above her like a tongue of flame.

She had been in love—and she tried to think herself still in love until at last there was no possibility of mistake—with John Trainor when, ten years before, at twenty-one, she had married him.

There was something very taking about the young purser then, bronzed, clean-cut, affable, courteous and joyful. A hundred men had envied him the rapture of her love. She poured it about him like a fragrant April shower. But little by little, when she began noticing that apprehensive, calculating, secretive look in his eyes, she began to feel lost and bewildered. She lost, as it were, her spiritual handclasp with him. She fought to get it back. She wanted to know what was wrong. In a thousand ways she tried to discover the cause of it. But a woman cannot tell her husband to put a mean, secretive look from his eyes. She mustn't notice, and even had she been brutal enough to put it into words, what would Trainor have done? One can see him indignantly disclaiming anything of the kind.

"I wish I knew what was wrong with him," she would say plaintively to herself. "There's nothing in the world I wouldn't do to right it for him."

And then suddenly when she was with him she would put out her right hand and catch his and look at him searchingly.

"Is there anything wrong, John?" she would ask. "Tell me if there's anything wrong. If you're in any trouble. Perhaps I can help you out."

"There's nothing wrong," he would laugh. "What should be wrong?" But under the searching look of her face his eyes would falter and fall, and then she would sigh again, her long, plaintive sigh.

I think I can understand the terror through which she went, this poor woman, the feelings of panic, the long searches for light, the despair. It was as if her husband were attacked by some deadly, incurable disease. If it had been only a physical thing, if it had been anything from typhoid to leprosy, she would have stood by him and helped cure him or comforted him while dying. If it had only been some drug addiction, like morphine or opium, she would have fought with and wrestled and downed it. But she could do nothing against this, this spiritual and mental disease, which was more lethal than drugs or leprosy, which was rotting his spirit before her eyes and wearing away his soul in minute, implacable inroads.

And if he had been still in love with her it would have been perhaps all right, but his love for her had changed into a cut-and-dried, convention-made thing, out of which the fire and madness had gone. For an unclean man cannot have love any more than a blind man can see the sun.

Sooner or later she understood, as she could not help but understand. She knew his salary; she knew that the expenditures he made doubled and sometimes trebled it.

"John," she took it on herself to say—"John, you are spending a lot of money, much more than you earn."

"Nothing is too much for my little girl," he smiled blandly at her. She winced at the insincerity of the thing and at the smile and at the tone. Already the smile was too bland and the voice too oily. "I am making a little money on the side and can afford it."

"Yes, but how?" she persisted.

"Quite all right," he slipped the question. "A matter of business. Don't mind that, my dear; just take care of your clothes and your house. Business is not for women." And again his eyes faltered before her look, and again she sighed.

Gradually, with such subtle, minute inroads that had she not been watching for the thing with a hawk's eyes she could hardly have seen it expand and grow—although its ravages would in the end have been apparent to any one—the disease told in his eyes, told in his mouth, told in his whole demeanor. First the eyes, which had grown shifty, became callous and hard, grew suspicious. He looked at every one as though they were concealing unnamable sins, as if they would spring at him or do him some injury if he once removed the guard of his own gaze. The mouth grew weak and indulgent. The chin lost character. It showed in his conversation. He seemed to believe in no one. If a statesman were mentioned he dismissed the man with a contemptuous epithet, charging him with insincerity and venal interest. "Faker" was a favorite word of his. No man could perform a disinterested act without his seeking some motive behind it.

"He doesn't do that for nothing," he would say; "he's got something up his sleeve."

And in Millicent Trainor's heart there grew a great feeling of contempt for this state of mind. She fought against her contempt every hour, but in spite of her it grew and rankled.

"I wish he wouldn't say things like that," she would cry to herself passionately. "I wish he wouldn't."

One by one she saw his friends go. They stopped coming to his house. They stopped asking him to theirs. Her also they dropped, because one cannot, after all, keep on good terms with a wife while condemning the husband. And certainly she wished to be out of it, too, for her loyalty would not permit her to associate with them, feeling as they did toward him. She did not blame them, for one cannot be cordial to a man whose eyes regard you as a detective looks at a criminal, or rather as one criminal looks at another. One cannot like a man who pours cheap contempt on every ideal in the world, who reckons everything in dollars and cents, and sees behind every clean door a rotten dive.

What galled her most was that she knew she was being pitied. The maids who opened doors for her and the tradesmen delivering goods all knew of her husband's shortcomings. Twice she overheard criticisms of him. Once she sat behind two of her neighbors in a train.

"This man Trainor is a case in point," one of them, a white-haired bank official, told the other. "You can see from his face that he's crooked and dishonest. It always shows. They'll get him in the end."

"He's a clever man," the other, a tubby, jolly silk mercer, broke in; "and he's careful. He plays a safe game."

"You never get away with it," the bank president replied; "it always finds you out in the end. It will come some day as sure as water runs and grass grows."

"I'll be sorry for him when it does," the silk mercer philosophized. "It will be merciless."

"I'll not," the bank president shook his head. "I'll be sorry for his wife. I'm sorry for her now. I believe she's as clean as they are made."

And as she sat there, listening, her face grew as red as the red-plush seats of the car. Her heart seemed to wither up like a flower before frost. Shame struck at her with merciless blows until she

wished the ground would open into a black yawn-
ing chasm and engulf her. Silently, with the stealth
of a thief, she crept from the carriage and made
her way to the back of the train, where she sat
with her head bowed and her cheeks flaming like
banners of scarlet.

On another occasion she was less strong. It was
at a country club. Two women on the veranda
were talking as she stood in the shadows.

"Where's your husband?" one of them asked.

"He went off to get a drink with Mr. Trainor,"
the other replied.

"I didn't know he was a friend of Mr.
Trainor's. I thought he didn't like him."

"Neither does he," replied the second; "he
loathes the man. But he couldn't get out of it. He
thinks Trainor one of the most contemptible
grafters in New York."

There was a moment's silence. Millicent
Trainor tried to steal away, but a sort of hypnosis
kept her feet rooted to the spot. The first woman
spoke suddenly.

"I wonder how the man's wife stands him," she
broke out heatedly. "Why doesn't she leave him?
Run away from him? Do something?"

"Oh," said the second, "I suppose she doesn't
see it. Wives never do. But everybody else can
see it."

She broke away from where she was standing

and ran forward with little stumbling steps into
the inviting space and darkness of the big golf
course. It didn't matter to her that a light mist
was falling and that she wore an evening frock.
She raced forward with a wild, mad energy, until
she felt she was sufficiently alone. Then great panting sobs shook her.

"O God, what can I do?" she wept. "What can
I do? What can I do?"

When she came back, an hour later, and hurriedly and secretly slipped into her cloak and
found her husband, he looked at her with unseeing
indifference.

"Been out?" he asked.

"I had a little walk," she answered. "Let us
go home now."

It was about that time, too, when Trainor's
decent friends were leaving him, that he provided
himself with a new set—"a live gang," he called
it—a crowd of men with the same earmarks as
his, with unctuous presences and servile smiles
and hard, distrustful eyes. She hated those, did
Millicent Trainor; she loathed them. The deceit-
ful appearance of them made her gorge rise. But
what could she do? I think that in those days she
would have gone mad or committed some very
desperate and very foolish deed if it had not been
for young Joseph Ligatt. I see Ligatt as a young,
callow thing, immature in spite of his thirty years,

more like a boy, with his mouse-colored brown hair and straggling mustache, and big eyes that looked at you with a discomforting, searching quality. I see him now, very pale and very much in earnest, weedy and tall. He was rather a pathetic figure, without sufficient ability to do anything big and with sufficient money to abstain from doing anything small. He had two virtues—his white, fiery soul, and his love for Millicent Trainor, and I hope she is happy with him wherever they are.

He had never until now spoken to her about love. He had never achieved any close, outward intimacy with her. They had talked together about this and that, about books and poetry, about men and occurrences of the day. They liked each other most when silent. Only when they were silent he looked at her furtively out of dumb, admiring eyes. One afternoon on the front lawn of her house he came upon her. They spoke for a few moments. They were silent; suddenly he noticed her eyes were full of tears.

"I'll kill him. I'll tear him limb from limb," he cried passionately, blindly.

It seemed as if by some supernal feat they had both bridged a vast chasm and were standing together on the same intimate ground. Dumbly she shook her head.

"Listen," he said: "Come out of this hell. Come away with me. It's killing me to see you unhappy.

It's tearing my body and soul apart. Come away
and leave it. We'll both be happy. You'll be happy.
If giving you every breath I take and every pul-
sation of my heart and every thought of my mind
will make you happy."

She looked at him for a moment, and she saw
the distraught agony in his eyes. She put her hand
on his shoulder.

"You poor boy!" she said after a moment.
"You poor, poor boy!"

IV

He very seldom went out now in the evening,
John Trainor, not because he had nowhere to go,
but for the reason that he was becoming lethargic
and comfortable. He took on a likeness to an extremely ugly and untrustworthy pet dog that
spends most of its time dozing in its kennel. After
dinner he would sit in an easy-chair and doze over
a paper until the clock struck ten and it was time
for him to go to bed. What was the use of going
out, he said—you only met grafters and bums and
people who were trying to do you. Theaters were
con games where they stung you for two dollars.
And if you went to see any one else you were under
an obligation to them and you would have to kick
in sooner or later—so what was the use of going
out?

He was very drowsy and very comfortable as he sat that night in his comfortable arm-chair, dreaming of the future. Dinner was over and his wife was in some portion of the house, where he didn't know. He sat back with a shipping periodical on his knees and a short, obese cigar between his lips. If he could only get his hands on some stock of the company's; if he could only get an interest, a wedge in—

His wife came into the room. There was something curiously deliberate about her movements. Her mouth was set firmly and there was a queer, determined look in her orange-flecked eyes.

"John," she said, "I want to talk to you."

"Yes?" he said. The sound of her voice waked him and he began turning over the pages of the review on his knees.

"I want to ask you again about your business," she said a trifle nervously. "I want to ask you— do you think everything is all right?"

"Yes," he drawled lazily. "Everything's all right."

"John," she began deliberately. There was a little uncertainty in her voice and the suspicion of panting, as if she were laboring under a great strain. "You know how I look at things—at these commissions of yours. I don't think they're straight—not honest."

He gave a mock groan. "Are you beginning again!"

"It's not honest," she went on as if she didn't hear him. Her deliberate words had the ring of one who is stating a case. "If everything is right, as you say, there is no need for these commissions. If men are selling you things at a fair price they can't afford to give you commissions. It seems to me that the loser is the line; that the line is taken advantage of. John, these commissions are—are —dishonest bribes."

"For God's sake, leave it alone," he snarled.

"I am right, John, am I not?" she said with great simplicity. "These are bribes, dishonest bribes?"

"It's business," he snapped; "it's done everywhere. Mind your house and let me run my business."

"It's not, John," she said again. "Be honest. There are thousands of business men in your position who would knock a man down if he offered the thing you're taking. It's not business."

He said nothing. He began reading his periodical nonchalantly, because he had a theory that it was the best thing to do with a woman, to take no notice of her little brain-storms. Women were not logical, he said. When they got on to a subject the best thing to do was to let them run their gamut and to pay no attention.

"John," she began again appealingly, and she looked at him with that queer straight look of hers. "Forget everything until now. Put it all aside. Come to me and begin anew. Be straight about things. If I can help I am here to do it. Straight, John! Honest!"

"I am honest," he growled suddenly, with a touch of a snarl. He was beginning to lose his temper. He caught himself with an effort.

"Oh, John, you're not." She wreathed her fingers nervously. "Lately, for some time past, there's—there's—there's a mean look in your face, John. Put it out of your eyes."

He felt like boiling over with rage. He felt cut to the quick as by a whip. But he remembered in time his philosophy, that she was only a woman and must not be answered back. Say nothing. In the morning she would be sorry for this. Women were not the same as men. They had queer crises, queer viewpoints and no logic. It was the way of a big man to let things go by, to forget. In the morning she would make a pretty, shamefaced apology, and he would chuck her under the chin as she handed him his hat and coat, and she would admire him all the more.

"Listen to me, John Trainor!" Her voice rang out suddenly.

She had drawn herself up, he saw as his eyes lifted from the pages before him at the imperial tone of her voice, her head raised, her hands behind her, and even his clodded heart thrilled a little as he looked at her. The red-shaded electric lights struck iridescent gleams in her great mass of hair and brought out strangely the orange flashes in her eyes. It brought out every line of her strong, supple figure as she stood there, big, heroically big, unconsciously poised, like the Winged Victory of Samothrace, or like a bird preparing to ascend in the clear air. One could imagine a great background behind, such as the depth of a Roman Temple, or the delicate fleece of a cloud, or a wall of high black rocks. Her voice rang out, muscular though musical and very tense, like a staccato ringing on a bronze bell.

"John," she said, "I am young and handsome and alive—so much alive! And I want love. No, stay where you are. I want the love of a clean man, of a man who is not afraid to look the world in the face—the love of a big, honest man."

He looked at her a little askance. This was a new turn things were taking. She had never spoken like this before.

"John," she began again, "I want you to choose and to choose now. Will you give me that, and give it to me from an honest and clean spirit— will you make yourself honest and clean—or must I look for it somewhere else? for"—her voice trembled suddenly and her hands trembled and her

cheeks grew red to the color of rowan berries—
"so help me God, I will have it from another
man!"

He laughed low to himself in relief, for now he
understood that it was merely a touch of hysterics.
Another man! The thing was ridiculous. She must
be stirred up very much to say a thing like that.
The best thing was to take no notice. To be gentle,
that was the part to play. In the morning she
would be ashamed of herself. He rose with a
smile and placed his plump hands on her shoulders
and smiled with self-possessed assurance into her
eyes.

"You are all wrought up, darling," he said
pleasantly, "and you don't know what you're saying. You're nervous and tired. You had better go
to bed now. We'll talk about it to-morrow. Don't
mind to-night." He kissed her on the cheek and
smiled again. "There now, good night. Sleep
well."

She looked at him intently. Her lips made a
motion as though she were about to speak again,
but she was silent for a minute.

"Faugh!" she said suddenly, and disgust rang
out in her voice, cold and ugly and bare. Her
hands struck her sides in token of defeat, and turning on her heel slowly she walked out of the room
with long, swinging, Artemisian strides.

V

He felt well that morning. His face, clean-shaven and pink, radiated pleasantness and affability. His well-manicured hand tapped the desk in front and showed up shining and delicate against the green of the office blotter. The little salesman, with the intent gray eyes and short-cropped mustache, radiated, too, for he felt that business was in the offing. And he smiled back in grateful appreciation of the purchasing agent's affability. Through the window of the office building the breadth and bridges of the East River, the lines of steamers and sailing ships at the piers, the bulk of sky-scrapers, and across the way the drab outline of Brooklyn showed up with the distinctness of a fine etching, and the June sunshine crept through in a splendid golden mellow warmth.

"Your oil, you say," Trainor smiled, "is not quite up to the standards set by the Albany people, but it's good enough for any marine engine. Well, there's a good deal to that, Mr.—"

"Mr. Raines," the little salesman prompted. It was his first visit to the Azure Star Line and the prospects were bright.

"—Mr. Raines," Trainor nodded. "Well, we may be able to do business. Now, let's see—"

The door opened and a messenger boy entered.

He came forward to the desk with the shuffling stride of the broken-arched. He pushed his oilskin-peaked cap on the back of his head and produced a letter and receipt form.

"Trainor?" he asked.

"Here." The buyer looked up, puzzled.

"Sign here." The boy pushed the letter and blank toward him.

He looked at the letter for a moment in amazement. On its envelop he could see his own name, "John Trainor, Esq., Azure Star Line," written in his wife's big, curving hand. What was she writing to him about? She had never done anything like that before. And sending it by express messenger too? He ripped open the envelop.

"Excuse me," he muttered to the little salesman.

He smiled to himself a little smugly, for he understood at last, he thought. She had not, as he had expected, said anything to him that morning in apology for the outburst of the previous night, but had gone round with an air of curious deliberation. He had been a little offended and hurt, but the letter he held in his hand, he knew, was a plea for forgiveness. It was a pretty thought. He pulled out the folded paper. He read it once. He read it again. His brows gathered together and the pupils of his eyes dilated. He half rose in his chair and he sat down again.

"John," she had written, "I gave you your last chance last night. I told you I wanted the love of a clean, good man. I think I have it. I am leaving for Italy with Joseph Ligatt. By the time you have this letter the liner will be in the bay. I couldn't go ahead with you. This grafting business is too much for me. It has killed you and conquered you. It is in every pore of your mind and body, and it shows in your face like a disease." Just that and no more.

He sat for a moment stunned and mortified. His wife had run away with another man, had put on him the last supreme insult. A vicious, snarling rage filled him. What would he say to people? And graft? This abandoned hussy had spoken to him about graft! By heaven, he'd show her!

The little salesman rose, his kindly gray eyes brimming with sympathy.

"I'm afraid you've had some bad news, Mr. Trainor," he said. "I'll come again."

"No." Trainor's teeth clicked together. He tore up his wife's letter into minute white pieces and glanced out of the window. She was down the bay, and to blazes with her! He'd divorce her and get a new one, not one of the whining, Puritanical kind. He swung round. "I'm going to place an order for twenty-five thousand dollars' worth with you," he said.

"We'll do everything we possibly can," the little

salesman beamed, "to justify your confidence in us."

But Trainor wasn't listening to him. He was thinking of that wife of his. He reconstructed a scene in which she was standing in his office looking on now. He would show her something. He wanted to be as brutally vicious as he could. He wanted to shock her, hurt her, horrify her.

"How much?" he said suddenly. His voice was nearly a shout.

"How much?" the little salesman repeated in wonder.

"Yes. Hurry up. Quick! How much do I get out of this?"

"But I don't understand you." The little man's eyes looked abashed and dense.

"Ah, cut that out," Trainor shouted. "You know what I mean all right. If you people want that contract you've got to come across to me. Is that plain? You don't think I'm giving you this because I like you? Now what are you going to do about it? What's the figure?"

The little man pushed back his chair. He snapped his order book to. He rose and looked at Trainor. He was very red and his gray eyes blazed with unexpected fire.

"Well, damn you!" he said quietly, "for a stinking rascal. You low, unprincipled, grafting crook!" He spoke each word clearly and distinctly, and the accents dropped from his lips like globules of acid from the end of a pipette. "You tin-horn swindler, jail is too good a place for you!"

"Get out of here!" Trainor bellowed in rage. "Get out of here!"

"I'll get out of here when I've finished saying what I think of you, you rotten cad! 'Come across!' That's not the way we do business. I've got a good mind to swing one at you—"

"Get out of here," Trainor roared again, "before I have you thrown out! Go on! Get out!"

"I might have known you for a grafter, you sleek hound," the little salesman went on. "I might have seen it in your face. It's there for all to read—"

The door to the outer office opened and the tall bulk of the owner of the line stood in it like a portrait in a frame. Six feet of knickerbockered tweeds, with round, swelling calves to the legs; a flowing white mustache, glistening like fine carded wool; a plump, well-colored face; two blue eyes like a June sky—old Elias Dyer.

"What is the trouble here?" he asked in his mellow, full voice. The little salesman turned on him with purple rage.

"What's the trouble here?" he raved. "The trouble is that I thought I came into a reputable business office to sell oil, and instead of it I've wandered into the worst crooks' and thieves' and grafters' den I've ever seen—that's the trouble!"

"What is this? What is this?" the proprietor sputtered.

"This crook of a purchasing agent of yours will give me a contract if I 'come across,' grease his palm, give him a bribe," the little salesman thundered. "Let me get out of this!"

"Wait a moment." The proprietor raised his hand. His face had gone very stern and white. "Wait a moment. Is this true, Mr. Trainor?"

The purchasing agent rose and held on to the edge of his desk. Everything about him was a vapid, tumbling dream—the stern, Jehovah-like face of the old sporting proprietor, whose mouth had narrowed suddenly, and whose eyes took on the cold, white glint of hoar-frost; the wild, berserker rage of the little salesman, on whose brow anger had brought out little pearl-like beads of perspiration. And in his fancy, too, his wife was in the room, tall, heroic, with cold contempt showing in her orange-flecked eyes and her nostrils quivering like a blood mare's. A sudden blind rage shook him like an ague.

"Is this true; Mr. Trainor?" Dyer thundered again.

"It is true," Trainor answered back snarlingly. He was like a rat fighting back venomously at the dogs running it to earth. It seemed to him that instead of answering accusations made now he was answering that wife of his who had left him. "It's all right. It's the custom." His eyes were blood-shot and a little froth collected at the corners of his mouth. "Everybody does it. It does no one any harm. It's just like a tip, do you see? Don't you understand? Why shouldn't I, just like every one else? Why shouldn't—"

"Has this ever happened before?" Dyer asked calmly. "Is this the first time?"

The purchasing agent caught his reply in time. He was giving himself away in his blind rage. He paused before replying. The owner cut in again.

"This has happened before," he said, and a rage passed over his features in a convulsive spasm. "This is a habitual thing."

"But no one can prove anything," Trainor pro-tested. "No one has anything on me. No one—"

"I don't need any proof," the owner said with a cold contempt that was worse than rage. "My eyes are proof enough. I can see it in your face."

He put his hand on the salesman's shoulder and turned toward the door of the inner office.

"Come with me, young man," he said. He looked at Trainor. "As for you," he continued, "I should put you in jail, but you're in jail already. No one will have anything to do with you. Get out of here within five minutes or I'll have you thrown out." And the door slammed.

He sat still at his desk for a few instants, his

mouth open and teeth stripped in that impotent, ugly snarl of his, his eyes staring blankly in consternation. What was wrong? His wife had gone —ah, well, to blazes with her, he swore savagely. And they had thrown him out of the office. They said he was a grafter. They could see it in his face.

He opened the drawer of his desk quickly and delved there until he found a discolored photograph—a group of ship's officers in white duck on the boat deck of a liner. He picked himself out among them, a thin, bronzed young man with a pleasant smile. He turned to a cupboard on the wall and looked at himself in a mirror there. He watched the snarling mouth, the small eyes, the pendulous and fat chin for a moment. "There's no difference," he said. "There's nothing to it."

He threw the picture down and grasped his hat, for the five minutes' warning was pricking him on subconsciously. He tried to walk through the outer office jauntily, but he broke down before a quarter of the space was covered and he finished in a quick shuffle. All eyes were fixed upon him, like mosquitoes tormenting him. He breathed when outside and pressed the elevator button. But somehow he was afraid to meet the elevator boy's eyes, and he tore down the fireproof stairway at a run.

"They never gave me a chance," he whined, in a cry that was more of a sob.

He stopped outside the door for a minute and thought bitterly. His wife had run away from him. She was living in sin, he phrased it, and she gave as excuse that he was a grafter. And his chief had thrown him out of doors because he said he was a grafter. And they would keep him from getting another job anywhere because they said he was a grafter.

The midday rush was on in Broad and Wall Streets. A vast mass of people milled to and fro like ripples on a whirlpool—stenographers, business men, telegraph messengers, office boys. A great golden sun threw white spaces and black shadows in the maze of streets. The curb brokers chanted in a sudden frenzy. The only calm thing in view was an office-boy eating his lunch on the steps of the Mint.

"Never gave me a chance." He shook his head bitterly.

The clergyman called the Bishop of Wall Street mounted his stand. He opened his book. In clear, sonorous tones he gave his text for the day:

"For what shall it profit a man, if he shall gain the whole world, and lose his own soul? Or what shall a man give in exchange for his soul?"

A spasm of angry contempt passed over Trainor's face.

"That kind of thing makes me sick!" he said. He turned down Wall Street aimlessly and walked toward the docks. At Pearl Street he stopped at the corner and looked at a saloon. He paused for a moment, and then with a shuffling grimace he pushed the swinging doors open and disappeared inside, as something might disappear when tossed overboard into the middle of an ocean.

VI

AND DID THOSE FEET—

I

B EFORE the war each of them had occupied a
position of solidity in his little world. Niblett was known to have been the best house-painter
in Middleford. Porky was supposed to have had
two butcher shops in the Midlands. Le Gros had
been a gamekeeper. Napper, the business man, had
been for a year at a public school. Denton, whom
the war had left without arms, had been chauffeur
to a great financier. Strangways was a master barber.

With the exception of Porky, who had been too
old for the war and whose ruin had been drink,
the war had, in their own phrase, done them in.
Only one had achieved profit out of it, and that
was Jerusalem, who had gained the Victoria Cross
for valor at Gallipoli. These were the main potentates of the County Club. They kept also, as a sort
of mascot, the boy who was called alternately Razor and Lightning. As Razor was the harmless
type of village idiot not uncommon in England, the

reason for his nickname is obvious. Still, Razor had his uses.

The caddie house was a sort of cellar near the professional's shop, with very little light in it, and warmed in the center by a huge iron stove, the fuel for which the caddies had to provide themselves. When the caddie-master, the professional's son, called a name, one of the club peeped through a spy hole to see what sort of prospect the player was. If he did not please the outer guard, no caddie was forthcoming, and the player had to take a small boy or carry his own clubs.

The caddie-master—and the professional himself, for the matter of that—had too much respect for the members of the County Club to force any of them to caddie. The professional had tried it once, but the night of that occurrence all the windows in his house had been broken and his fowl run denuded of life. Of course a fox may have taken his chickens; but there were strange stories of a midnight feasting on the Barley Downs, and on the morrow the County Club seemed replete and pleasant, and marvelously sympathetic. The professional, who was a Scotsman and therefore a philosopher, cut his losses and said no more.

But if the outer guard proclaimed that the visitor was all present and correct, the member of the club whose turn it was came out and stood blinking in the light. Niblett, the former house-painter, invariably caddied in a derby-hat, and smoked a clay pipe while caddying. Porky was the most picturesquely dressed of them all. He had trousers of tweed, an aged and greasy coat of the type called in America a Prince Albert, a double-breasted white waistcoat, and a stiff white shirt without a collar or tie. The frock coat was a reminder of the days when he was a capitalist and had two white and shining shops. His daughter, one of the town laundresses, used to fit him out on Sunday morning with shirt and waistcoat, but as the week went by they lost their glossiness, until by Saturday night they were a blue gray from drizzling rain, with brown splotches of beer lost through unsteadiness of hand or gesticulation in debate.

Napper, the business man, wore in all weathers, dark January or flaming June, an overcoat which had started by being black but was now a dreadful green. The sleeves of the overcoat hardly passed his elbows, but the skirts were down to his heels. The barber was a dapper little man, with his hair done in a wave. Denton, the former chauffeur, was always decently dressed, with his two armless sleeves pinned across his chest. The boy Razor looked as if a suit of reach-me-downs had been flung on him any way.

Jerusalem, the young V.C., always was clean

and sprightly, with the stilted walk of the horseman. Even in his face there was something of the
alert look of a horseman. He seemed to be listening silently to a trainer giving him instructions:
"Just breeze him over the last three hurdles, Joe,
and push him along up the stretch. If he pigs it,
hit him once, and no more." Jerusalem always
seemed to be listening to an invisible trainer giving him orders about an invisible horse. When he
walked he started away crisply, as if going to his
mount.

Le Gros, the gamekeeper, always caddied in
leggings, and his sleepy small green eyes missed
nothing. The County Club relied on him for their
weather forecast.

Of them all, good caddies, splendid judges of
distance and condition of ground, Jerusalem was
by far the best. He had won two open artisans'
meetings, and it was known that he could give the
pro one up and a beating on his own course, though
the pro was no mean player. His peculiar nickname was from his singing of Elgar's setting of
Blake's beautiful poem:

> And did those feet in ancient time
>   Walk upon England's mountains green?
> And was the Holy Lamb of God
>   On England's pleasant pastures seen?

And did the countenance divine
  Shine forth upon our clouded hills?
And was Jerusalem builded here
  Among those dark Satanic mills?

I will not cease from mental fight,
  Nor shall my sword sleep in my hand,
Till we have built Jerusalem
  In England's green and pleasant land.

The clients of the County Club, as the County Club called the players on the Middleford Links, considered Jerusalem to be a pure patriot, and were glad that England produced such men as this—men who could win the Victoria Cross, and were not pessimistic about their country, as so many old soldiers were. But the truth was that the County Club was as fine a collection of ruffians as the shire could boast, and that Jerusalem was their presiding spirit.

When the players had finished, or there were no players, the caddie house became a secret place. Young non-serious caddies were driven forth, and only an occasional visiting tramp was allowed to remain. Then a strange ritual took place. And the secrets that master caddies seek were not lost secrets.

They dealt mainly with the abstraction of iron clubs from bags and the proper losing of balls;

of prospects who would pay cheerfully for holing out in one on the blind seventeenth, where the boy Lightning lay in the bushes; of stealing dogs from old ladies by means of liver in the calf of the trousers, and of bringing them back for a reward of information as to racing jobs, heard from jockeys; of poaching; of new "pizzies," who are detectives; and "flags" who are policemen. And hushed talk, too, which would appal the members of the golf-club proper, of a day when the rich would not be rich and the poor poor, and you would not have to say "Sir" to every Tom, Dick and Harry with a golf-bag, and stand their impatience and—worst of all—applaud their womanish shots.

II

Each of the County Club had a client for whom he caddied regularly. Strangways, the barber, caddied for the parson, for Strangways had a strong religious strain in him; and though he would suffer any amount of cursing in the caddie house, yet for a client whose language was vehement he would not caddie at all. Le Gros carried for the local surgeon, in whose house he also cleaned boots and kitchen knives.

Porky attached himself to a former officer of the Brigade of Guards, broken through drink. Drink was never mentioned between them, but

that each knew a terrible land haunted by demons
was a tacit bond. Razor caddied for the low-
handicap man of the club, a solicitor's clerk, who
believed that the idiot boy brought him luck in
tournaments.

Napper, the business man, considered the sporting dentist his peculiar property. The business man
carried on an extensive correspondence as a tipster on races, following the fortunes of a couple
of small stables in the South of England. He had
been and was still on occasion a ticktack signaler
on the race-course. When a book-maker in the Silver Ring found himself overlaid against a horse,
he would bet on that horse with the big book-
maker at Tattersall's. He would give his bet to
the head of the ticktack men, and that would be
coded across to a runner in the Big Ring. Sometimes the Big Ring would ticktack across bets to
the Silver Ring, for though pounds and fifties and
hundreds are bet in Tattersall's, yet the Silver
Ring took in immense quantities in half-crowns
and half-sovereigns.

A ticktack man was paid well—three pounds a
day—but Napper's own failing was betting, and
as he owed so much to every book-maker, he could
hardly show his face on a course. So he had to
fall back on the profession of tipster. He took his
tipstering very, very seriously, claiming it was
strictly a business. There might be periods of bad

luck in it, as there might be in the building trade, but nevertheless, it was a business.

He lived in a small hotel, "for business men," out of which he was always being driven for lack of room rent. The other business men at the Shepherd and Flock were small peddlers, ruffians employed by mock auctioneers, two railroad porters and a drunken compositor in the Shire Gazette, who took precedence of the others as being in the literary business.

The armless chauffeur caddied for an American gentleman who had taken up residence in England, and who was not above picking his own club out of the bag, making his own tee and lifting his ball out of the tin when it succeeded in getting there. The fee for the round was one shilling and sixpence, which included cleaning the clubs, but the American gentleman always gave five shillings. When Denton came in with the clubs Jerusalem would take them from him with a sharp " 'Ere, you!" and clean them. Denton always wished to split his tip, but Jerusalem would have none of it. "Shut your fice! You've 'elped me. I 'elp you." The occasion on which the chauffeur helped the V.C. was when Jerusalem had got a "buckshee," or "free" motor-cycle. He had picked it up outside a pub in Putney, and Denton had helped him disguise it so its maker wouldn't know it. Denton also advised Jerusalem as to where he would find

purchasers for brand-new tires he found, which
he claimed to have fallen off the racks of motor-
cars.

Jerusalem himself had two regular clients, Lord
Kirkoswald, the captain of the club, and his daughter, the Honorable Ishbel Bruce.

III

Every member of the County Club knew about
the private affairs of the others—more so, perhaps, than the man whose affairs they were. They
knew, for instance, that Porky's daughter had two
professions, and they admired her for clinging to
that of laundress instead of giving up hard work
for the easier. They knew, too, that of the second
Porky was ignorant. The boy Razor had no private affairs except in his own mind, and they were
too dark and contorted to be of interest to sane
philosophical men.

Napper, the business man, might sit writing to
his clients from the caddie house: "Dere Friend,
Our run of bad luck has been impresendented but
I am confident that I have Discovert one wich will
come home spinning next time out."

His clients might smile at the misspelling, but
the County Club knew that Napper could spell if
he wanted to. They knew he had been for a year
at Eton before his old man had come a purler in

the Hooley business. They knew also he had been in a military prison during the last part of the war. That shambling gait, that dreadful mottled face, that lank gray hair, told their own story. A civilian or a regular officer might call Napper harsh names, but they had all been through hell, and they knew some could stand it and some couldn't. Napper couldn't—that was all. He might have let down his country, but he never let down a pal.

The drama in Denton's life they knew, though Denton didn't. The girl to whom he was engaged had insisted on marrying him in spite of the loss of his arms, and had taken a job as typist in a big garage. She was a bouncing, emotional girl, but she had become the garage man's mistress. The County Club didn't blame her. Yet she took care of Old Stumps. The man to be blamed was the garage man. There was a dog for you.

Niblett's Rabelaisian amours among the hop pickers and the pseudo gypsies on Epsom Downs were all too public for a private life. Le Gros, the gamekeeper, was known to have a warm bank account. He was paid well for the trout and hares and grouse he provided for the swank butcher. Still, he always had a pint for a pal.

And as to Jerusalem—every one knew that Jerusalem was Lord Kirkoswald's natural son. The old man himself knew it. The County Club knew it. But none ever mentioned it, gentlefolk being reticent.

IV

The Middleford Golf Links on the Barley Downs was of considerable antiquity. It dated from a time when people of means in knicker-bockers, red coats, caps too small for the modern school-boy, and spats, played with a gutty ball and wooden clubs faced with leather. Before that it had harbored a race-course, where stakes with equal value with those of Newmarket and of the Curragh of Kildare were offered. But now the race-course was only remembered by old sporting prints.

There was about the whole of the Barley Downs a feeling of failure. On one part of it was a great hollow chalk pit, which antiquarians in-sisted had been a stable of Roman cavalry, and that gave a feeling of loneliness, for even great Rome had failed here. The Barley Downs were common land, but the lord of the manor had cer-tain rights over it. The lord of the manor had given, with the consent of the House of Lords, the right to play over it to the golf-club. But the townspeople resented this, and there were con-tinual wrangles about it. The feeling about the golf-links was one of unrest and contention. A player could not drive a ball while any one was in the fairway. Whether any one had the right to play without paying was also moot.

The links themselves were ridiculously out of date. The holes had not been lengthened since the introduction of the elastic-wound ball. Great giants of golf-links were close by—Worplesden with its vast greens, Sunningdale with its terrain of gorse and heather. To the young school of hard hitters, each hole of Barley Downs was a drive, or drive and chip. At most a drive and pitch. But the greens were so small, the bunkers so contracted, the fairway at such an angle, the rough more like a matted jungle than rough, that the scratch golfer from a great links made a ridiculously poor score on it. The home players, with two staccato hacks, a bumpy running-up shot with some sort of iron, and a putt mean and effective as a bailiff's writ, got their par or bogey figures, while the visitor's golf-ball went to and fro, over and back over the green like a tennis-ball. Not a long course, y'know, but frightfully sporty.

The majority of the members of the Barley Downs were former civil servants in the colonies, former managers of small branch banks abroad, retired officers of worthy but socially unimportant regiments, people who had spent their lives in the service off somebody else and were now spending

their remaining days on a pittance, in England because it was home, in the South of England because
the climate was equable.

These men viewed with dismay the motor-
bicycles and silk dresses of what they called the
lower classes. Their remedy for labor troubles was
quick and drastic. They were certain that England
was going to the dogs, and equally certain that it
was the greatest power the world had ever seen,
or, for the matter of that, would ever see. They
voted conservative to a man, not being mentally
able to afford liberalism, and played bridge for
threepence a hundred. They were careful to explain to everybody that they used the Barley
Downs links while waiting to be elected to one of
the great clubs. The period of waiting for one
of them might be five or six years, and even then
it was a ten-to-one chance against their making
it. In their hearts they were satisfied with the
Barley Downs.

A second class of men belonging to the local
club were rich men who could easily make the
bigger clubs, but for whom the long carries, the
subtle bunkering, the greens large as a small garden, were too difficult. They complained bitterly
that these links were made for scratch men. Chief
of these latter was Lord Kirkoswald. Although
he had been a stone-mason in his youth and was a

Scotsman by birth—his native county was Ayrshire—yet he could only achieve less than mediocrity in the ancient Scottish game. Arms, no matter how powerful, if used in one's young manhood for short chopping blows, cannot get the long sweep of the good golfer or the timing of the crisp iron shot.

In his old age he had no amusement but golf, yachting not attracting him; and coming from a stock to whom horses are either drudges or wild animals, not methods of conveyance in a hunt, he did not take the interest in racing and breeding that many of his fellow peers and fellow millionaires did. All his life had been concentrated in hard work and in the recognition of opportunity. And now that hard work was no longer possible and opportunity no more to him than an autumn-driven leaf, only this baffling, maddening game of golf was left him.

The old man was tall and spare and fierce, and although three and sixty years of age, there was a great handsomeness about him. His eye was sea-colored, a blue nearly green. It looked at you from under white brows in a sort of baffled anger. You were never certain whether his hair was white from age or naturally the color of ripe corn. For all that he was a peer of the realm and a millionaire, yet there was a dreadful rage about him. He had found the world no granite set to be chipped and shaped. What he wanted no man knew, but whatever it was, he hadn't achieved it.

Two things gave away his plebeian birth—his accent, which was the harsh Scots of the Ayrshire workingman, not the speech of the Caledonian aristocrat, who loves the tongue of Allan Ramsay and James I and Drummond of Hawthornden, and despises English as a genteel language, but that dreadful Lowland rasp that is a physical defect, and a warning; also, his hands were splayed and clumsy, and no washing would take out that fine pattern of stone dust that labor had worked into the wrinkles of his hands as gold is worked into a Damascus blade.

Had Lord Kirkoswald been proud of these, or had they not mattered, they would have been no defect. But he despised any man who worked with his hands as being a fool. Also, he had never been in Scotland since early manhood. He had taken the name of the town of his birth merely to satisfy his vanity over the town for the slights he had received as a youth.

He had been quick to perceive that the Scotsman's road to fortune is the London road. He had argued that there must be profit in a man's work or none could hire him. Then if there were profit in one, what about fifty, a thousand, ten thousand? He arrived in London at a time when the gray, dignified city began to put on a portly abdomen of villas on the Surrey side, and finding a Scottish partner as shrewd if not as hard as himself, had launched into contracting.

One of his first great successes was around Middleford. Railways had begun to rob the shire capital of its importance as a commercial center, but railways were now making the dreamy southern town the haven of the head clerk and the small city man, fleeing from the fog and smoke of London to the downs. For this class Alexander Bruce, Esquire, Builder, flung up villas with astonishing cynicism.

It was during his first stay in Middleford that he met Jerusalem's mother. He was staying in a boarding-house kept by English people who for four generations had been coming down in the world, but about whom clung the sense of gentlefolk, like the faint scent of verbena. Jerusalem's mother Lord Kirkoswald could hardly remember, except that she was a very romantic woman. She had called him her gray, Scottish deerhound. Her love and her complaisance Kirkoswald had accepted like any other weakness of the boarding-house, like an extra egg at breakfast or a free fire in his bedroom. When she told him she was going to have a child, he was quite firm that he was not going to marry her or do anything for her.

She was a sensible woman; she made no scene.

Only her face drained of blood, like the face of a guillotined man. She said nothing; only looked at him. It took him some time to forget that face, but in the end he succeeded in forgetting it, as he succeeded in everything. She wanted romance and she had to pay for it in realism, just as in any economic dispensation. Later on he knew he had a son by her. She had become a dressmaker in Saturday Street, near Middleford. The local clergyman, seeing that she was in straits, and thinking of the child's future, had come to see the father at Westbourne, where he was building a new civic hall.

But Kirkoswald had been firm. He admitted no responsibility. He wouldn't have minded a five-pound note, but give people of that indigent class a finger and they'd take the whole of your hand. "No, no! How do I ken the bairn's mine? And besides, as yourself says often, no doubt the Laird will provide." He could not forbear a slap at the clergyman, who belonged to a class, he considered, of privileged paupers and loafers. But the clergyman did not fight back. He was silent a moment. "I think," he finished quietly—"I think the Lord will."

Three years later he married the daughter of a great brewer whom he met at Westbourne. She, too, was a very romantic woman. Her family were very much against the union, but as she was a rich woman in her own right, no parental interference discouraged Bruce. Her father was a shrewd business man and recognized in his son-in-law the elements of a great success. With her money and his own savings, he began a big career in building. He was bold and unscrupulous. Civic politics in England are quite as venal as anywhere else in the world, but they are managed with a dignity and reserve that chill the heart of the agitator. Moreover, ninety-nine out of a hundred agitators agitate only until bought in. The English mentality is somewhat slow, and when a fact is accomplished the ordinary tax-paying citizen accepts it with a fatalism which would make an Arab envious. He may grumble in his pub in the evenings, but he burnishes up on Sunday and goes to church and sings the lilting hymn:

> All things bright and beautiful,
>   All things great and small,
> All things wise and wonderful,
>   The Lord God made them all.

> The rich man in his castle,
>   The poor man at this gate,
> God made them high and lowly
>   And ordered their estate.

V

In the years before the German war England's prosperity was so universal that everybody became a Liberal. Labor was so well fed as to forget the dream of revolutions, and Toryism was lulled to a pleasant drowsiness by port and good will. A Celtic visionary, seizing his opportunity, pushed through in a constitutional manner a caste revolution as thorough as the bloody labor of France. Party politics, coinciding with his schemes of private gain, made Bruce so heavy a donor to the party as to earmark him for one of the new peerages, and when the war came, with the necessity for new barracks and camps, it not only made him a millionaire many times over but a great patriot. He became Lord Kirkoswald.

His wife died in the dark early days of the war, and his daughter Isabella—Ishbel now, in the old Scottish fashion—had grown up to be a grave and, as far as expression went, a beautiful girl. Kirkoswald bought a great place in Surrey from an impoverished family and decided to settle there. He might have married again, but he found himself, what with his own money, his wife's and father-in-law's money, beyond the necessity of an alliance for gain. He was too canny to marry a young woman for her beauty. He had had so much beauty free.

He found himself now in this position that he had all the money he wanted, and there was nothing he wanted to do with it. He found himself ennobled, but still an outsider to families whose nobility was recorded for half a hundred generations. Once he had achieved his peerage, he was quick to cut free from the party which had given it to him. But the caste system of England was not to be done away with legally. He could never quite understand the old crowd. Their women were outspoken as navvies, free and easy in their manner. But underneath this their virtue was like chilled steel.

One does not let Crusader Fathers down. A woman of another class who aped their verbal indiscretions would be only vulgar. As to the men, their reserve infuriated the old man. Their courtesy was terrible. An only beloved son died for his country. The father said nothing. His hair was whiter, but his back was straighter. An outsider could no more speak about it to the father than he could ask a Perfect Ashlar about the secrets of the craft.

Death duties and post-war conditions made bankrupt the old families. They accepted it quietly. They got up from England as a man of breeding might get up from the gambling-table where he had lost his last sovereign. A nod, a smile, a casual word, and they went off to Australia, to Canada, to South Africa, and settled down to farming, marrying some colonist's capable daughter, and the Garter and the Lyon and the Ulster King's-at-Arms knew them no more.

The daughter Ishbel had as kindly brown eyes as any one would wish to see, and a sweet mouth. You wouldn't call her fat, but too plump for beauty. She was the sort of woman of whom you say, "There's a lot in her." She had the quiet air of one accustomed to money. But a stickler for breeding would not waste two looks at her.

VI

The parish priest of Saturday Street was now a white-haired old parson whom a quarter of a century of work had worn to a shadow. His chaplaincy during the war had helped to age, so that he seemed more a man of seventy than of fifty. At any rate, there was very little left of the young high-church curate who had asked aid from the growing builder for an illegitimate child.

Yet once again he came to Kirkoswald on the same matter, but the difficulty this time was not that Kirkoswald might be ungenerous but that the boy might not receive. He told the millionaire how the boy had been brought up on charity, but had got employment with a small racing-stable in Berkshire. He had been too heavy for a jockey, but was, at the outbreak of the war, head man to the old Irish trainer. The stable brought off on the average a dozen good *coups* in the year, and what with stakes and money bet, and now and again a shrewd sale and a shrewd purchase, did quite well. It had never captured but one great classic, and that was the Stewards' Cup at Goodwood, but was always dangerous at Kempton and Windsor and the smaller races at Epsom.

On the outbreak of the war Jerusalem, as he was known even then, had enlisted in a cavalry regiment, was promptly dismounted and made a machine-gunner. He had been a very reliable soldier, but one to whom his officers did not take quite kindly. His demeanor and action were in accord with military regulations, but his cold blue eye was not. An officer could find nothing wrong with the man but that his look made him uncomfortable, and you can't quite barrack a man for that. All you can do is, when promotion opens, to give the rank to a more sympathetic if less able man.

At Gallipoli, Jerusalem had distinguished himself so valiantly as to be given the Victoria Cross. Under a demoniacal, hysterical spray of machine-guns he had crawled five hundred yards to where his company friend lay wounded, and began drag-

ging him in. When the enemy saw what he was doing, the Turkish officer gave the signal to cease
fire, and the Australian riflemen broke into cheer-
ing. His own battalion took it up. So daring and
gallant an episode bleak Gallipoli had never seen.

The incident was mentioned in despatches by
the brigadier and seized on by the papers. No
mention was made of the Turks' chivalrous ges-
ture, for propaganda must see to it that there is
nothing in the enemy to admire. Jerusalem got
his decoration "for valor," with that pension of
fifteen pounds a year considered an adequate return for bravery. The authorities considered it a
sound investment. It bucked up Berkshire.

The war over, Jerusalem had thought to re-
sume his occupation with the racing-stable. But
the racing-stable was gone. War had hit the sport
in England a blow from which it could never re-
cover, and only the great establishments, run as
efficiently and as heartlessly as department stores,
weathered it. The small stable had been patronized by minor owners who did not feel justified in
keeping their horses in the dark days. Now they
flung the animals on the market, and old Breen,
who had loved his string, lived with and for them,
brought them in himself.

Horses which you have known from yearlings,
which have run great-hearted races for you—the
Irish get fond of them. The buying in of them

voided a bank account which had never been of a notable fullness. He tried to carry on quietly, but could not. The civil cruelty of the war was greater than the military. He could go nowhere for help, because his point of view would not be sympathized with. Also, Irishmen were anything but popular in England. Forgetting the hundreds of thousands of that race with the home and with dominion forces, the country seemed only to remember with bitterness the pathetic revolt of Easter in '16.

One afternoon in December he discharged the few remaining employees and saw them off the training ground. Then loosing the horses out of stalls and boxes, he hanged himself with a stirrup leather, putting the iron in a saddle hook. A verdict of suicide while of unsound mind was brought in, his insanity being patent from the evidence of former employees, who stated that while the horses were fed and employees paid, the old man was starving. The horses were rounded up and sold, but as old Breen seemed to have no relatives and died intestate, the prices brought went to the crown.

When Jerusalem was demobilized he returned to Berkshire. Undoubtedly a place could have been found for him, in some capacity, at one of the neighboring stables, but as he said himself, he was fed up with Berkshire. He decided to return

to the southern whale-backed down, to Middleford, or to Saturday Street, dreaming in the holly
lanes. Before he went he paid a visit to the grave
of his old employer.

"No luck, guv'nor!" he said, standing at the
foot. " 'Ere!" he said, and looked around. He
found a small slate, blown from the church roof.
"Objection sustained," he muttered, and digging
in the grave whereabout the man's breast might
be, he buried a small bronze Maltese cross, marked
"For Valor."

VII

At Middleford he was offered various employment. Many men in comfortable circumstances offered him the position of valet. Many old ladies
wanted him to be their chauffeur, not knowing
that valor is a hundred-to-one shot in recklessness
which comes off. A cinema theater offered him the
position of doorman, with a comfortable wage,
the certainty of tips and a uniform of maroon and
gold stripes. But not only did he refuse these
offers but was incensed by them, which made pros-
perous folk more and more certain that the war
had spoiled the lower orders. When he went
caddying for a living he ceased to be an object of
admiration and became an object of distress.
When one thought of one's own relatives, fine
young officers, who had received no recognition,

and to whom the V.C. would have been so much value in the scramble for billets in a post-war world—disgraceful, some of them called it privately.

Between Lord Kirkoswald and himself there was a bond which both of them recognized and of which neither spoke. Once the old Scotsman had tried to mention it.

"I don't suppose you know—" the old man had begun, with many preliminary hees and haws.

"I knows my own business, which is caddying," Jerusalem had said, in such a cold and dangerous tone that the subject died conversationally and forever. He was, in a way, proud of the old man, and the old man proud of him. He bore no malice to the peer. The thing had occurred and was occurring so often in Jerusalem's world. Heroics were for the upper classes. You had no time for heroics if you had to work hard for your hot cup o' tea and your kipper. Besides—"I've done well enough wifout him, and"—he grinned—"he ain't done so well wifout me, if you know what I mean."

At times he felt a rough tenderness for the old man. In a very futile patch of the old man's bad golf, he would break in and take the club from his hands. " 'Ere, bring your left shoulder around, slow-like, and then, click, let your 'ands go out!" And he showed his own perfect shot. "Now try it. Slow back! Keep your eye on the ball!" But the old man would repeat his fault. "All right, 'ave it your own way!"

At times something Jerusalem would say would infuriate the old man, and no words would pass between them for weeks except such as would pass between a taciturn golfer and an uninterested caddie. For instance, the old man liked to talk of Gallipoli.

"It would have looked better, laddie," the old man thought and said, "if you had rescued your officer instead of an ordinar' private."

"I wouldn't walk from 'ere to that bunker on a sunny day to save an orficer," Jerusalem laughed. "But Bill, 'e was my chum."

"I tell you, man," Kirkoswald roared, "you're a red—a low, lousy, r-r-r-red!"

"Yes, I'm a red. So's everybody. Leastways everybody with guts, and no money, and no chance to make it."

"You've had every chance."

"I'm all right. Maybe I don't need money. When my 'at's on, my 'ead's covered. I see some folks 'as money isn't much use to."

"We'll go in from here," said Kirkoswald with outraged dignity. But he was back the next day, silent and bitter.

Once or twice their disagreements had been terrific. On one occasion the old man, in a flaring temper over some fancied slight from a country family, struck Jerusalem. Very quietly, Jerusalem broke the beautiful wooden clubs over his knee, smashed the irons and flung them, with the golf bag, into the pond, or rather puddle, at the thirteenth hole and walked in. The old man turned up four days later with a new golfing outfit. Jerusalem shouldered the clubs. Nothing was said of the disagreeable incident.

VIII

The bond between the old man and Jerusalem was weak. It held only by common agreement. But the bond between Jerusalem and his half sister was simple and compelling. Though they never spoke of it, though the barrier of illegitimacy was between them, each knew of the other's feeling. They were victims of the old man's iron selfishness. When they were on the golf-links, and Jerusalem not looking at her, her grave eyes were always on him, full of a burning sympathy. His eyes on her, when she was not looking, glowed with adoration.

A man fond of horses has always in him an unsullied pool of love for womankind. One's heart rises high at the thought of the colt that, grazing Tattenham Corner, unleashes a fire of speed uphill home to win the Derby stakes, but one's heart goes out to the filly that wins the Oaks. Great

beauties, great artists, die and are forgotten, but
the memory of Shotover, of Pretty Polly, of Sig-
norinetta, exists forever. No mother with child in
arms has, for many men, the heart-moving appeal
of a young dam with foal at foot.

Something of this love for a gallant filly was in
Jerusalem for his sister. Something, too, of a love
he once had for a young springer bitch which had
been closer to him than any human being in his
life. And with that, too, something tremendously
personal.

She never called him Jerusalem. She called him
Joe. To him she was always Miss Ishbel. The
"Miss" both of them recognized had to be. She
was never any good at golf, never would be. But
he did his best to make her game into some form.

"You see, Joe, I'm no good." It was very evi-
dent.

"Well, what does it matter?" he said.

Sometimes the club professional paired with the
secretary, and himself paired with his sister,
would play a four-ball match. For these occasions
Jerusalem lived. Once in this match Jerusalem
made the incredible score of sixty-three—thirty
out and thirty-three home—beating the pro's
record by five shots.

"I was lucky, dead lucky," Jerusalem said, and
his sister smiled, remembering the mounting tee
shots, the irons crisp as the crack of a whip, the

bold, confident putts. "Like I always was," added Jerusalem, and his sister's eyes filled suddenly with tears.

He could take only one present from her—a photograph. "It brings a bit of light into my rat hole," he told himself. This and the post cards she sent him from abroad were his chief treasures. Of her life he knew more than she thought, for he could imagine the dominating personality of the old man in a house.

Once he was able to help her. The old man had gone on a royal commission to South Africa to investigate the possibilities of emigration.

"The poverty of 'er 'eroes," Jerusalem explained it to the County Club, "is breaking old England's 'eart. So she wants us to go off where she won't see us. And she wants us to go off to a British possession, so's when the next war comes she can find the 'Earts of Oak. No work at 'ome. 'Oo the 'ell wants work? We done enough work in four years to last us the rest of our lives. That's where I stand, if you know what I mean."

The old man went off on his ungrateful task. But as the commission took no women along, Ishbel was sent for the winter to Mentone. She returned in February.

"Been to Monte Carlo too," Jerusalem opined. She smiled a little wryly. "Took it by the roots?"

She nodded. Back of her smile there was a little

apprehension. She flubbed a shot to the easy third green.

"Got to keep your head down. . . . Much?"

"Thousand."

"Francs?"

"Quid."

"Gaw!"

He was silent for a couple of holes, and then he burst out: "The way I figures is this—you had to let out a wrap and breeze along, if you know what I mean; boil over a bit like."

"I boiled the lid off, Joe."

"That roulette, I knows it," he said. "Give me horses and a form book, and I knows where I'm at. But thirty-six numbers, with zero thirty-seven! Thirty-seven starters, and all of them triers—that ain't gambling; that's murder. Still, you 'ad to do it," he told her. "I'm glad-like you went for it. We ain't the sort what picks up tuppences and threepences if you know what I mean."

At the end of the round he looked at her straight. "I don't suppose you've got fifty pounds loose?"

A pang went through her that the first time her brother had asked for money, she hadn't got it. She pulled from her finger a diamond ring that had been her mother's.

"Will that help, Joe?" she said.

"That'll do." He said no more. She didn't see

him until after the Lincolnshire. Every time she came up the boy Razor caddied for her. None of the caddies knew where he was. He had gone north, they said. Where was he? They didn't know. He was "staying private."

She got a message from Razor to come up to the golf-club for practice. Jerusalem was there with her bag. He said nothing until they were on the seventeenth green.

" 'Ere's the ring," he said. She looked at him in wonder. " 'Ere's a thousand pounds." And he handed her a vast bundle of treasury notes.

"What have you done, Joe?" Her face was white.

"I've 'urt a few bookies, if you know what I mean," he told her. "I put the ring up the spout and went up to the Lincoln and got in on a couple of open-and-shuts. The man wot rides the horses is the man wot knows most about it, and often wot a jockey knows 'e don't tell his guv'nor; 'e tells his pals. Then you use your head, if you understand."

He shut her speech off curtly. "If a man can't help his—his friend, if you know what I mean. See," he told her, "you can't let down before the old man."

She put her arms around his neck and kissed him.

"Gaw! If any one saw!"

"Let them see!" said Ishbel proudly.

IX

The old man returned from South Africa with the firm conviction that the empire was not the solid thing that government-inspired newspapers would have the public believe. Canada was notoriously chary of English emigration. Australia selfishly refused to take mill hands out of work, but required agricultural laborers and would take as many of these as England could supply. But then, England was not an agricultural country. And now South Africa, with its illimitable resources, wanted only men who would work like giants to make the Union another America. It refused very solidly to be the dumping ground for men whom the home country could not use. The sons of the Boers did not accept their fathers' defeat in that smiling modesty which is the essence of cricket. They loved their veldt, and though they could see that the Colonial Office might be of use to them, yet they could not see their home as an appanage of the colonial officer. If any one wished to come to South Africa, let him come, but let him bring some money with him to develop the resources of the Union. Unfortunately, the men whom England wished to send out were, by some curious circumstance, men who had no money at all.

The old man told his conclusions openly and

honestly, and found himself vastly unpopular. The
old man was a shrewd business man, but no politician. He should have known better. Small capital-
ists, who draw their living from Malayan rubber,
from Kimberley diamond fields, from Canadian
paper mills, mustn't be disturbed in their minds.
The old man heard himself being laughed at, saw
himself being avoided, and trembled with a cold,
speechless rage. He immediately conceived the
project of living in France, and spoke of it freely.
Among the details of his life, as he saw it, was a
French son-in-law for his daughter. He saw Ishbel
as Madame la Comtesse of some place or other,
and a little grandson who would be vicomte. The
origin of his title would not be looked into as
harshly as in England. The climate was good.

"How would you like to come to France, my
lad?" he asked Jerusalem.

"My pals as were in France got their bellyful."

"It's no' a bad country, and I'd look after you."

"You weren't thinking of racing horses?" Jerusalem looked at him.

"Na, na. Yon's a mug's game."

"What would I do in France?"

"There's caddying," said the old man, "and
lodging's cheap. There's a chance you might become professional at one of the resorts."

"Lodging's cheapest of all in hell," said Jerusalem. "And I'm a gambler. I don't want chances. I

want a sure thing. England owes us men a lot. I think we'll stay and collect."

"You'll collect a hanging, I'm thinking."

Jerusalem laughed. "Even the plute system won't hang a V.C. It looks too bad. That's where I hedged good."

The talk about France worried Jerusalem, for he had heard of the old man's plans about a French son-in-law. Kirkoswald's sanctimonious-looking butler was a heavy gambler in his way, and was about three evenings a week, from ten o'clock until closing time, a client of the Hand and Flower, whose owner had been connected with a stable in Salisbury and who still was one of the men used for a job. He could organize a raid to the extent of five hundred pounds on the starting-price offices. There most of the punting crowd collected in the back room. It was from the butler that Jerusalem got the word about the projected marriage.

"He'll do it too," the butler said. "Mark me, he'll make her."

"What about the other?"

"Him, he'll scratch. Well, you knows the old man. Ain't he had his own way up to now?"

" 'E 'as. And wot's 'e got?"

"He's got the brass, boy, and he's got the title."

" 'E ain't got as much as we 'ave. You've got content and I've got freedom."

"I ain't doing so badly, thank you," the butler smiled. "But what's this freedom?"

"If you ain't got it in your 'eart I can't tell you."

"The other" Jerusalem knew about was the last of a local county family—"so-called"—Napper, the business man, had explained, "because they 'ave to count their last ha'pennies." About the romance Jerusalem knew little, but he knew it existed; and because he felt it was his duty, had investigated the man. He was a lean young man from over the Hog's Back, where his family had farmed and bred horses for generations. But now there was practically nothing in farming, the big milk companies having smashed the small routes and London getting its food supplies from Ireland and Canada in cattle on the hoof, from the Channel Islands and Brittany in fruit and vegetables. The Bowmans had in the last generation bred half-Shire horses for haulage, but the advent of the motor-truck had killed that business. Young Bowman had served four years in the war and got the rank of major in the artillery. When he returned, the farm had all but died, and what profit he had made out of selling horses to the army disappeared in his attempt to put it on its feet again. He was now looking for a post as land agent. But these jobs were difficult to get.

Jerusalem went for information to ex-service

men around Farnham. "This 'ere Bowman—this major—'ow is 'e?"

"What do you mean, Jerusalem—'ow is 'e?"

"I mean, is 'e all right?"

" 'E's all right, 'e is. What I mean, 'e won't let you down, 'e won't. 'E ain't got nothing, but what I mean is, if 'e 'ad somethink, 'e'd still be all right."

"Then 'e's all right?"

" 'E's all right."

He saw in the distance one day young Bowman and his sister riding with the Chittingwold Hunt. He liked the way Bowman handled his aged mount. " 'E's got 'ands!" Jerusalem decided; but he clucked in pity at his sister's horsemanship. She had not that wise sense of balance which is essential for horsemanship, and she took the small fences clumsily. She'd look well in a little gig driving to the hunt, he thought. "She's a 'ouse-and-garden girl," he decided, "and there ain't many of them. 'Ell! Hunting is a man's business, and golfing is a man's business, but a 'ome is a woman's business. That girl needs a 'ome."

Often when she came to the links now there were dark circles under her eyes and a strained look about her mouth that told a story of weeping. Jerusalem felt he could help her in anything about money, but where the heart was concerned you were out, you couldn't help. That's a road every one must go on their own, he knew. One had to be philosophical about it. Still, it worried him, and the County Club knew he was worried.

"I've a good mind," he told Razor, "to give you an 'iding."

"What for?" the idiot grinned. "I ain't done nothink."

"No, you ain't done nothink. But if you was to do somethink, 'onest, I'd do you in, I would."

One day his sister came up to practise, she said, and with her was young Bowman. There was a redness to Ishbel's eyes that betokened a storm passed through. Bowman and Jerusalem looked at each other. They liked each other. Bowman's eyes were good eyes, true eyes, eyes that smiled all the time. He couldn't play golf, he told Jerusalem. Played a little polo, but those days were over. There was silence on the round.

Coming home, Ishbel looked at young Bowman. "Norman—" she said.

He turned to Jerusalem. "What I came up for was this: I'm off to New Zealand in about a month. Emigration and all that. I'm buying a place there—sheep and cattle and all that. Few horses too. Not a big place, y'know, but with a possibility."

Jerusalem looked at him.

"I just thought, in a way, I'd like some one with me. And"—he looked helpless for an instant—

"Miss Ishbel," he went on, "suggested you might come. We'd get along all right, I think. I'm— I'm not supposed to be a bad sort. But I'd like to have you. The cattlemen out there are a hard-bitten lot. I'd need help and all that. Now wait. This isn't a job. A quarter interest would be fair —what?"

They looked at Jerusalem silently.

"You're going alone?"

"Alone," Bowman answered. Ishbel turned away.

"It's 'andsome," Jerusalem told him. He flicked at a clump of heather with a putter. "It's uncommon 'andsome, if you know what I mean. You wouldn't think," he said, "of starting a little racing-stable here at 'ome. I could 'elp you there. There's money in it. I ain't a-wanting to 'ang medals on myself, but my old guv'nor, what taught me all I know, was getting old, and it was me readied Banshee for the Molyneux Cup—we done uncommon well there, with the stakes and what we got out of the ring. And when Damozel won the Breeders' Stakes at Sandown, I raised that filly by 'and. I did, and it was the job of the year. You wouldn't think of that?"

"I'd give my eye for the chance, but, Joe, it wouldn't run to it. You've got to have money and patience, and there's always the chance of your bad luck coming first, and all that."

"Well, major," Jerusalem said, "you don't want me to say offhand, do you?"

"Any time before I go, Joe. Tell you what. Come up to the farm some night and we'll go over it. I'll show you my plans."

Ishbel took him aside a minute. "I'd be happy if you were both out there. I don't suppose you've noticed anything, Joe, but I like him. And if you were with him, I know he'd be all right."

" 'E ain't gone yet," said Jerusalem.

x

He tackled the business man. "Napper," he said, "if I was to go into some night-school stable, d'you think I could talk sort of 'uman?"

"You can read, can't you?"

"I can read the papers."

"Write?"

"Write and figure, sort of. But my talk is rough-like. Not for the parlor, what I mean. 'Ell! I don't want to talk like an actor, but I don't want to be dropping me aitches like a drunk man drops his money."

"A night school would fix you. What's worrying you?"

"Thinking of settling down, maybe."

"I had a wife myself once, for a while," said

Napper, and his fat gray face trembled. "Oh, let good enough alone, Jerusalem."

A certain picture Jerusalem had in his head was obstinate in remaining there. Bowman and his sister married, a small racing stable of which he was private trainer. "Maybe we wouldn't make Dick Dawson and George Lambton look up!" The rolling stretch of Newbury and the hard pull of Ascot came into his eye, and his sister looking on while their horses bolted gamely along. "When she sees her own colors come first past the post!" He wouldn't worry then, he knew. Nobody need know he was her brother. " 'Ell, it ain't 'er fault, is it?" She would be happy. Bowman would be happy. He would be happy. The only person to be unhappy would be the old man.

Another alternative came into his mind, and he spoke of it to her when she came again to the golf-links. "Major Bowman," he said, " 'e's all right."

"I'm glad you know it, Joe."

"If 'e was going out to New Zealand, and I liked him, and I was a woman, I'd go too. I'd bolt if I 'ad to."

"I haven't the courage," she said with a wan smile. "And besides, I can't leave the old man; all he has is me."

"It's your life or his. His is over."

"I know, but I can't. It isn't in me to be brave like that."

"I know," Jerusalem said. "Something may turn up."

He knew she was dreaming, as women will, of a day when all things will come right. For all the money of the family, for all the ephemeral peerage, she was no more than a woman of an artisan, a girl standing by the door of a clean-swept cottage. She might dream of her lover in New Zealand and make a resolve to be true to him, and, indeed, she might be true in her heart, but what her father directed she would not have the courage to oppose. So one day, after a flood of silent and lonely tears, she would go to the altar with the man of her father's choice. The memory of the far-away lover would be like the odor of verbena in her life.

"She can't stay the course. 'Ell! A mare can't run against a railroad engine."

The old man's decision to go to France was hastened by the rumors of coming labor troubles. A general strike of the year before had been broken in less than two weeks by preparation and organization. A vast bitterness remained. The secret councils of action had decided that the next strike, local or general, would hurt. The government agents, posing as rabid communists, had discovered plots in which dynamite was the chief factor. The last strike had been smashed by transit. Well, you might get scabs to drive trains and amateurs to drive, but if the bridges were down and the roads mined, where were you? The government decided to move slowly.

The old man knew that if there were to be mad, dangerous work, somewhere near the center of it Jerusalem would be found. He decided to pump Jerusalem.

"I hear," he said, "there's to be dirty work in the future." He winked portentously. "Capital and labor."

"There's always been dirty work between capital and labor," Jerusalem added. "Without capital couldn't exist."

"I hear talk of dynamite," the old man queried; "bloody Fenian stuff."

"I take no interest in politics," said Jerusalem. And he moved on toward the ball, humming as he went:

> "Bring me my bow of burning gold!
>   Bring me my arrows of desire!
> Bring me my spear! Oh, clouds, unfold!
>   Bring me my chariot of fire!"

"Don't take the cleek," he said; "you know you can't use a cleek. Take the deep-faced spoon. Keep your eye on the ball."

"I will not cease from mental fight,
    Nor shall my sword sleep in my hand,
    Till we have built Jerusalem—"

"Oho!" old Kirkoswald laughed.

"In England's green and pleasant land."

"You've told me," said the old peer.

"I've told you nothing." Jerusalem looked at him blankly.

"You've told me enough to start my flittin' at once."

"Won't you be up again?"

"Och, aye!" said the old man. "I'll be up for ma last game."

XI

The old man was playing well, for him, smacking a nice little ball, dribbling it up with an iron, dropping an occasional good putt.

"Man, ye're nervous," he told the caddie. "You walk like a cat. You lay down the clubs as if they were the royal insignia. What's biting you?"

"Oh, nothing," said Jerusalem.

"I thought you wouldn't be up the day," said Kirkoswald. "You were late."

"I had to go to London this morning," Jerusalem told him.

"Politics, I'll be bound," Kirkoswald said shrewdly. "Ah, well! I'm through with those. I'm off to France to-morrow." He threw the club toward Jerusalem. Jerusalem caught it in mid-air. He breathed heavily, white for an instant.

"I shouldn't be surprised," said the old man, "if I did an eighty-five the day."

He went out in forty-two and got a five on the difficult tenth.

"I suppose Miss Ishbel will marry over there."

"Aye, and she'll do well. I shouldn't be surprised if she got a duke. What do you think of that?"

"Froggies are all right," said Jerusalem. "I was beside the First Regiment of the Legion at Salonica. They can fight. They breed good horses. But marriage! They've got queer ideas, Froggies. . . . No, take the jigger and play to the left."

"I suppose," sneered the old man, "you've got the English idea of marrying for love."

"Something-like," said Jerusalem. "She might have a fancy over here."

"Hoot!" said the old man. "I know my own affairs."

"And hers?"

"If I wasn't playing so well," said Kirkoswald, "I'd send you in for your impertinence."

"Don't take the pitcher," said Jerusalem.

"Take the mashie. Even if you top it, you'll get on."

He putted out and moved to the next tee.

"There's some one she has an interest in over here."

"I know that," said Kirkoswald, "but interest is as far as it will go."

Jerusalem looked at the ground a minute. "Women's hearts break," he said.

"Heigh, but you're sentimental!" cackled the old man. "I thought the Scots blood in you would have killed that."

The eyes of Jerusalem were light blue, cold as ice. "There's no Scots blood in me," he said quietly.

But the old man could be insulting too. His smile was dreadful. "Oh, aye," he said, as if he were remembering something, "I could easily have been fooled."

Though it was a coldish day, the face of Jerusalem was wet with perspiration. He wiped it carefully. At the sixteenth tee the old man was held up. A couple with caddies were before him. The old man fumed with impatience. He had three fives for an eighty-three.

The sixteenth at Barley Downs is a dog-leg hole. A hundred yards from the tee a wedge of oak wood comes out in a little copse, and this must be either cleared on the drive or avoided by hitting to the left. A sliced drive will find its way into a bunker from which the green cannot be seen, at such an inclination, from left to right, is the fairway. Jerusalem handed him his driver.

"I'll go ahead," he told the old man. He vanished around the promontory of oaks.

The old man drove with his nasty little click, keeping well to the left. "You'll be good," he decided, but when he got up, he found Jerusalem looking at the ball, a glimmer of white in the bunker.

"It took a bad kick," said Jerusalem. "It's not lying so bad, though," he considered. "A good shot will put you on the green." But he offered no club.

"You won't change your mind," Jerusalem said, "about France and Miss Ishbel?"

"It's my pride," said the old man, "that I never change my mind."

Jerusalem whipped the niblick out of the bag like a man whinging a rapier from a scabbard.

"I'll go ahead," he said, "and shout when they're off the green. Keep your eye on the ball."

He strode off to the left, standing on the shoulder of the down where he could see the green. The couple ahead had putted out and were standing marking a card.

"Fore!" he called. They looked up and waved him on, moving aside from the green. "All right!" Jerusalem called.

The old man's niblick twinkled in the air. The earth of the bunker burst suddenly into a fountain. It hung in the air like some strange dark flower. Then the monstrous bellow of the explosion rushed blindly across the downs.

XII

It seemed to Jerusalem as he walked down the High Street of Middleford that no more scrofulous spring had ever crept into England. Muddy roads and soggy land, and though May was here, there was in the air the feeling of snow. After the old man's death, due, it appeared from the coroner's remarks, to his having struck a communist dump of ammunition, the government had taken quick steps to quell disaffection. Though there had been a strike, all public opinion was against it, and the people who had taken part in it were worse off than before. Niblett, the painter, had been killed in it. An omnibus, which had charged into a party of strikers and their sympathizers, had run over him, breaking his back, and gone on.

The old County Club had broken up; there seemed to be a curse on it. Porky was under sentence of death for killing one of his daughter's friends with a meat ax. He had discovered that all her earnings had not come from laundering. A brilliant young advocate, prosecuting for the crown, had made it seem impossible for him not to have known. "Where did he get the money to get drunk? Drunkenness costs something nowadays!" So old Porky—old Porky was going to get his.

The armless chauffeur had gone into the river one cold night, and armless men cannot swim. He must have found out too. "What else could he do?" the ex-service men asked. "An armless man —'ell, 'e can't pull a trigger!" And so the garage proprietor went unscathed. Poor Napper, the business man, had had a run of good luck backing horses, and then starting as a bookie on Newmarket Heath, his luck had deserted him. He had welshed on the last day, but the crowd catching him, he had been badly mauled, and on top of that the magistrate had given him a year's hard labor as an old lag.

Strangways, the master barber, had been caught in a minor burglary and sent up. Even the boy Razor had not escaped. Some busybody had appealed to the authorities, and he was taken from the caddie house, where he was quite happy, and put in a home for the mentally deficient. Only one member of the club had gone up in the world, and that was the ex-gamekeeper, who had seduced and married the daughter of the owner of the Mainsail and Jib, and would inherit the business. " 'E's an artful one, 'e is. But 'e's a swine!"

Bowman had gone off to New Zealand, but was returning almost immediately, and Ishbel had followed him. They were to be married out there and spend the honeymoon on the return voyage to Tilbury. They had done their best to make Jerusalem come along, but he would have none of it.

"I'll be 'ere when you come back, all right," he had grinned. Besides, he was on a horse for the Derby. He had backed it on the winter books at a hundred and at sixty-six to one, and he considered it the easiest money he had ever touched. But a week before, at exercise, it had thrown the boy who was riding it, and escaping from the training grounds had run a mile until it collided with a motor-car and broken both forelegs. It had to be shot.

Jerusalem, with the old crowd gone, could no longer abide the caddie house. And even if he had been in the mood to accept menial occupation, he doubted if he could find it. His V.C. would not help him much. People were now sick of the war and didn't wish to be reminded of it.

As he walked down the High Street, he was sick of it all. The tragedy of the Derby outsider seemed to him the culminating point of bad.

"Thirteen hundred quid I stood to win on that moke, and now—*na poo!*" Spring was a mockery. The scant primroses, huddling beside dirty crusts of snow, fair turned your stummick! The drab population of the town, the hopeless faces, the cobblestones wet with mist, gave him the hump. And all he had was fourpence.

He picked up a brick from a pile where masons were building a new sixpenny-and-threepenny shop, and walking down, looked around. He stood in the middle of the street and looked at Fairweather the Spiritualist jeweler's shop. Old Honest but Rich, Fairweather was called. He sang:

"And did those feet in ancient time
    Walk upon England's mountains green?
And was the Holy Lamb of God
    On England's pleasant pastures seen?

" 'Ere, you bloody ghost-twister"—he spat on the brick—" 'ere's a manifestation for you.' He flung it like a Mills bomb. The crack of glass resounded through the street. O'Rourke, the big Irish policeman, who had been a Connaught Ranger, hurried up.

"Cripes, Jerusalem, what did you do that for?"

"I don't know, Jack. I'm fed up."

"You did it," O'Rourke prompted, "to protest against the prosperity of the middle classes."

"That's it."

"Then it's two months in the second division for you, me bye. Political prisoner; photygraph in th' paper."

"Gorn!"

" 'S truth. Ham and eggs for breakfast."

"Ham and eggs, Gaw!"

"Whist drives."

"Chance o' making expenses."

"Come on, Jerusalem me bye." A small crowd began to follow them. A thick yellow mist came rolling up from the river. Near by, an ex-service man groaned as he pushed along a barrel organ. He stopped and looked at the crowd with optimism, and turning the handle with his one hand, his other sleeve being empty, began to grind out the strains of a popular hymn: "There's a land that is fairer than day."

VII

THE THING CALLED GRATITUDE

NOWHERE, in those authorities on political economy, so far as I can remember, will you find a disquisition on commercialized gambling. You will find an interminable list of things which can happen to money, from the payment of public debts to the loss by the wear on milled edges, but gambling as a business is dismissed among the vices. And yet it has its curves of probability; it is governed by the laws of permutation and combination; and in the hands of professionals it produces a gain as infallible as the gain on legitimate business skilfully handled.

I imagine that Meyer Fine knew and worked on that principle every day of his life until four years before that cracking automatic shot in the spine hurled him into the next world he so much feared.

"If there weren't money in this, do you think I'd be in it?" he used to say.

And if he looked at you with that shrewd glance he sometimes used, with his black, beady, somewhat reptilian eyes flashing sideways above the flattened beak of his nose, you would have believed it. There

have always been two opinions about Meyer Fine
—the one that he was a shrewd, shifty, grasping,
merciless vampire; the other that he was a square
and honest sportsman. I knew Meyer Fine. I knew
the many times he was a level sportsman. I liked
Meyer Fine, but I know of times when he was the
other thing.

Now that he is dead and gone, and cannot con-
tradict them, there are men in New York who will
tell you they knew him in his youth, when he was
a newsboy on Broome Street, and they will tell
you how he scrimped and saved until he bought a
share in a shoe-black privilege in a barber-shop on
Third Avenue.

"And he did the Greek down there, too. Can you
get that? Doing a Greek?" Rather a notable
achievement, I must admit.

From that the trail runs to the partnership he
held with Irwin Eckstein in a series of stuss games
along the East Side. "Gee, he was lucky!" they will
tell you. "No wonder he got his"—referring to the
superstition that a man who meets death violently
is notably fortunate in things of chance. "He got
in then with a bunch playing poker and bridge up
and down the coastwise lines, from New York to
Savannah and Jacksonville and New Orleans. He
didn't play, but he found out which passengers had
money and were good sports. That was his job.
He had his nerve with him. Gee! He'd ask a man

how much he made a week and how much he had
on him, and he'd get away with it. They'd tell him.
They'd tell him right out. If they didn't they'd
give him a line on it somehow—and then he'd put
the gang wise. Good night, sucker! He played the
races down South for a while. Then he came to
New York and set up for himself—a swell joint on
Thirty-ninth Street between Fifth and Sixth Av-
enues. There's many a roll was lost there—judges
and everything. And never a pinch made. He was
in all right, I guess!"

And they were right, too, for judges came to that
silent house in Thirty-ninth Street—Congressmen,
lawyers; business men who in the placid waters of
success yearned for one more gallant fight in the
troubled waters of fortune, and got a thrill behind
the close-barred doors of Meyer Fine. Came a few
divines also, if a former Police Commissioner is to
be believed. Within, the rattle of honest business
without shut off as by the walls of a vault, the
roulette wheel whirred and clicked; the poker chips
rattled; the dice thrummed. Beneath a Bouguereau
picture solid citizens played bridge at twenty-five
cents a point, while immaculate stewards moved to
and fro with wine-cups, with fruit and sandwiches.
And the play went on from evening until dawn, and
sometimes from dawn until evening, and until dawn
again.

On all sides he was protected, by the vice of the

high men who patronized him, by the blindness of the police whom he had corrupted. Very boldly he used to stand at Forty-second Street and Broadway, on sunny afternoons, watching the motley crowd go north and south, go east and west. A stocky figure of a man, of average height, dressed well in the current fashion of Broadway, with here and there a touch that hinted of Oriental ostentation—a large and flashing stick-pin, large and flashing rings, a cravat not loud but not correct.

Occasionally, at some slight incident of the street —a fat man running grotesquely to catch a car, a woman dressed ridiculously and unaware of it, the smart trick of some gutter urchin—the saturnine look would leave his face, and on it would beam a smile like a trusting child's, a thing to evoke sympathy in all about him, a thing to love him for. And then in an instant it would disappear again. . . .

You can, if you will cast your mind back a few short years, remember Minna Fenton. You will remember her as the wife of one of the biggest scoundrels unhanged—a tragical figure, whom New York took to its sentimental bosom when James Fenton died, shot in a bar-room quarrel, leaving her penniless. You will remember her brief sojourn on the vaudeville stage, where she sang a few numbers, "Carry Me Back to Old Virginny" and the like, in a mediocre, rather thin voice. New

York did not want to hear her sing—there are many decent singers at the Opera House—but it wanted to see her. It could have gone on looking at her for years, reckless of her meager attainments.

But behind those green eyes and those creamy regular features, behind that abundant bosom and plump, somewhat languorous figure, there was a spirit in Minna Fenton combined of whalebone and of steel, a great blazing pride and a hunger in her for a love that would be worthy of it. She wanted to love magnificently the man who she felt could be husband and mate and master of her.

Casually and unwittingly Meyer Fine went to see Minna Fenton, as men go to the biggest things in their lives. He saw that face on the stage, as fair and as forceful as the one for which Troy went mad. There and then he fell in love with Minna Fenton, not sentimentally, not passionately as we understand the word in these days, but terribly, intolerably. There is something about these Orientals that we of the West cannot understand, and that is their torrid, lightning love-affairs. A glimpse of a face seen through a veil, and they will droop and well-nigh die for love of it—a remnant of the ancient days in torrid, tropical lands. Consider David. Consider Solomon. Consider Amnon, and Tamar, David's daughter. And Meyer Fine was Oriental, in spite of his New York birth, the centuries his family had spent in the Ghetto of Kazan—Oriental, heart and body, mind and soul.

He was introduced to her by John Necker, sportsman and square man. He asked her to lunch with him at Delmonico's.

"Your friend Fine has asked me to lunch," she told the Nevada sportsman.

"Meyer's all right!" was his succinct answer. She went.

There was something about the man that intrigued her—his powerful silence, his meticulous if florid courtesy; his naïve way of bringing great bunches of flowers to her; his embarrassment in her presence, and never a word of love.

She saw strength behind that grim and sinister countenance, and sympathetically, as every one did, she smiled in accord with that cherubic, golden smile of his. There is in women a great sympathy for men who are without the law. A common gambler, the statutes would call Meyer Fine, but in him she saw what she might have seen in a great filibuster or a noted romantic rebel. In danger all the time, he seemed, and still he abode in it warily. The man troubled her. She saw in him great tenderness and she thought him a big, strong figure. If he had made love to her all would have been over. But he never did. He, with his gambler's sixth sense, felt what she thought him to be, as he could feel what his opponent was thinking of in a poker bluff.

Came the night he proposed to her. It was at dinner at Delmonico's. A little silence, and he leaned across the table.

"Do you think you could marry me?" he asked her bluntly, as though calling a hand. He had been through hell thinking about her, but it never showed in his impassive face.

"I don't know," she said, embarrassed. She fingered a glass nervously.

"Perhaps it's on account of my race?" he said cleverly. "I've been hurt a lot about that."

She looked up at him suddenly. Her eyes were flashing through a faint haze of tears.

"Oh, how could you think that of me?" she cried aloud. "How could you!"

And so they were married, and she went to live with him very quietly in the upper part of the saturnine house in Thirty-ninth Street. He had furnished it for her in a way that can only be described as gorgeous. She went out very little. Quietly she lived there behind doors through which there never came the whirl and the clatter and the hum of things below stairs. She had found her ideal, and she was satisfied, and Meyer Fine acted up to that ideal harder than any mummer on the stage.

There was one question she put to him when she first came home.

"Myer," she asked him solemnly, "downstairs— is it on the square?"

"It is," he lied magnificently. There was a cunning electric device connected with the roulette wheel. His faro dealer was an expert. But thereafter on the level it was.

Big and powerful and generous, he walked through her life like some hero in a romantic book.

At times she would look at him with haggard eyes.

"If some day some one should kill you!" she would speak her fear aloud. "Or an accident should happen!"

"Why, it's all in the game, sweetheart," he told her. "Death, after all—" He spoke lightly.

And there Meyer Fine lied. One thing had haunted his life, and that was the fear of death. When an impressionable boy, he had seen his father die, a horrible choking and contortion of the body and strange blue features. He had seen a little brother of his crushed by a mail-wagon. Those things had kept at him all his days. Beyond Death he saw nothing, but the physical fact of it was torture. There is a name for it among medical men— a terrible disease. To think that one day up and down the gaudy streets men and women should pass laughing; the sun should shine in the sky and flowers bloom; while he would be lying in the cold earth or in some lonely vault in a place apart, in a wilderness of gray stones and clipped and mournful trees—a little earth, a little liquid, a great corruption. . . .

At the thought of that his face would go white and his hands shake and his eyes start out beneath perspiring brows. A moan of terror would break from his lips if he were alone. He would creep against the wall with his hands before his face. . . .

It was old man Hennessy, the railroad magnate, who decided to ruin Meyer Fine. Young Patrick Hennessy had gambled away his fortune and prospects in the house, and when he had done that thoroughly he neatly shot himself. There was no blame to Meyer Fine beyond giving him the opportunity, and that he could have had somewhere else. The game had been square, according to plumb and level. But old Hennessy was pardonably relentless, and old Hennessy's word went. The grand jury would act if he wanted it. He could, if it were necessary, make a holocaust of all New York. The only thing was to get reliable evidence.

It was on a Saturday night, about eleven, when Reynolds, the big politician, rushed up to Fine.

"Who the dickens let that man in—the man just gone—with the red camellia?"

"Oh, he's all right," Fine nodded. "He brought a card that was all right."

"You blasted idiot! Don't you know who that man was? That was Lovelace, the big operative from the Sheldon Bureau."

About the pair a crowd grouped quickly. There

were fifty immaculate reputations in that room which police-court evidence would ruin—there was the head of a great banking-house, a city executive, a score of society men, a candidate for governor. Meyer Fine wiped his forehead. The group murmured like excited bees.

"We've got to stop him!" Reynolds snapped. He rushed out.

A half-hour later Lovelace of the Sheldon Bureau was stopped very effectively. At the door of his Harlem apartment a whirling taxi drew up slowly as he came from the subway. Through the window of the car Lovelace was plugged neatly with two bullets in the head. . . .

Minna clung to Meyer in terror on hearing of the killing. She recoiled an instant, with a look of horror.

"Did you send those gangsters to get the man?" she demanded.

He told her no.

"But you're in danger. They'll indict you with the rest?"

He nodded.

"They may send you to the chair. Can't you get out of it—tell them who really did it?"

"Squeal?" He laughed grimly.

"But the chair! The electric chair! They may send you to it."

"Let them!" he answered calmly, although his

mind and soul were screaming with terror at the thought of the grim dawn, the dread procession, the horrible harness of leather and steel. "It's all in the game!"

She watched him for an instant in mute awe, and then she drew herself up proudly as a queen might when her royal husband has gone royally to the dreadful execution block, and in her heart a great pride thrummed, like the thrumming of majestic harps.

"My man!" she told herself. "My man!"

A big police official had brought John Lardner to Meyer Fine.

"The warden thinks that this bird has had a bum deal up till now," he said, talking of a famous reform executive of Sing Sing. "He's thirty now, and been in jail most of his life, but it's been for sneak-thieving. I don't think he could work. He's too scared. Nobody will give him a chance, and I don't blame them. Look at him." He pointed to the shivering figure. "Well, what about it, Meyer?"

"Oh, I'll take a chance with him," Fine laughed.

And so John Lardner became valet to Meyer Fine—a lean, cringing, nerve-broken lad, with something of the ship's steward in his deft facility for things, insignificant-faced, with a deprecating mouth, with eyebrows and eyelashes nearly invisible, and in his china-blue eyes the look of a kicked dog. An ordinary person would have nothing to do with the man, although he would pity him, but Meyer Fine did not mind.

"There's nothing to be scared of," Fine more than once reminded him. "You're all right here."

And John would nod his head in dumb recognition, and follow the big gambler with dumb, adoring eyes.

There is a sense of spiritual deformity about a valet. He has no personality. He is more invisible than a postman, more negligible than a waiter. From his master's clothes he draws a portion of his master's personality; from his trinkets a share of his foibles.

A queer affinity comes between them, as between a body and its shadow. He senses a man's mood more quickly than a wife would. Uncanny; somehow immodest!

More than ever any valet understood the feelings of a master, I think, his man John understood Meyer Fine. He, of all the world only, saw the inside of the big heroic person that strutted before his wife Minna, like some romantic figure in an antique tale. He alone saw the haunting horror that transfigured the man's face at a passing funeral, an obituary in a paper, a bunch of white lilies. He quivered and cringed in vicarious terror.

He wanted nothing for himself, nothing. He was content to stay within, polishing shoes, pressing trousers, putting studs in shirts. The only time he went out was when Fine sent him on an errand, and he would return shaking at the sight of the police-man in the street. Like some gray ghost he haunted Fine's rooms until even his friends protested.

"Why the blazes don't you let that lugubrious spaniel go," Richards once asked Fine—he didn't notice that John was right behind him—"and get a decent Jap?"

"Oh, that would never do," Fine laughed. He turned around to the valet. "We're too old friends, John and I!"

Toward Minna Fine the valet felt a queer sense of awe, as an attendant of a priest might toward the goddess of the priest's worship.

Vaguely, and yet in another sense acutely too, he understood what this glorious woman meant in Fine's life.

It was John who conducted Letherbridge, the keen hatchet-faced District Attorney to Fine's rooms one significant night. It was he who heard the official's parting words.

"I don't know how far you're implicated, but implicated you are. There were you, Reynolds, Big Kennedy, and Murray Richards. You sent down to Barney's for those two gunmen, and they did the job. There's no use trying to get the others unless through you. You've got to come through, or be the goat—and that means the chair. I expect your decision to-morrow night."

All night long the valet had heard Fine moaning and tossing. To him in the morning, haggard-eyed and terror-stricken, he had brought the coffee and rolls. Fine looked at him.

"Has Mrs. Fine come back yet?" he asked.

His wife had gone to spend a few days in Washington with a sister there. She had written she might come back that night.

"I'll see, sir," John answered. She had not.

All day long, through minutes that were like hours, through hours that were like weeks, he watched Fine go through an agony of fear. At times he would rush to his wife's bedroom and come out again, holding little things in his hands, a ribbon, a stocking, a trinket. Through keyholes, through curtains, by every expedient, the valet kept watch over him. At times he could hear him sob; choke the sobbing by closing his teeth on his hand; cry aloud.

"Minna! Minna! Minna!" he would cry.

Then for a minute he would throw up his head defiantly. He would be true to her ideal of him. The greatest thing in his life would end unspoiled.

"No!" he would snarl. "I won't! I won't!"

And then would come clear to his mind and imagination what his refusal meant; the march past the condemned men's cells, who were crying aloud

in terror; the rabbi's voice shaking and quavering
as he read; the buckling into the chair; the wan
faces of the witnesses; the electrician's rubber
gloves. . . . His hand would go out to the telephone, and then the trinket or the ribbon or the
glove would catch his eye, and again would come
agony.

All this the valet knew and understood, understood as though it were plain on a written page, or
thrown vividly on a cinema screen. He felt the great
love in the man that would be defiled and splotched
by this great cowardice. He understood the terror
of the man before the thought of death. Outside he
moaned in unison with him within.

At four he heard a cessation of the restless pacing and the muffled moans. He pushed the door a
little ajar. Fine was sitting at his desk, fumbling
with his revolver.

"It's the only way out!" he said aloud. "The
only way!"

He put the muzzle to his mouth and the barrel
rattled against his teeth, so great his terror was.
An instant later he flung it down.

"I haven't got the nerve," he sobbed. "God help
me! I haven't got the nerve!"

He leaned forward on the desk, his shoulders
shaking. The valet rapped on the door and
walked in.

"What is it?" Fine asked.

The valet walked toward him.

"Shall I lay out your dinner things, sir?" he asked.

"No! Don't mind!" Fine told him, his face averted.

Very firmly the man picked up the discarded revolver, firmly aimed it. Shots rang out like the breaking of small electric globes.

"So you bumped your boss off, eh?" Girondo, the detective who had made the arrest, was giving an unofficial third degree to the valet. "You bumped him off. You shot him in the back when he wasn't looking. What did you do that for?" he snarled.

"I never liked him," said the valet sullenly.

"He took you in when nobody would have you. He treated you fine. You wanted for nothing while you was with him. Blast you! You cell toad, did you never hear of a thing called gratitude?" He smashed him viciously across the face. . . .

VIII

THE SOUND OF MILLSTONES

I

FOR five years now he had been looking through the dingy pawnshop window into Second Avenue, and of that time there had not been one month, one week, one day even, but he had been gnawed by a terrible, relentless apathy.

Outside, the avenue ran past the shop southward in a boiling rapid of life. Overhead the elevated clanged by in a continuous rolling, like drums. The line of street hawkers on the curb opposite, with their push-carts loaded with vegetables, with socks, with bed and bedding; the slatternly women and dingy men who swarmed about them, like flies swarming about refuse; the grimy children stumbling against the legs of passers-by; the stuffy look of old furniture places and delicatessen shops; the garish red and white parasols flaunting above stores —all this left an evil sight in his eyes, as there might be as evil taste in his mouth after drinking polluted water.

About the shop itself there was something of a

dark and shameful intimacy that appalled him—
its dim light; its booths for the reception of customers of the better class; its heavy, shining safe;
its scales for weighing wedding-rings and jewelry;
and worst of all, its license, signed and counter-
signed by the city officials, that took away from the
store its character of being a business and hinted at
it being a base predatory thing, having to pay a
manner of blackmail for its very existence.

No matter how he turned, something crossed his
sight that shamed him. There in the window were
the unredeemed pledges offered for sale; women's
dresses, relics of ancient glorious days, pledged
with a pang of pride and lost in agony; blankets
that some one had bought to keep warm of nights
and now must go cold without; three score wedding-
rings thrust carelessly on a stick; a violin worn
where the chin and cheek had cuddled, so lovingly
and often had its owner played it; a heap of children's silver presents thrown together carelessly
and blackening with tarnish—none of these things
were, to his eyes, the stock of legitimate commerce.
They were shreds of souls, layed and torn off in
moments of dark tragedy.

A steady stream of customers flowed in and out
of his place. An occasional Italian, a few Poles and
Magyars, some of his own race, though these were
few. For the most part they were the Russian folks
of the vicinity—Little Russians, Esthonians, Cour-

landers and Finns, whitish haired, heavily-built, stolid, with dumb eyes. They brought in their clothes, their tools, their little jewelry; and because Ben Harris was generous with loans, was ready to grant extensions of time, and was not over-strict about interest, they liked him. Their stolid eyes would light up with a touch of appreciation and they would nod heavily and say: "Ben Harris! That's one good Jew. If they were all like him in Russia there would be no trouble; no pogroms; no Black Hundreds. Ben is all right."

But he could no longer feel even the thrill of helping out these people, of being as generous as possible toward them. Apathy was eating at his mind and heart as a disease might eat away the body.

Five years now, since he had come out of school, he had been telling his father he wanted to do something in the country, farming preferably. His father had listened carefully, trying to understand.

"But you can't make a good living in the country," old Aaron Harris had told him. "The farmers complain. There isn't anything. Why not business? Why not? Why not?"

One could understand old Aaron Harris saying that, because he was a good and religious man. Following his creed, he was as strict as a Karaite, and no Sabbath of his adult age had passed without his baring his soul in the synagogue. There, hooded, in his striped robe of white and black, he was a prophet and a great man among his race. And because of that, in Kiev, where he had lived as a young man, he had been almost martyred by his race's enemies. He had been forced to huckster and bargain, to let no opportunity for making a penny go by, in order that he might have some single thing solid beneath him—the solidity of money. For him two things existed—the dark mystery of religion and the stark fact of commerce. For him there was no borderland of subtleties, no obscure human tragedies. He stood up with his strong hooked nose and his long, strong, iron-black beard, and he faced the mystery of the next world and the fact of this boldly and courageously.

"For why?" he asked again about the country. "We're not farming people. We're business people."

"Not always," his son answered him.

"But why?" old Aaron persisted. "Look at your brothers, how well they are doing! Stephen with his dentistry business. And look at Sam. He has two barber-shops and three bootblack stands and the hat-checking in five hotels. And you—you've this business, and will have it when I'm gone. Fine business too. Good situation."

He couldn't tell the old man he didn't want the shop. The father was proud of the shop, which he

had built up against a terrible struggle with poverty. But his mother understood. She had come
from one of the rural communities in the Crimea,
and there was a strain of Tartar blood in her. One
saw that from the marked slant to her eyes and her
high cheek bones. To her he would speak of the
country.

"Fine horses and fine dogs!" she would breathe
in ecstatic memory. "Blue grass and the sun on it,
and trees! Ay, and the lapping of the water on the
Black Sea. I know! I know!"

After her speaking like that, he would go over
to Bryant Park, and the look of the grass and the
trees with the birds clamoring in them would
awaken a terrible nostalgia in his heart.

Perhaps it was the strain the mother had be-
queathed him that awoke in him the burning desire
for wide free spaces and clean air. Perhaps it was
nothing but the ancient country spirit in him that
his people had possessed before the Temple walls
had crumbled and the Babylonian king had driven
them into narrow ghettos and decaying cities. But
whatever it was, sitting in that dim city park with
Second Avenue behind him, grim and sordid, and
Third Avenue before him, lethargic and deserted,
he could see as on a biograph screen visions no
foundation for which had ever entered his life: the
free movements of horses and the eager jumping of

dogs, grass bending before the wind, and the wind from the sea, salt, stinging, turbulent. The visions would trouble him.

He would return home after an hour of that and his mother would talk to him.

"What is it?" she would ask. "What is it, little dove?"

"I want to go away," he would tell her. "I'm sick of the city. I'm sick of the pawnshop. If I can, I want to work somewhere away."

She would look at him carefully, at his slim, strong figure, heavy about the shoulders and the hips; at his broad, blunt hands covered with swarthy hair. From those she would glance into his face, handsome in its dark heavy way, with its strong nose and strong chin and big black eyes with earnestness in them. She would nod her head with pride.

"No one in the country could work like you," she would say. "You are strong and you want to. There is no one as fitted."

"And I would get on with the people, little mother?" he would ask eagerly.

"Why shouldn't you?" she would answer him evasively, but there would be a quick little shadow of fear in her eyes.

"But the old man!" he would object to himself. He knew how it would hurt the old pawnbroker for his son to leave him, and he shrank from it.

"Yes, the old man!" the mother would say with a touch of pathetic tenderness. There was too much fine loyalty in her to be true to her son at the expense of her husband. No, she would not counsel. If the son were to do anything, he should do it himself.

Yes, the old man was the obstacle, he thought to himself. If it hadn't been for the fear of hurting the old man, he would have been in the country three years ago. But in the intervals of attending customers in the pawnshop, of appraising their pledges, of writing out pawn-tickets and drying them in sand, and of handing across the counter greasy and torn green bills, he would think of how he might accomplish his dream. There was always in his mind the memory of the night he had met Hosea Tucker, the Long Island farmer, at the restaurant of the Metropole. The farmer was with Regan, one of the bosses of the district. They had been to school together. Regan called the young pawnbroker over and introduced him. Regan had the habit of promiscuous introductions.

"Ben," he announced, "meet my friend, Mr. Tucker. He's a farmer."

Harris glanced shrewdly at the farmer's face. He was a short, squat man, with a reddish-brown beard, reddish-brown hair, and a sly, uncertain look in his eyes. There was a pretentiousness of dress about him, as though he wished to show how much at home he was in a city restaurant, that jarred on the pawnbroker.

"I've just been telling Regan here," the farmer said a little loudly, "that I don't understand why a lot of you young city fellows don't come out and farm. Why, look at you, as sturdily built as any countryman—and more so, I tell you, more so. Aren't you ashamed to spend your life in a store?"

"I am," Harris answered with a smile.

"Why wouldn't you come out and work on a farm?"

"I would." Harris's smile became a trifle longing.

"If you would, you've come to the right man. I'd call your bluff. Come out and work for me." He banged the table.

"You mightn't want me." Harris's smile became a little sardonic.

"What's wrong with you?" The farmer raised his head and looked at him with a sort of elder's contempt. "I don't see anything wrong with you."

"There's nothing wrong with me," the pawnbroker smiled on, "but I'm a Jew."

"Look you here"—the farmer waved a fat hand: "That doesn't cut any ice with me. I'm not prejudiced about that. No, sir; I'm free from that kind of thing. A man's a man in my eyes. Why, do you know"—he raised his voice—"do you know that I've had rabbis come out and preach in our church? Yes, sir! Rabbis! That's how prejudiced I am."

"Well, maybe I'll take you up on that," Harris told him.

And over and over again as he sat in the seat by the window he pictured to himself what life out there would be like. Would the man keep his promise? Not a trustworthy man, Harris judged, but hardly a man to go back on a boast. Vanity would hold him to his bond. Perhaps some day—

A phrase out of Isaiah, that fierce, terrible old man, came to him once or twice as he dreamed there. Some prophecy of the fall of Zion, that there would be lacking the voice of mirth and the voice of gladness, and there would be lacking the sound of millstones and the light of the candle. How true that had become, he thought with a shade of bitterness. The sound of millstones! And that brought into his mind the vision of corn sprouting green on the blue Asian hills, of its turning little by little into a faint blue and then ripening goldenly. He could hear the whish of the sickle as it was cut, and the thrumming of flails at the threshing; the dull rumble of millstones as it was ground for baking, a loud and harshly harmonious sound that typified the being and end of all agriculture. That was gone. And gone, too, was the mellow golden glint from the tents and houses in the night-time. The old habits and occupations had gone from his people.

No longer were they shepherds in the hills, no longer tillers of the land, no longer owners of fleet horses and sleek kine. Now they tended sordid shops, like this shop of his, this bargaining place for tragedy, and from the hills and valleys of Beulah land they had swarmed into the sordid cañon of Second Avenue. The sound of millstones was silenced and extinct was the lighted candle!

The door of the shop opened with a hollow ping from the bell at the top and an old Italian woman entered. Her hair was white, but she was whiter still in the face, and its lack of color was made more startling by the still bright hues of her faded shawl. She did not lift her feet from the ground, but dragged them across the floor. Harris rose and went to the counter. She pushed a book across to him.

"Three dollars," she said—"three dollars on the book."

He picked the thing up and looked at it, a faded octavo volume, bound cheaply in brown and lettered cheaply in gold. Already the gilt was falling from it, disclosing gray patches in the letters. Lives of the Saints it seemed to be.

"Three dollars?" he said wonderingly. She answered nothing. She seemed to choke silently.

He looked at the flyleaf: "To Beppo Galli, from Father Tom, on his first communion, May 1,

1889." Beppo Galli? Beppo Galli? Who the deuce
was Beppo Galli? Suddenly it dawned on him—
and his skin prickled with a shiver, as though on a
June day a snowing wind had enveloped him
strangely—that the Beppo Galli of the book was
Beppo Galli the gunman who was to be electro-
cuted for murder on the morrow. They looked at
each other tragically across the counter.

"My boy," she said.

"God!" he breathed.

"Three dollars on the book," she pleaded, still
with dignity. "I'll come back for it. Yes, sure. I'll
come back. My boy's book."

He couldn't pick the words to say to her. He was
hypnotized for the moment by the figure before
him, so ghastily tragic it was.

"I go up to-day," she went on in a trembling
monotone. "I bring him something from his
mother. A little bottle of wine. A few cakes. Just
something from me. Three dollars. I'll come back.
I'll come back for the book."

He got a ten-dollar bill from his pocket and
thrust it toward her.

"I'll come back for the book. Give me the ticket,
the ticket for the book."

He handed the book back.

"I can't," he said. "That's all right."

She began crying softly and speaking as if to
herself.

"And from a Jew!" he heard her say. He slipped away to the back of the shop and stayed there until he heard the ping of the bell.

His father came up behind him.

"Not business, Benny," he reproved gently; "that was not business."

"How not?" the son answered shortly.

"To give her the money, Benny, that was fine. I do it myself. But, Benny, keep the book—you get the money back. That was business."

"That was business, was it?" He went toward the stairs at the back. "Well then, I'm through with business," he uttered savagely.

His mother came to him in his room, when he was packing a bag.

"Going away, *galoupshik*, going away?" she crooned. "The dogs and the horses! The wind amidst the grass!"

"Come away, *matushka*," he pleaded with her. "Come too. Let us all go!"

"I stay by my man," she nodded her head. "And for you, if you come back."

"No more business for me, not of this kind!" he answered contemptuously.

"Perhaps," she thought to herself with terrible wisdom. But to him she said: "No, Benny!"

His father met him as he went out.

"Where are you going, Benny?" the old man asked anxiously. "Where are you going, son?"

He dropped the bag for an instant and threw his arms out exultingly. His voice rang like a bell.

"I am going away, *batushka,*" he answered. "My little father, I am going away. I am going to hear the sound of millstones.

II

If you pass along the sea road from New York to Riverhead you cannot miss the old Tucker homestead at Setauket. A little to the left you will find it, a square-built white house, low-eaved, heavy-porched, hemmed about by tall, slim elm-trees. Right and left of it the ground rolls like a heavy-swelling sea, rising back of it to a sheer brown earth cliff, beneath which is the Sound, a white pebbly beach and a haze of blue water, with the dun vista of Connecticut beyond it, like a bank of threatening cloud—and always something be-tween them: a cargo boat with a smudge of brown smoke from her stacks; a schooner with her four jibs bellying to the breeze; a sloop, scuppers down; a line of barges like a school of porpoise.

On the square-built colonial porch Hosea Tucker received him. There was something in the man's foxlike eyes and hair that jarred on Harris more in his new surroundings than it had done in the Metropole. He seemed out of place in all this fresh world, so confiding, so natural, so sweet.

The old farmer had thrown his head back slyly.

"So you came down for a summer holiday," he said shrewdly. "You came down to put one over on old Hosea."

"I came down, Mr. Tucker, to work," Harris answered succinctly. "I came down for no holiday. I'll work as hard in winter as I'll work now. You offered me a job and here I am. Do you want me?"

"Hosea Tucker never went back on his word," the farmer told him. "If you want work you'll have it. When I say a thing I mean it."

"That suits me," Harris told him.

It suited Tucker, too, after a few days, when he saw how much in earnest young Harris was. He showed him about the big byres, where the dozen cows were that were to be cleaned every day. He taught him how to milk them, and showed him the different breeds—the big, fine-boned Ayreshires, dappled in white and red; the tractable Jerseys, yellow like buttercups; the Holsteins, rugged cattle and great milkers, with their irregular markings; the few Dutch, with their peculiar belts of white. He showed how to harness and drive a team, for part of his work, after helping to gather the garden produce, was to drive in to the station. That and a thousand jobs constituted his day.

"You're wanting to work on a farm," Hosea told him. "Well, it ain't no picnic. What do you think of it?"

"It suits me," was all Harris answered.

On Second Avenue he had been somewhat of a dude in dress, inclining, with a touch of Oriental grandiosity, to marvelous vests and tight-fitting clothes, and it astonished him how glad he was to put all that aside and clothe himself in a flannel shirt and khaki trousers. He had never believed a human being could be so tired as he was after a day's work about the farm. At nine he was asleep in the low, gabled attic that had been given him, a bare, healthy room, with the salt Sound breezes blowing through it. On Second Avenue he had been in the habit of lying awake at night full of bitterness, but here something was lulling him to sleep with the drowsy cadence of a cradle song.

"The sound of millstones," he would say to himself.

He had come down with a peculiar feeling toward the people he was coming among, the feeling of a sentry who challenges an unknown man in the dark, bayonet lowered and finger on the trigger, uncertain whether the person be foe or friend; but this was wearing off. Toward Hosea himself, even though the farmer's pretentious sentences still jarred a little on him, he began to feel an affectionate tolerance. With the motherless son and daughter he was getting along well. Frank, a tall lad of twenty-four, with his father's suspicious look, couldn't understand why he came away from the city.

"Can't make it out," he would say to Harris. "Appears to me you got a better time up there— theaters, and hotels, and everything. Moment I can get a little money I'm not going to stay here. Not on your life!"

"I like this better," Harris would laugh.

He was too wise in his generation to attempt to explain things to one who couldn't understand.

"Police aren't after you?" Frank would hint sheepishly.

"Not that I know of," would be the answer.

The daughter, Mildred, a thin anemic girl, tall as her brother, white in the face, with large blue eyes, overhigh forehead and scant hair, would smile demurely at him as he brought in the milk foaming in its pails night and morning. Between him and her there was little said.

"It must be a great change from the city," she would suggest.

"Thank God it is!" he would say fervently.

The few neighbors round seemed to regard him with tolerant suspicion; old Sam Robideau, for example, eighty years old and tough as oak, a little runt of a man with a short beard; and Captain Martin, half landsman and half sailor.

"I suppose you come down to work on a farm

so's you take an examination on that Board of Agriculture?" they would try to sound him.

"I came down to be a farmer," he would tell them brusquely. But they would not believe him.

May had gone and June had come, a glowing, golden month with still a touch of cold in the air. At night now for a half hour or so he would go out to the top of the cliff behind the house and look over the Sound. A soft, velvety dusk would come up a half hour after sundown, and through it he could see distinctly the lights of the traffic on the water. A little after nine the passenger boats would go up to New England from New York— three of them, flashing with yellow light, and looking like three golden argosies off on some mystic voyage. The haze of the Bridgeport lights would reflect itself dimly in the sky, and from somewhere across the water a lighthouse revolved solemnly with a swinging saffron gleam. From beneath him would rise the little chantey of the waves on the beach, a delicate minor of sound that suggested somehow the chink of silver.

A great feeling of happiness and freedom would sweep over him, something that he did not attempt to formulate but was content to feel, something big and comforting and balmy, like the smell of pine-trees; and occasionally when he felt so he would think of the days on Second Avenue, and the thought of them would sear him like a burning iron. Thank God all that was behind him, he would say, and never again to be opened! At last he was in the light of the candle and at last hearing the millstones' sound.

He would return to the house, past the little millpond where the bullfrogs croaked unceasingly through the night—a queer, unharmonious sound that he liked, broken only by the whang of some mysterious bird and the soft plud of turtles as they splashed from the bank or from logs into the water, or the rustle of a rabbit through the grass —and at times he would stretch his arms out and come near to sobbing, so great was the happiness in him and so far away was Second Avenue.

He was passing through the kitchen one night on returning from the cliff when he heard voices in the living-room.

"Sure can work," Frank was agreeing with some one.

"What did I say?" Hosea asked exultantly.

"Queer how he handles that horse," the son ruminated. "It sure will do things for him it won't do for me; and Bill"—Bill was the Irish terrier, an aggressive, uncertain dog with a great barrel of a chest and a fine muzzle—"Bill has certainly taken a shine to him. Follows him round like he belonged to him. Took a bite out of my leg last time I tried to take him out."

"It appears queer to me," old Sam Robideau broke in with his high falsetto, "him being a pawn-broker, as you say, and a Jew—"

"That'll be all," Hosea raised his voice. "None of that, Sam. None of that. A man's a man, and when I meet a man I take off my hat to him; I do, sir. That boy is as good as me and you, Sam, and I won't hear anything to the contrary. I'm broadminded—"

Harris didn't go in. He crept upstairs to sleep, and somewhere about his heart there was a warm glow, as of a comfortable fire, and the faint note of music, like the chiming of delicate bells.

She was not beautiful, that daughter of Hosea Tucker's, and Harris knew that. She had little mentality; his own mind was too incisive for him not to recognize it. But to him she symbolized the fresh air, the green fields, and the rocks among the trees, even as Ceres typified the growing corn and the fruitfulness of earth, for every ideal must have a human embodiment. Along Second Avenue there had been none of that freshness; there had been sophistication. It was, in the main, innocent; but it existed. And to him it came home, with the force of a climax in a play, that here was a woman who used no coloring on her cheeks but what Nature had given her; who was ignorant of the seductions of dress; who knew nothing of the uses of lip-stick, or eyebrow pencil, or enamel for the skin, or paste to gloss the nails. This was woman, he thought, as God made her; not the artificial product of the beauty parlor; the helper of, not the lure to, the male.

It was only natural that alone there for months, and undergoing, as he was, this violent sea-change, surcharged with emotion and vibrant as an electric medium, he should unconsciously have sought some object to cling to. And suddenly he found himself thinking about her nearly all the day. It was refreshing to see her in the morning bustling about the spotless kitchen; to return to the house for meals, to find her waiting there for her father and brother and himself. A little mist of glamour interposed itself between his eyes and her features, until it had refined away the anemic whiteness of her face, making it only pure; had taken the harshness from the high brow, until he saw there only lack of artifice in dressing her hair; had changed the expression of her eyes, which were as furtive and suspicious as her father's were, into one of modesty and timidity.

Her father had strong ideas about her marrying.

"I have figured it out," he said in that large way of his, "and Mildred is going to marry a man, a man from the feet up. She's not going to marry one of your city dudes. No, sir! If a millionaire

came round here to-morrow I'd say to him: 'Get
out of here. You're half dead. I don't want you.'
I want that girl of mine to marry some one who's
a man. He may be a carpenter, a farm hand, a
road laborer, but he must be hard-working and a
man. I've got no fool ideas."

"I think you're right there," Harris would
agree.

"To be sure I'm right," the farmer would tell
him.

And he thought of her in a new light after that,
as a guerdon to be won for manliness and sincer-
ity, as difficult of attainment and as desirable as
the king's daughters, whose hands were for the
victors in the tourneys and joustings, for the captains who saved their nations in war, for the
knights who slew dragons.

She would thank him for doing little errands,
jobs for her, in that low voice of hers, and give
him a demure glance from underneath her brows,
and he would feel a little thrill at that.

"There's simplicity for you," he would say to
himself. "In New York they've lost that."

He was affected, too, when after a hard day's
work she would press his supper on him.

"Go ahead and eat," she would tell him.
"You've been working all day. You need it."

That was perfectly good farm economics, but

he read into it a certain personal tenderness for himself that struck harmony in him, like a delicate touch on harp-strings.

Occasionally, as they grew to know each other better, she would ask him about New York. She had never been there. Hosea Tucker—although twice or oftener in the year he made a visit to New York and investigated Broadway completely and with elaborate detail—would never allow his son or daughter to go up. New York was no place for a young man or woman. That was one of the things he had figured out. But in her there burned a fierce and consuming desire to know the city she read of in the papers—its lights and gaiety, its skilfully dressed men and beautiful women, its theaters and its cabarets. She would have thrown away her comfort at home to go to New York and work there endlessly at the most menial occupation, simply to be there and of it. But she had not the courage to gainsay her father and assert herself.

"Tell me something of New York," she would ask with careful distraction. There was that in her, and from her father she got it, which urged her to conceal her feelings, when concealment was unnecessary; a quality of vanity which believed that the world was meddling with her affairs; the inherent strain of deceit.

"You should see Fifth Avenue on Saturday

afternoon," he would begin, and then he would tell her of the crowd that swarmed like an army with banners. He would tell her of Second Avenue at night, with its line of hawkers' carts illumined by sputtering naphtha torches, and strange commodities being offered for sale in strange, discordant tongues. Eloquently he would tell her of Broadway, noisy and a-glitter; of the brooding river beside the Drive; of the hooting traffic in the harbor; of the great bridges of stone and steel. He liked telling her of these things, to amuse her and to pass her time, as one might tell a child a fairy-story, like the story of the Sleeping Beauty in the Wood, or of Aladdin and the Potent Lamp, or of the Caliph and the Kalendars of Bagdad.

"Is that so?" she would comment blankly, biting short her sewing thread. That was all.

"She doesn't care for it," he told himself exultantly. "She's content where she is. Thank God, there's one woman who doesn't want excitement and cabarets!"

A certain intimacy was growing up between them, an intimacy of gaiety and banter. Once or twice their hands met over the milking-pails; once they clasped while he was driving her into Port in the buggy. Each time she blushed, but said nothing.

"Why aren't you married?" he questioned her jokingly.

"Nobody asked me," she smiled at him.

"Supposing I were to?" he smiled back.

"Oh, I don't know," she answered, and she laughed gaily. A sudden resolution took him, but he checked it.

From then on, for a few days only, he ceased to joke with her. The thought of marriage appalled him. For that one of the prejudices of his race, high as a walled city and impregnable as a tower of brass, still clung to him in a thin but unbroken thread. If he married this girl of an alien people, he would cut himself loose from his own. His father would call down the lightnings of Sinai to strike him. His mother would hardly dare think of him. To the whole of his family his name would be silent, like the name of one ignobly dead. He must live alone and die alone.

"But is it right?" he asked himself quickly. "Is it right?"

He couldn't decide about that, but of this one thing he was sure—that for himself, at least, it was only proper to drop the ancient prejudice. He had come out here as a man, to do a man's work, and to adopt the customs of the folk with whom he was. If this girl were of his own race, would there be any obstacle? There would be none. Well, then, let the obstacle not exist! It had been, he felt, that offensive defense of his people against the outer races which had narrowed them into the back streets of Europe; that clinging to provincial habit and ethics which had singled them out and drawn attention through the ages. He might be wrong, he granted, but so it appeared to him.

He met her at the gateway of the orchard and spoke to her as she was coming through.

"About that question," he said: "I'm going to ask it of you."

"What question?" she asked furtively. He did not notice the furtiveness. He thought it only modesty.

"I am going to ask you to marry me, Mildred," he told her with simple directness.

"You must ask father," she said nervously, and ran into the house.

Hosea was not home yet. He had been to the county fair at Riverhead, with Frank and old Sam Robideau, and might return at any minute. September had come in now, with a touch of cold in the air, and over the ridge of the hills westward the harvest moon was rising like a great gold coin. It seemed to flood the country with a golden light that was like a liquid, and cut the porch of the house into a sharp chiaroscuro of object and shadow. In the woods about the house the katydids were chattering incoherently, a presage of frost. Here and there in the darkest corners could be seen the faint red glow of fireflies, like the sparkle of minute rubies.

Harris moved unconsciously toward the shore of the Sound, passing the little pool from which a misty haze was rising, like some misty emanation from a sacred well. The high elm-trees threw shadows before him that seemed like great logs thrown in his way. He came to the brink of the cliff and stopped.

Before him the Sound lay, a great stretch of glass-like water, calm and cold beneath the moon. Beneath him he could hear the lick and swish of the incoming tide and the faint grinding of pebbles.

So the die was cast, he said to himself. There was no going back now—not that he wished to. He was to marry this girl, this wholesome country maiden, fresh as the springtime itself; and there close to the land he would live with her to the end of his days, well-ordered, healthy, happy. Forever the grinding chaos of Second Avenue was put away. Here he would take a wife and live.

" 'The voice of the bridegroom, and the voice of the bride' "—he quoted to himself softly— " 'The sound of the millstones, and the light of the candle.' "

He looked round at the swelling hills behind him, silvered by the moon, at the tall trees and the fruitful fields. He at last had found Zion.

"Zion!" he murmured to himself, awed by the great name.

And then suddenly the idea exploded within his brain that here was not only his Zion, but the Zion of his people. Not in Africa, not in the Mesopotamian valleys, but here in America, by the land and sea. Not in the gullies of the East Side nor in the sweat-shops of Williamsburg, but right here by the kindly earth. Here were fields as fruitful as the olive gardens of Bethlehem; trees as mighty as ever grew by Lebanon hill; fish-ponds as well stocked as any of Heshbon; grazing land as bounteous as any by Kerith stream. Here might they till their fields and tend their kine. Here might they grow in grace and favor, loving and well beloved.

"Zion!" he shouted aloud in ecstasy. "Zion!"

He would go forth to his people, he said, go forth and preach to them. He would go down into Second Avenue and lead them out. He would take them from the sweat-shops and the peddlers' carts. No longer should they dream of a torrid home in Africa or dicker for an Asian valley. No longer should the terrible litany be recited at the Temple's wall. They would come here in peace and good will, leaving aside their ancient prejudices and intensive cult, and mingling with the dwellers in the new land.

"Zion!" his voice rang over water and wood like the trumpet of Jericho. "Zion!"

And she would be with him in his work—she,

the white and ruddy one! A great flood of tenderness and love and adoration swept over him. Fair as the moon she was, clear as the sun. As a bundle of myrrh she was to him. Behold, she was fair, his beloved; she was fair; she had dove's eyes. . . .

As he passed through the kitchen he could hear and distinguish the voices in the living-room—the booming and inflated tones of the farmer, the shallow baritone of his son, and the mellow, salty voice of old Robideau. The farmer was speaking:

"I'll allow I was wrong in that first trotting contest. I'll allow I was wrong. When I'm wrong I give in. I'm not stubborn or bigoted. Yes, sir, that horse was a surprise to me—"

Harris strode into the room.

"Well, Ben boy?" Tucker greeted him. "What's on your mind?"

In the center of the room on the table the big green-shaded lamp threw a circle of yellow light and faintly illuminated the remainder of the room outside it. The heavy old furniture loomed up in bulky shadows here and there. The sea-beached logs in the great fireplace flared up with sudden spurts of yellow and green and purple. Beside the fire old Robideau sat, leaning on his oak stick with his gnarled brown hands. The farmer sat by the table, with Frank across the way from him. In the

shadows Mildred was knitting. She looked up, a
little startled, when he came in.

"Mr. Tucker," he said boldly, "I want to marry
your daughter Mildred."

"Eh?" The farmer looked at him in a puzzled
way, as if he had not heard aright.

"I want to marry Mildred."

"You want to marry Mildred!" Tucker repeated with his mouth agape.

"Yes," Harris nodded. "I do."

The farmer got up slowly and looked at him.
Suddenly the gaping look passed from his face.
The mouth closed and the corners drew back. The
eyes narrowed and the false geniality went from
them, and an expression came into them like the
expression of an untrustworthy dog.

"You want to marry Mildred!" he repeated.
"Well, of all the damned impertinence!"

He turned to the old man at the fire and
laughed raucously.

"I knew it would come to this," he said. "I
knew it! I pick this thing out of the gutter. I take
it down here. I give it a home. And now it wants
to marry Mildred!"

"You did none of these things," Harris snapped
back at him; "and why shouldn't I marry Mildred?"

Tucker's face became purple with passion. His

eyes protruded and he beat furiously on the table with his hands.

"Why shouldn't you marry my girl? Is that what you ask?" he thundered. "Do you know who you are and what you are? And you want to marry my daughter? Go back to your own kind, you scut! You and your flea-bitten, dirty, cheating tribe come over here and eat the country up. Keep to your filthy pawnshop—that's the place for you."

He paused for a moment, out of breath. His son had risen and stood beside him, threateningly. In the shadows the girl still rested immobile. The old man by the fire laughed with a horrible, wheezing cynicism.

"Do you know anything about this?" Tucker asked of his daughter fiercely. "Did he say anything to you?"

"No," she answered frightenedly. "He said nothing."

"Get out of here!" the farmer shouted at him. "Get out of here before I kick you out! I've a mind to get the horsewhip for you. Get out!"

"Go back to your pawnshop," the son snarled at him, and again the old man laughed.

He stood for an instant looking at the four of them with a glance so fierce that it stopped the words in their mouths like a drawn sword, and

then turning on his heel slowly, dignifiedly, carelessly, he went out through the door.

A minute it might be he stood in the moonlight,
dazed, before starting on the road to the station.
The high voices inside still rose passionately. Once
more the old man laughed in his grating, grinding
way, and it seemed to Harris as he listened to that
cynical cacophony that somewhere was the sound
of millstones revolving, and that he was only a
grain of corn being crushed to powder beneath
their ponderous, unrelenting motion.

III

Old Aaron Harris cannot understand why his
son should so suddenly have become reconciled to
business. Above all, he cannot understand how
Ben, who used to be so lax about the proper valu-
ation of pledges, about the lapsing of tickets,
about the four per cent per month interest, should
turn so fiercely shrewd in driving bargains and so
savagely implacable in his demand for the fulfil-
ment of the bond. No, he can find no explanation
for that.

But the folk of the vicinity, the Little Russians,
Esthonians, Courlanders and Finns—that whitish-
haired, heavily built, stolid people with dumb eyes,
who bring in their clothes, their tools, their jew-

elry to pawn—they have an explanation. "It is the Jew breaking out in him," they say, and their features become distorted with futile rage. "If he were only in Russia now," they snarl—"the Black Hundred. . . ."

IX

THE BRIDE'S PLAY

ABOVE, in the dining-hall, for a long time now, the clatter of dishes had ceased. For over an hour no sound had been heard but the plaintive Dvořák melody Lady Nan was playing on the antiquated grand piano in the music-room. Below in the great kitchen the wizened huntsman leaned toward the portly, ancient butler.

"Sir Fergus may be a great one for the old customs, but do you think he'll have the bride's play?"

"And hasn't the family had the bride's play for three hundred years? And why shouldn't Sir Fergus have it?"

Old Paudeen Rafferty hung the little kettle on the crane over the fire, for Sir Fergus's punch.

"I'm not so old as many people think, but I can remember Miss Enid's bride's play, and the time there was that day with O'Brien of Fews going wild, and the poor Miss Enid crying her eyes out. On the lawn they had it, the second Sunday after the marriage, following the old custom—I wonder is himself coming in at all to-night," Paudeen broke off for an instant, watching the kettle. "They stood out on the lawn, Miss Enid that was, and her husband, Mr. Johnson, and all the tenants were there, and the pipes piped up a reel. When the reel was danced the bride made the round of the people, looking for him she loved best. Instead of turning to her husband, she turns to O'Brien of Fews and she pitches herself into his arms, crying her eyes out—"

"Look out! Herself has stopped," the huntsman broke in.

The music above had ceased. There was the rumble of a male voice, deep and sonorous, as though some one were rubbing a drum. A woman's voice chimed in—a slender voice, clear and musical as a flute.

"She's coming to hurry us up herself, begor!" Rafferty hustled around the fireplace, swinging forward the crane.

There was the patter of feet on the stairs, spirited, impatient feet, and Nan Cassidy came into the room—a tall woman, tall as a tall man, slightly built, with a face purely molded on a regular Saxon type, with eyes blue as ice and hair like corn. There seemed to be too much spirit in Sir Fergus's wife for a woman. She might have been a great actress or a great queen, as she stood there, only for the fleeting dimples about her mouth that could only have belonged to a young woman.

"Well, Keogh! Well, Rafferty!"

The butler rushed about, taking the kettle down, putting it on a tray, looking for the lemons and sugar.

"Lady Nan, Your Honor!" Keogh, the huntsman, pulled at his forelock. "Is there to be the bride's play?"

"Hurry up, Rafferty! The master is waiting," went the crisp, flutelike tones. "The bride's play? Of course there'll be the bride's play." She turned and slipped up the stairs with a nod.

"As supple as a hare," Keogh's eyes followed her in admiration, "or as the finest horse in Ireland. I wonder now."

"You wonder what?" Rafferty was hoisting himself painfully up the balustrade of the stair, with the toddy things.

"If Master Bulmer turns up at the bride's play, as O'Brien of Fews turned up for Miss Enid's—"

"Begorra, if he does"—old Rafferty turned around, his red, kindly face set into stern, anxious lines—"begorra, if he does, he's a dead man!"

They will tell you, the tenants of the Cassidy estate, that the lords of the manor first came to Ireland from Spain, three thousand years ago, with the Iberian invasion. Sir Fergus himself will tell you that he believes—he is not certain, because he never tells a lie—that the Cassidys fought against the Danes at Clontarf. But what is certain is that they received the rights to the stronghold of Killevy from King John, and that they have held it in undying succession since.

"As long as grass grows and water runs there will be a Cassidy of Killevy," goes the popular belief.

If there is such a thing as royalty in Ireland, it is the lords of Killevy, small as that kingdom is, not more than four hundred acres. And they look it, too—Sir Fergus to-day, Sir John before, Sir Brian in the past; huge men, six feet six inches tall, built like the giants who were before the deluge, or the sons of Anak later; men with great, hairy, well-kept hands, with the noses of eagles and the eagle's look in their black eyes; slow-aroused men, who can be quick as a cat if occasion demands it; and young until their dying day.

He is old now, Sir Fergus, sixty-five years old, and, except for the grayness of his hair, one would hardly take him for a day over forty. He lunges along in his gray homespun tweeds, with the trout flies in his hat, his old face set in that stern expression which is the mask of good nature, and by his side, only twenty-five years old, goes Lady Nan, and none take them for father and daughter. One sees respectfully that they are man and wife, and there are none who are not glad.

Now, when John Barrett, he who owned every granite quarry in Ulster, died and left his daughter Nan alone in the world, there were few who were not anxious, not that she was left without money, but that she was left by herself. If the opinion of the hard-headed Scotch-Irish is worth anything, it was like leaving a rare flower in a public garden for the first passer-by to pick up, wear for a while until it died on the air, then throw away. There is protection for flowers in public gardens—the police look after that—but there was no protection for John Barrett's daughter. She was all alone. And she was hot-tempered. She would have nothing to do with protection.

"She'll go her own gait and she'll have a fall— and oh, the poor girl!" the Bishop of Down said.

Bishops know a lot about human nature. They were once ordinary parsons and saw much of it, much more than doctors do.

If Nan Barrett had been an ordinary girl, for all her hot spirit and her face and figure, there would have been nothing to worry about. If she had grown up in the quietness of Newry, that little backwater of a town with its granite quarries and sea docks, where the Norwegian vessels wait for their cargoes at the pier, Newry might never have noticed her. But John Barrett had, after his wife died, no love or interest in the world beyond his daughter. He was a little bit insane—that man!

"I'm going to give her an education and a time fit for a queen," he told his cronies.

He sent her to Brussels, to a convent there, where she was treated as a princess, so much did he insist upon it, and so much did he spend. From there he sent her to Paris, accompanied by a chaperon, and from there to Germany and Italy. And all the time he sat at home, befuddling himself with liquor.

"There isn't a commoner's daughter in the world," he told his friends, "having the time my girl is having. No, nor the lord-lieutenant's either"—and he would pour whisky into his tea. "And isn't she worth it, the heart of corn!"

Not because she was John Barrett's daughter but because she was a myth in the little town, every time she returned from abroad her entry was the event of the month. There were balls and fêtes given her. There were special hunts of the foxhounds. Everything in the town was at her feet. There was nobody who had not asked her to marry him. She was very honest and blunt with them all.

"I cannot," she told them straight. "There is nothing but admiration in my heart for you, but I do not love you."

"What do you mean by love?" a major of the King's Scottish asked her hotly.

"I don't know," she said, "but I think it's a great madness."

The dapper little officer looked at her with his soul standing worriedly in his eyes.

"God help you, Nan, when it comes, then."

And so around the town, where she was loved and venerated as no saint has ever been, the word went, and men and women grew anxious. She would never die an old maid, they knew that—their intuition told them so. But she would marry, and would a great loveliness of soul be murdered?

"If she's hurt inside," the bishop pondered over his port, "she dies."

And then John Barrett died, and she was left alone in the world, without a husband, without a lover, without anything, until Bulmer Meade, the poet, who was called the D'Annunzio of Ireland, came and saw her.

Where is Meade now, I wonder? In some drunken gutter, where he belongs? But in those days he was the star of hope of literary Ireland —a great poet undoubtedly, so everybody says— the people who should know. I can see him now, brown eyes with wavy hair, a fine figure of a man with his monocle at the end of a black silk ribbon, with his cloak, such as a naval officer wears, buttoned with his silver clasps at the neck; with his voice ringing like a clarion as he declaimed his verses. A fine figure he knew himself to be, with every pose studied as an actor would study it.

He went through Paris, a dramatic figure; London lay at his feet. He went to Constantinople to write, as he admitted it, a greater novel than Loti's. He came back—the atmosphere jarred on him, he explained, and to write novels or poems one must have the right atmosphere. And all good men despised him, and all women came at his beck and call.

"After all," he said, when he was taxed with laziness, "to live poems is much more than to write them."

So he lived them. He lived them at every one's expense. He broke the heart of poor Moleska in Paris, the greatest Polish actress the world has ever seen. He estranged the husband of the Comtesse de Lèches. He patted them on the shoulder; he put his arm around them.

"Listen!" he would tell them. "You and I are going to Damascus, where the sword-blades come from. The city is like a strange picture, in the dawn. There are red colors in the air, mauve, dark green. Story-tellers sit in the streets telling the story of Ganem, the Slave of Love. Everywhere there are camels with tinkling bells and Nubians with slaves. In three months' time we will go." In a month's time he was gone, God knows whither, without saying good-by. And broken-hearted, distraught, the women mourned for him. Poor Gretchen Davis, the dancer, threw herself into the Seine. They recognized that all they had been to Meade was lay figures to post against and talk to —and they had given their hearts and souls to him, and some their bodies, to be dropped as a toy is dropped and broken by an irresponsible child. . . .

He left Dublin to come to the north, where, he told his admirers, the gods still were, by the green sea and purple mountains. He would go into the wilderness for forty days, he had decided in his blasphemous phrase. He came up to the Hills' of Newry, his cousins, who still believed in him, and there he met Nan Barrett—a new thrill.

I don't think that Bulmer Meade could any more keep away from a fine woman than a dipsomaniac can keep away from a glass of drink. Other men may be the same—many a one. But where they play with a woman's heart, Meade played with her soul, the most sacred thing in the world.

He met Nan Barrett at a dance at the Foxes', where she and he were the lions of the evening. The band had ceased playing for a moment and about him were grouped the women who had heard of his reputation and were drawn to him as moths are drawn by the danger of flame. Suddenly he saw Nan pass.

"Who is that magnificent woman?" he pulled his host aside to ask.

"That? That's Miss Barrett." Fox, an ex-officer of dragoons, was none too keen on Meade's knowing her.

"I should like to meet her," Meade said, and there was nothing to do but introduce them.

She knew him by reputation of his writings—as who did not?—"The Garden of the Yews," "The Harp of Seven Strings." And he looked to her as a poet should look, a magnificent specimen from some unknown world. His brown eyes talked to her, adored her, and her heart went a-flutter like a swallow's wing. They spoke only the usual ballroom amenities but that night she did not sleep.

By next morning he had sent her flowers for her rising and by afternoon he called.

"I know it's not convention," he told her, "but neither you nor I are made for convention—I just came."

She blushed for the first time in her life, but could find nothing to say.

"And neither is this convention." His voice trembled. "For the first time in my life I love a woman."

All things went dark for her for a minute. In her ears worlds droned. He caught her hands.

From his oil-painting on the wall of what had been his favorite room, the spirit of John Barrett must have wrestled with its death bonds to jump to the rescue of his daughter.

"Do you know what you are saying?" she asked him. "Have you gone mad?"

"I know what I'm saying, *a-hagur*." His voice began that violin-playing of its own. "And you know it, too. I love you. I love you. I love you!"

He never kissed her. That was not his way. He did not want the lips. He wanted to play on the heart and soul. That semi-insane dramatic sense of his, wanted elbow-room. And it got it.

He left the room abruptly, in a stage exit. That evening he met her with the Hills' motor-car, which he had borrowed. He drove her out to Slievegullion Hill. He never spoke until they had passed Camlough Lake. He stopped the car and took her in his arms.

"I love you!" he whispered into her corn-colored hair. "Look!"

Northward the low, brown hills of Slievegullion rose like the back of a nesting bird—a place of great loneliness, dotted with three cottage lights. Behind it, white like a Chinese lamp, rose the round disk of the October moon. A little wind was out, and it rippled the waters of the lake to their left, so that they shone with scales of silver and gold. To the right of them the forest of pine-trees rustled like a bride's dress. Forward, the white, ribbonlike road crept like a wounded snake. Over the water a lone bittern boomed like a drum. And high on the mountaintops somewhere an eagle barked like a dog.

"Listen, love," he said, "unto that mountain, Finn MacCool came when he followed the brown woman he loved over hill and dale through all Ireland. From that mountain Cuchulain went to Skye to discover the Amazon queen he loved. To the right of us, miles away, is the sea where the daughters of Lir were enchanted into swans—for love. All around us are great love stories." He held her now closely in his arms. "But all of them together in their loves had not the tithe of my love for you. O fairer than Helen of Troy! O sweeter than Niamh! O lovelier than Deirdre, for whom five hundred men died! Can you love me? Will you love me?"

Against his shoulder her bosom fluttered; her throat swelled.

"I think I can," she whispered.

"Do you?"

She said nothing, but he could see her head nod. An hour of vague, incoherent mutterings, and he drove her home.

And for days this went on; for weeks; for a month. And as he poured out purple prose and poetry to her, her own voice found itself and she told him how she cared for him.

"If this goes on, Bulmer, I shall die. If it stops I shall die too. I never knew love could be anything like this." Tears wet the lashes of her eyes. "O man of mine, poet of mine! How can such a person as you love poor Nan so?"

He did not love her long. He came out of his emotional debauch as a drunkard comes out of liquor. He had left her at the gate of her garden one starry night, and she had given him a rose in his hand. He went to his room at the Hills'; laughed; tossed the rose out of the window; and was gone by the first train.

She hunted him wildly about Newry, wondering what had become of him. She thought of having the canal dragged, fearing that by mischance he had fallen in. She went down to Dublin, thinking, perhaps, he had become offended at some stray word of hers. She drove up, haggard and anxious, to the publishers of his poems.

Ryan, the rosy-cheeked old man of the world, had seen this thing before. He knew how to handle it.

"If you go and see Miss Gallagher-Reynolds," he blinked, "at 89 Mount Street, she will be able to give you news."

She didn't understand what the old man meant, but she went to the Georgian house on Mount Street. A woman of thirty, pretty, old-eyed, hard-jawed, swept into the room. Nan rose.

"I beg your pardon for coming," she said, "but I was sent here to see if you have some news of my fiancé, Mr. Bulmer Meade."

"You had better sit down," Miss Gallagher-Reynolds advised. Into her hard eyes there had crept pity.

"He is not dead?" Nan had grown white and faint.

"He is not dead, though he deserves to be. Now listen to me, girl, and set your jaw. . . ."

She was no longer now the care of Newry—the child that the town had to be anxious about. She was its pride. There was no woman in Ulster who could lift a cob over a four-foot wall as deftly as she. There was none with a finer eye for a dog or a horse. Spiritedly she went through the town, and whipped the stream for trout. And there was a look in her eyes like the look of a thoroughbred horse.

"It was that affair with the poet made a woman out of her," the wiseacres said. "I wonder what has become of him now. I wonder, will he ever turn up again?"

But she had little thought of Meade any longer.

She was studying a man, what to her mind was a real man figure. Since she had given her whole mind and spirit to sport, she spent most of her time with Sir Fergus Cassidy. The great old feudal landlord appeared to her as some Roman of old-time might, with his pride that he was father of his peasants, no better than they, conforming to their customs, wearing their dress of homespun, though made by a good tailor; their brogues, though the bootmaker to the King had designed those—speaking even a little of the kindly Gaelic. And she was proud and happy to be with him.

They were whipping Camlough Lake for trout —a long graceful cast, and the flies rippling the water in steady, infinitesimal jerks. Suddenly Sir Fergus laid his rod down.

"If I were not an old man—" he said abruptly.

Nan turned to him.

"But you are not an old man, sir."

"If I were not such an old man," he went on, "I should ask you to marry me and come to my house."

She bent her head.

"I was once infatuated with a vain popinjay," she murmured. "Do you know about that?"

"I do," the old squire said. "That was nothing. I want you to marry me."

She raised her spirited head, and tried to keep back the tears.

"I shall be a proud and happy woman," she told him.

"A marriage has been arranged and will take place on June the first," read the society columns of a great London weekly, "between Sir Fergus Cassidy of Killevy Castle, and Miss Nan Barrett of Newry. Sir Fergus is one of the remaining Jacobite adherents in Ulster. . . . There are many quaint customs in the family, including the peasant custom of the Bride's Play, which takes place on the second Sunday after the ceremony. . . . The happy pair go out on the lawn and to the music of bagpipes dance in company with their friends and tenants. When this is over the bride goes the rounds of those present with the purpose of finding out who she loves, but, eventually turning to her husband. . . . The custom undoubtedly originated to show friends that the married pair had made a happy choice. . . . It is refreshing to find, in these days of liberalism, a nobleman who is keen on retaining the quaint traditions of his family." And so on.

Bulmer Meade, sitting in a café in Budapest, sipping absinthe while the orchestra played a piece he had chosen, read the paragraph. The brooding look came into his eyes.

"The Bride's Play!" he smiled to himself. "The Bride's Play!"

For a half-hour now the blind piper's fingers had been jigging over the silver keys of the union pipes like a dancer's feet, and, laughingly, the assembly on the lawn, more accustomed to ball-room dances than the reel and *rinnce fada,* had been merrily attempting the intricacies of the Irish steps. Around about ran Rafferty the butler, and his two black-clad maids, bringing sherry and biscuits to all the guests. Sir Fergus stood aside, speaking to Widger, the horse expert. Nan, in her bride's dress, went over and touched him on the arm.

"Now for the play," she laughed.

The company scattered in a circle. The piper, at a touch from Rafferty, began to ripple out a tune. Nan went slowly over to the old butler.

"Are you the one I love the best, Rafferty?"

"I hope so, Lady Nan," the old man replied, gallantly.

"You are not, Rafferty."

She tripped to the first in the line, Major Barrett.

"Are you the one?" she laughed, and passed on.

A jaunting-car had come up the drive, and across the lawn Meade, in his cloak and soft hat, came walking into the circle. There was none who noticed him particularly, except Nan. She touched Powers of Orior on the shoulder.

"Are you the one? . . . No!"

She had gone the round until she came to the black figure. She asked no questions, but became white and set in her face. Meade put his arms out.

"I am the one, *agra*—"

Sir Fergus came slouching forward, his great shoulders set.

"Who is this, Nan?"

"It's nobody, Fergus. Just leave him to me. Please, Fergus, don't kill him."

She tapped Meade on the shoulder.

"Are you the one I love the best?" Her voice never faltered.

"I am, Nan." Meade's violin tones came throbbing and passionate. "Come with me."

She held her husband back with her hand.

Then bending down quickly, she slipped her shoe off, and, standing up again and holding it by the toe, she smashed him across the mouth.

"There's a situation for you." Her voice bit like acid. She caught her husband's arm. "And here's a man!"

She turned her husband toward the house and went in with him, while the guests stood around, white and silent and horrified. The figure in the cloak staggered away toward the car, all its jauntiness and mummery gone, with something broken inside it. The blind piper, who sensed something wrong, worked his bellows unconsciously, and from nervousness fingered the keys, but no tune came from drone and chanter, only a long-drawn wail, like a funeral note.

X

A WOMAN IN THE HOUSE

I

HE reined in the big gray gelding for an instant while he watched his son and the girl take the fence together. There was a hard thunder of hoofs, like a hammering of bass drums, as they raced neck and neck; and then suddenly the great chestnut hunter that the boy rode and the girl's fine black mare were over lightly, like swallows whipping over water.

He brought the gray across easily, with a quick lift of his knees, and leisurely took in the scene before him. Three hundred yards away, up the hill, between the bright yellow of the gorse and the grayish brown of the winter grass, he could see the red streak of the old dog fox as he headed warily for the copse above; then came the flying squadron of the dappled pack, heads forward and tails stiff, silently intent; and after that Tim, the old huntsman, in faded red broadcloth and brown corduroy, on his mare Pegeen. Then again came the girl and his son, tall, lithe figures on their mounts. Behind him straggled the rest of the hunt, motley in red broadcloth and gray tweed.

He brought the gelding down to a walk, and for the first time in many years he let his eye wander from the quarry and the pack. His glance was on the girl ahead, in her trim habit and bowler hat. And he wondered to himself how it was that, of the thousand times he had seen her, it was only on the last three or four occasions she had engrossed his attention. He had always known her for a little beauty, and he had laughed at every dare-devil feat of hers that had evoked the applause of the country-side. But somehow he had never thought of her as a woman until a few days ago; and yet she was twenty-five.

"The little Heart of Corn!" he said to himself tenderly, repeating the name that the peasantry had given her.

And then suddenly, as though he had been storing up memory subconsciously these ten years or more, there rushed into his brain a flood of remembrances of her. It seemed to him that he had always been looking into that imperfect oval face, with its tinge of olive color, its full gray eyes, and straight black hair. He could always remember her swift boyish stride and hunched shoulders; the mannish hunting dress; the little spurred feet in the top boots—and, above all, that pert, inquiring, challenging look of hers, that made one uncertain, a fox-hunting parson had said, whether to thrash her or kiss her.

And how often had he laughed at Tim the huntsman's description of her!

"She's a rare young devil—Miss Hester!" Tim would say. "Ah, but she's the little Heart of Corn!"

That morning at the meet she had greeted him pertly, sitting there beside that son of his, who seemed less of a son than a younger brother.

"I doubt, Sir Patrick," she had said in that touch of brogue that was hers, "you're getting old. I heard your bones creak, and you climbing into the saddle."

"Huh!" her father, old Colonel O'Donnell, had snorted. "Boyd's younger than his overgrown son, and he rides harder; and harder than you, too, miss."

And he could, too, at forty-six, outride his son Harry, who was only twenty-three; and her, too, though she was the best horsewoman of the county.

A host of new and disturbing ideas had come into his head since he had begun noticing her, now that there was the fleeting expression in her eyes that betokened she was woman as well as tomboy, capable of loving as much as of riding to hounds. He remarked the trim tidiness of her, and it oc-

curred to him, with a sense of shock, how much in
need of attention his house and gardens were,
which had had no woman to care about them now
for two-and-twenty years, except for a doddering
housekeeper and a couple of maids who would be
more at home milking cattle than polishing
furniture.

That old house of his, now, for example, resting at the foot of Slievegullion—how much she
could have done with that! There in the great
dining-room, where the portraits of the Boyds
looked down mellowly from the wall—the Boyd
who had fought with Cromwell, and "Boyd of
the Boyne," and the Boyd who had stood by Grat-
tan against Castlereagh—those and a dozen of
others, soldiers and statesmen—would there never
again be a gathering of beautiful women and stal-
wart men? In the drawing-room, with its noble
depth and height, with its virginal, which a queen
had given his father, with damascened weapons
on the walls, would there never be a woman to
brighten it, to place flowers here and there, to
warm it into the intimacy of life? Every corner of
the house was cluttered with fishing-rods, with
guns and saddles. A pair of spurs lay on the antique
sideboard in the dining-room. An otter dog dozed
in the depths of a brocaded couch.

And that garden, too, with its walks that should

be graveled and its flower-beds that should be
trimmed; the little lake, where swans should be,
with their throats raised exultantly—would there
be never again a beautiful woman in clinging white
to pass down its alleys in the full of the moon?

The red fox had taken cover in the copse, and
about it the pack was circling busily, with shrill
impatient yelps. The whipper-in was herding them
together, making his lash crack like a rifle. Boyd
watched the girl as she sat back easily, waiting for
the leader to give tongue.

"A woman in the house!" Boyd thought to himself. "We need a woman in the house."

And for his son, too, something was needed. In
spite of the boy's years at Harrow and Dublin,
there was lacking a polish to him—due undoubtedly to the lack of mother care, the lack of mixing
with women. In a while, Boyd felt, the lad might
become a boorish type of country gentleman, like
old Squire Boyley, who spoke of nothing but the
points of cattle and the vintages of port. No; there
must be a refining somewhere.

The fox had broken cover and was careering uphill gaily. The hounds broke into a passion of
crying, and tore along in a wavering piebald
stream. The girl was after them like an arrow.

"The little Heart of Corn!" Boyd repeated as
he watched her; he nodded his head in conviction.
"That's what we need—a woman in the house."

II

If you had been present—say, three years ago—
at one of the formal levees at Dublin Castle, your
eye would have wandered past the gorgeous Vice-
roy; past the Ulster King at Arms, with his four
heralds; past the be-medaled generals and Knights
of Saint Patrick, in their long cloaks, with their
swords and stars—and it would have fixed on a
tall, young-looking man in modest court dress, knee
breeches and sword, standing apart, with his back
against the wall his arms folded. You would have
been certain to ask his name.

"That is Sir Patrick Boyd," the answer would
have come, with a note of deference at the name.

A tall, lean figure of a man, I remember him,
six feet or thereabouts, and spare as a lance. He
impressed you as a sheaf of sinew, something like
a panther. Surmounting that came the lean, aqui-
line face, with its over-big nose and its over-long
jaw; the chestnut hair, with just the faintest gray
at the temples; the cool, calm, fearless brown eyes.
If it had not been for the eyes one might have
thought him to be some official, aged thirty-two;
but the look in them showed that he was a man
who had lived long enough to gain poise and authority. Still and all, one would hardly have
thought him to be forty-six years old, and to have
a son of twenty-three.

It means very little in England—that name,
Boyd of Beltana. It means nothing in Europe. In
America it has hardly ever been heard. But in Ireland it means a great and gallant sportsman, a
credit to his country; one of those last figures of
Irish gentlemen who resemble, in a way, the old
noblesse of France—like the White Knight, the
Knight of Glyn, O'Conor Don, and McGillicuddy
of the Ricks. It means all that; and it does more—
it recalls a tragedy.

They will tell you, old country gentlemen in
rough tweeds and blue poplin stocks, disappointed
diplomats in third-rate capitals, officers of the
Rifles and the Fusiliers, sunburnt from India—all
who had been to Trinity with him—that they cannot understand how Boyd married her.

"You could see she was that sort," they say.
"You could see it with half an eye."

They alluded to little Ada Breguel, that turbulent French dancer, who whirled across the stage
of the Empire, shook Dublin out of its lethargy,
and captured the hearts of a field marshal and a
chancery judge in ten minutes. A woman who
looked like a child, is the description I get of her,
with her pert flashing face, her mass of black curls
and her slight figure.

Boyd met her after the theater and in one week
they were married. It was his perfect courtesy, his
respect for her, for whom few others had respect,

and a clean, wholesome manner of wooing that
gained her. He was twenty-two then, and a student
at Trinity.

His father, blunt old sportsman, took it philo-
sophically.

"Well, it's done now. Let's make the best of
it," he said. "Thank God his mother isn't alive to
see it! She was such a stickler for family!"

Nor did he last to see the worst of it. A week
later they brought him home on a door from the
hunting field; and the men's heads were bared.

She had thought she would enjoy being Lady
Boyd of Beltana; of having a recognized position
in society; of having a husband who treated her
with deference. She had all the *gamin's* love for a
title and lands. She would escape, she thought, the
muck of dressing-rooms, the tyranny of hours, the
need for giving every ounce of herself every moment to keep her hold on the public.

But she found the North sad. The hunting and
the fishing did not interest her. She discovered, to
her amazement that a duchess was only a charming elderly lady, such as a butcher's wife might be.
The two peeresses she met never wore their coro-
nets, and one of them swore like a trooper. At the
Punchestown races none paid attention to dress, as
they did at the Grand Prix. They watched the
horses. She was bored.

"There are no smart people here, Patrick," she

would complain to him. "Let's go to Paris and live."

"But I can't, dear," he would explain patiently. "I've got my responsibilities here; my tenants— everything."

"I'm so sick of it," she would tell him.

This frame of mind occupied her for a year, at the end of which their son Henry was born. As soon as she could get round she packed her trunks.

"I'm sick of you," she told Boyd. "I'm sick of your place. I'm sick of your people. I'm going back to something with life in it."

Nothing could hold her; arguments, affection— not even threats. The dregs of Paris were in her, and they suppurated now into an ulcer of discontent. She had never wanted horses and dogs, flowing water and blossoming heather, a house surrounded by purple mountains. She had wanted an *hôtel* on the Avenue Kléber, the adulation of bankers, the intrigue of music-halls. A fierce nostalgia for them seized and paralyzed her.

"I don't want your child," was her final word.

She died in Paris a few years later. How, nobody but Boyd knew; and he never spoke of it. Even he could find nothing good to say of the dead. So he said nothing at all.

The boy grew up. Out of the indiscriminate features of childhood emerged the hooked Boyd nose, the heavy Boyd jaw. Out of the cooing clamor of infancy emerged the wonderful Boyd dignity and the Boyd calm. There was nothing in him of his mother—not one speck.

"A miracle of God!" the friends of the family judged it. But of that they mentioned no word to Sir Patrick. He was not the sort of man who allowed criticism of his wife, no matter what she had been.

Tall and lithe and straight he grew, while his father watched him with a care a mother could not have equaled. He taught him to ride and shoot straight; the ethics of sport; the duties of a landlord to his tenants; the duties of a gentleman to his dependents and his peers. And little by little they came to resemble each other, until the boy seemed but a pocket edition of his father.

"I'd know him out of his father anywhere," Tim the huntsman would say. "The same high head and the same eyes. Aye, and the same way of looking at you. The dead spit of the Boyds—God bless him!"

To Harrow the father sent him, going over to England to be near him, and forsaking, for the time, the furze-clad hills and ditches of his hunting country for the sodden plowed fields and elaborate social meets of the Saxon. Carefully he guided him through Trinity, in Dublin; and then Harry came home.

"What is it to be, Hal?" the father asked him. "Army, navy, diplomacy, church?"

"I'd rather stay at home, sir," he said, "and help you with the estate. If we look after our own people the Empire can look after itself."

"I'm glad," his father said simply; but his heart leaped at the thought that, for another generation at least, the Boyd tradition would be carried on; that another link in the chain would remain to care for the people and govern the estate well and justly.

Together they rode to the hunt and back from it. They visited cottages; planned improvements; heard complaints and investigated them. There was always the kind word for the children, and an occasional phrase of the vanishing Gaelic for the white-haired women sunning themselves at the doors. There was a joke for the fox-hunting parson and a chat over politics for the parish priest.

"Listen to me, my friend," old Father Kelly told a member of Parliament who had journeyed North during the agrarian discussion with an eye to the disaffection of the neighborhood; the member had spoken violently about "landlords' spawn," as he put it. "Listen to me: You may shoot landlords in Kerry and ambush them in Roscommon. But if you advise that here you'll go home on a stretcher. And it won't be the landlords will send you. It'll be the tenants. I'm just telling you!"

And it wasn't alone their sense of justice and honor that made this man and boy popular in the Barony of Oriel. It was the deep bond between them that called forth the sympathy in every one. Even old men's eyes grew dim as they saw the admiration and the near-worship of the son for the father; his happiness when they were together; his pride in the elder man's strength and endurance, handsome face and proud carriage.

And women with children smiled tenderly in understanding as they watched the baronet's concealed solicitude for the boy's welfare, the careful training, the inculcation of ideals. They understood even more his patient waiting for the boy's return when away on a visit, or on a trip to Dublin, or a round of the fairs, looking after stock. Patiently the baronet sat and waited on the terrace for his return, like David, sitting between two gates, waiting for tidings of Absalom, his son.

III

A great line of Boyds there had been since De Courcy clanked into Ulster at the head of his Norman band; and of all that line there had not been one who was a famous lover. They were not uxorious men—women in the main had no attraction for them; but it seemed their custom to pick out one woman and to lavish their lives on her. It was their boast that they picked out wives of high ideals and tried to live up to them.

"A grand eye for a horse, they've got," the country people would say; "aye, and a grand eye for a woman. 'Tis better for a girl to be married to one of them than to be a queen, with crown and jewels. A better thing, surely."

There had been few of them who had married outside their own Province of Ulster. They mated with the O'Donnells and O'Neills, overlords of the North; with the O'Hanlon women, those red-haired strapping amazons; with the De Lacys and D'Arcys, tall, commanding women who still retained the Norman manner. A Boyd had stolen a King of Spain's daughter, and another Boyd had brought home an Austrian; but that had been all— that and the defection of Sir Patrick, who had married the dancer from Paris.

"A queer thing for him to do!" the tenantry puzzled. " 'Tis many the hearts were sore and broken on that same day."

That was dead and gone, now; buried in the oblivion of twenty-three years, until it seemed no more to the squire than a tragic story that had happened to some one else. For twenty years the stream of affection that was in him had been dammed by the caring for his son; and now that the boy was no longer a stripling, but a man, the

stream flowed over the bulwarks and was prepared to take its natural course.

If there was one woman who would have suited
him in the whole world it was Hester O'Donnell.
He liked everything about her—that quick and
boyish stride that was always carrying her swiftly
somewhere; those raised eyebrows that gave the
impression she was eternally puzzling over something. More still, he even liked her way of walking
along the road, her left hand in the pocket of her
tweed coat.

And then came the daily, ever-dramatic change
from the hoyden of the mannish stride to the gracious, well-gowned woman who presided over her
father's table—a slim, soft beauty, to the manner
born. That was the thing which fascinated him.

"A sportswoman and a great lady," Boyd told
himself. "There's only one in a million!"

He had noticed her watch himself quizzically,
and with a little tenderness in her eyes. She could
not feel anything particular for him, he thought;
but she might be receptive toward his courtship.
Her father, old Colonel O'Donnell, would be only
too pleased at the alliance. Indeed, he had once
hinted at it himself.

"I wish I had some one to look after that child,"
the colonel had said—"some one like yourself,
Boyd."

"She'll find a young man some of these days," the baronet had answered; "my kind are too old."

"You're good for twenty-five years in the saddle yet," O'Donnell chaffed; "and she's not exactly an infant. She's twenty-five years old."

Whom else could she marry? Boyd tried to think. Two or three seasons she had been to London and Dublin; but from both of them she had come back heart-whole apparently. For the officers of the near-by garrison she seemed to have no liking. There were few of the old stock left from whom she could choose. She was too much of "a fine woman," as the phrase went, to be taken by the younger whippersnappers she might meet. She would want a whole man—mind, body and soul.

"I can't think of any one she could care for." The baronet shook his head.

Well, then, if that were so, why shouldn't he have his chance as well as the next? An old name and a fine estate, a constitution ten years younger than his age, there might be a possibility of the match appealing to her. And then there was the boy. She seemed to like him, from their companionship together. How happy they could be, all three of them! And how the old house would brighten up, as it used to be under every one of the Boyds until his tragedy had occurred! Again there would be the laughing parties there, the balls, the hunt breakfasts—everything as the old tradition had it, the tradition of his hospitable, openhanded ancestry.

It was getting toward evening now. The sun had dropped behind the crest of Slievegullion, and a great golden light, like a liquid, bathed the mountainsides. Beneath it the lake lay, a placid winding pool bordered on each side by pine-trees. As he stood by the open French window and watched it across the garden with the stripped rhododendron-trees, the baronet wondered to himself how the boy would take it. A great flight of wild geese went clamoring by, and Showk, the red setter, raised his head as though he heard something. He trotted down the avenue of chestnut-trees. A moment later Boyd could hear his son's strong barytone ringing out:

"I cautiously saluted her, and I viewed her o'er and o'er;
  And I says: 'Are you Aurora bright, descending here
    below?'
  'Oh, no, kind sir,' this maiden fair, she modestly replied;
  'I daily labor for my bread down by the tanyard side.' "

The boy swung round the side path to the back of the house. He had been duck shooting, the baronet remembered, and he was probably going round to leave his gun and bag before coming up. He could hear the old housekeeper greet him:

"Yerra, Master Henry, and 'tis you is the ele-

gant shot. Eight of them, and you not gone upward of an hour!"

"Not so bad for a young one—eh, Margaret?"

And then his voice rang out again:

"Her golden hair in ringlets rare hung down her shapely
    neck,
And the killing glances of her eye would save a ship from
    wreck.
Her cheeks like fair Hypatia's, and her teeth so waxy
    white,
Would have made Napoleon her slave down by the tan-
    yard side."

He swung into the room easily, with his shot-
gun beneath his arm. His hair was tousled under
the tweed hat, and the pockets of his golf-coat
were bulging with cartridges. His hands were in
the pockets of his riding-breeches. There was so
much wholesomeness to the devil-may-care look of
him that Boyd's heart jumped with pride.

"Dreaming, Father?" he asked laughingly. He
put his hat upon the muzzle of the gun and
propped the barrel carefully against the wall. "A
penny for your thoughts, sir."

"I was thinking, Hal— What would you say
if some fine day I were to get married?"

"Success to you, sir, a thousand times! And I'll
dance at the wedding until the dawn of day." He
paused for an instant and his voice grew anxious:

"Why, sir, you've not been worrying about me, have you? Sure, I'd only be too glad of anything that would make you happy. Who is it, sir? Lady Alice Sellingham?"

"No."

"Mrs. Brown-Abott?"

"No."

"Surely it's not Miss Reddy? It couldn't be she!"

"It isn't," his father laughed back.

"Who is it, sir? Don't tease me about it."

"Hal," his father said softly—he kept his head averted with some sense of embarrassment—"it's Hester O'Donnell I want to ask to marry me."

"Hester O'Donnell!" The name seemed to be more gasped than spoken.

The elder man was noticing nothing. His mind was full of relief and tenderness at the son's quick delight at his happiness. He didn't notice the long spaces that came now between his remarks or how white he had suddenly become.

"Have you asked her yet, Father?"

"Not yet, Hal."

Another long pause. The son moved toward him at last.

"I wish you every success, sir. If you get her you'll be getting the best girl in the world; and I've often said that the woman you'd marry would lack for nothing. Success again, sir."

"Thanks, Hal."

The boy straightened up and moved toward the door.

"I'll be taking the gray down the road for a gallop," he said. "He's not been out to-day."

Hal swung off quickly. His father stood there motionless. He couldn't trust himself to speak, so moved did he feel. How happy they three would be together, he thought! He listened for his son's voice to break into the country-side ballad again. The boy did so much like the last verse. The baronet repeated it to himself with an amused smile:

"Farewell, my aged parents; to you I bid adieu;
    I am crossing the main ocean, my love, for love of you.
    And if ever I return again I will make that girl my bride,
    And I'll roll her in my arms down by the tanyard side."

But no swinging barytone arose, lilting the grace notes of the Come-all-you. The only sound the baronet heard was the shuffle of the gray hunter at the stable door; and then, an instant later, the thunder of his hoofs along the road.

IV

It seemed to Boyd, in those three days, that there had always been a gray cloud over Slieve-gullion Mountain, and that the lake had always been misty and desolate, with no sound from it.

but the hollow and lonely booming of the bitterns. About the house the servants came and went with the furtive, exaggeratedly careful step that seems to go with the presence of Death—as though that were a light sleep, instead of being the heaviest of all. Riordan, the butler, for instance—his ruddy cheeks seemed to have suddenly gone gray. Margaret, the housekeeper, was ever wiping a tear from her eye. The stable-boys' loudness was hushed, and the maids whispered together in a stealthy susurrus that was more irritating than if they had shrieked aloud. Even the dogs whined, as though they knew something was wrong.

Where had his son gone? the baronet demanded of himself, fiercely. And why? There had been no news of him beyond that which came with the man who brought the horse back from Goraghwood Station, and who said the boy had got into the Derry train. To every station on the line Boyd had wired; but no news came from any.

"He can't be dead!" the baronet told himself over and over again, fighting against the fear that was rising in him; and as he began pacing about he noticed himself in the glass, and he saw suddenly how aged he had become in the few days. His face was haggard, and great rings showed about the eyes from sleeplessness. He had become old overnight, like Ossian of the Fianna, who had touched earth after living in the Enchanted Isle.

Why had the lad done it? he asked himself, going over the thing again like a foxhound searching a covert. Why? He had seemed glad that the father was about to marry. There seemed no objection to that—

Riordan, the butler, came into the room.

"Miss Hester O'Donnell to see you, Sir Patrick," he announced.

"Show her in, Riordan," Boyd told him.

There was no need for Riordan to show her in. She was behind him like a flash.

Her face blazed into the baronet's.

"Where is my boy, Sir Patrick?" she cried to him. "What have you done to my boy?"

He looked at her in amazement. A great color had mounted to her cheeks and her gray eyes were flashing in little sparks of vindictive light. Her ride over had blown a strand of black hair across her brow, and in her right hand she held her riding-crop fiercely, as though at any moment she might strike him with it.

"Your boy?" he asked faintly.

"Yes; my boy," she told him. "My boy! Nobody's but mine."

"I see!" He felt a little faint for an instant; but he pulled himself together quickly. "Hester, did you care for Hal?"

"I did," she told him boldly. "And he for me."

"Why didn't he tell me?" Boyd asked. "Why didn't he tell me?"

"He would have," she answered—"in a few days."

He must have gone very white then, for the eager fire went out of her face and a look of anxiety came into it as she watched him. He went over to the fireplace and leaned heavily on the mantel.

"Sir Patrick," she whispered—"he's not dead?"

"No; he's not dead."

There was a pause in which it seemed to each of them that they could hear the other's heart beat, and that they each could feel the other's mind and soul struggle with a gray, shapeless fear.

"Why? Why did he go?" Hester O'Donnell asked breathlessly.

He did not answer for a minute; it seemed such a hard thing to say, such a terribly violent, blasphemous thing in the face of what he had just heard. But it had to be done.

"I'll tell you, little Hester," he explained: "I told him I was going to propose marriage to somebody. I thought it would be good for him to have the house as it ought to be—to have a woman in it, who would look after him. I was afraid of his going wild. Do you see? Do you understand?"

"Yes; but why should he go away?" she demanded. "What is there in that to make him go away?"

He kept silent and watched her as she bit her lips and knit her brows, trying to puzzle it out. She raised her head to ask him again, to demand an answer; and they looked at each other without saying anything. The color faded from her cheeks and she recoiled slightly.

"You wanted to marry me?" she cried out.

"And to put it absolutely brutally"—he lied with a wry smile—"the only reason I had for wanting to marry you was my son's good. I never thought of him as being anything but a child; never thought of his marrying."

"At his age you had a son a year old," she told him. She took a quick turn about the room, head down, thinking. "I know where he is," she said suddenly: "he's in America. He's taken the Derry boat for New York. He was always saying, if anything went wrong— Oh, I know it in my bones— he's there!"

"I'll go look," Boyd told her. "I'll find him for you."

"Listen!" she asked him fiercely: "What you said to me—that the only reason you had for marrying me was for his sake—is that true?"

"Absolutely true."

"I don't know," she said. "On your word of honor as an Irish gentleman, is that true?"

"On my word of honor as an Irish gentleman," he answered smilingly, "it's true."

"Oh, then it is true!" she said in relief; and, letting herself break down, she cried in his arms.

v

The police had failed and the private detectives had failed to find any trace of his son in the week that the baronet had been in New York. There was nothing else to be done, they told him, shrugging their shoulders. People disappeared every day, and no trace was ever found of them. Perhaps the son was at home now. Perhaps it was only some boyish escapade, some hiding of himself out of pique. But Sir Patrick knew better; he knew the boy.

Disconsolately, night after night and day after day, he roamed the streets. He watched the quays, with the longshoremen loading cargo by sun and incandescent light. He watched the subway workers crawl out of their cave, shift by shift; but no Harry was among them. He searched among the structural workers who clambored like pygmies up and down the great iron columns. And yet there was no sign.

"Give it over," the police told him. "There's not a chance in the world. If he's to be found we'd have got him."

"He's here," the baronet replied doggedly. "I know it in my heart. He's here!"

The porters at the Grand Central came to know him, sitting there forlornly in the great main hall, waiting for the boy to pass through. The men at the Pennsylvania offered sympathy as the police told the story. He would thank them politely and, after hours of waiting, go away.

"I know he's here!" he would tell himself. "I know he's here! We both feel it—Hester and I."

It was eight o'clock now. Somewhere the strokes rang out from a near-by church as he crossed Herald Square from Sixth Avenue. The theater crowd of motors whirred into Broadway, their horns snarling like dogs. The elevated road lumbered by overhead with a thunder like bass drums. Here and there horses picked their way through the maze of cars and pillars with the adroitness of trick skaters upon ice.

All about him advertising devices twinkled and flashed—a red star; a pelican opening and closing its beak; a chariot snorting along, the horses' nostrils distended, the driver flogging viciously at their flanks; a pair of boxers leading and countering, with absurd mechanical gestures. It all seemed a vast pandemonium of sound and light.

Sir Patrick saw none of it, heard none of it, as he blundered his way across as calmly as though he were walking across his own moor. A shrill whistle cut into the air like a knife. From a street near by came the loud, insistent clang of a bell.

The automobiles stopped short as if turned to stone. A huge furniture wagon, with two figures on the driver's seat, drew up within a foot of him. The clamorous bell was nearer. It was fifty yards away.

"Hi, you!" a policeman shouted from a distance. "Where do you think you're going? Get back!" The baronet did not hear him.

A slight figure in overalls and a flannel shirt sprang from the furniture van. It caught the baronet by the shoulder and swung him into safety. The fire engine whipped by in a streak of red.

"A narrow shave, sir!" he heard said behind him. "Did I hurt you?"

He turned round unbelievingly, and caught the figure by the arm.

"Harry! Is it you, Harry?"

The boy went white. He tottered and nearly fell.

"It's I, Father," he said.

"Hey, yous!" the policeman bawled. "What do you think you are? A pair of statues?"

"Is Hester with you?"

"She's not, lad. She's at home, waiting for you."

"Cut it out, kid!" the driver called. "Get into the van. For the love of Mike, get into the van!"

"Boy, I only wanted to marry her for your sake —to have a woman in the house. That was all."

"Do you want to get pinched?" The policeman

came over to them. "Come through with the idea! Where do you get this statue stuff?"

"I'll have to get on the van, father, and deliver the furniture. I'll call down to-night and talk."

"No, you won't!" Sir Patrick said. "I'll get on the van and deliver the furniture too."

They had talked long into the night, and three o'clock was ringing as Sir Patrick left his son in his room at the hotel.

"So that's settled," the baronet said. "You go home to-morrow and get married as soon as she'll let you."

"But why won't you come along, Father?" the boy asked.

"Now listen to me, my lad," Sir Patrick said with mock solemnity. "I've been taking care of you for twenty-three years, and I'm through with it. You've got somebody else to look after you now. I'm going to take three or four years to look round this country. I like it. Good night."

"Good night, Father." He watched Sir Patrick move toward the door. "Listen, sir," he said. "Tell me honestly: Was that the only reason you had for wanting to marry Hester—for my sake—to have a woman in the house?"

"The only reason."

"On the one unbreakable oath?"

"On the honor of an Irish gentleman!" The baronet bowed.

"Oh, then that's all right!" his son said.

The elder man walked down the corridor and, pausing for a minute at a window, he looked out on the sleeping city. Very cold and lonely it appeared to him, for all its electric bulbs and humming traffic and lighted windows—a place he could never be at home in; a place that cared nothing for him or his people or his old traditions.

And in contrast to it, in his mind's eye there arose the yellow hills of Oriel, with the sun glinting on the gorse, and the sparkle of the frosty roads. He could see the hunt in the morning, the fine horses and the gallant riders, and the cunning dog fox streaking redly away.

"Never again!" he murmured heartbrokenly. "Never again!"

And then, following on that splendid picture, the face of Hester O'Donnell flashed before him— the sparkling gray eyes; the dusky hair; the knotted brows.

"Little Heart of Corn!" he whispered hoarsely. "Oh, little Heart of Corn!"

He straightened himself up suddenly and went down the corridor, his head high and his shoulders square, as a great man should march off into exile for a lost cause.

XI

A WIFE OF NO IMPORTANCE

I

WERE you to seek the whole land over, you
would find nothing more deserted, more
sordid or more sinister than the Sunnybrae Golf
Club from the fifteenth of October until April.

Above the Sound the club-house, a dingy
weather-beaten gray, broad like an owl, surrounded by sickly trees that have never bloomed.
The roads in front of it are in metallic ruts during
frost and in puddles of slush in a thaw. Hardly
ever does even a postman come up that road. The
lawn is choked with a thick layer of yellow de-
cayed leaves, with here and there flecks of grass
that is nohow green, and a great white numeral
showing grotesquely, where the clock golf course
is buried under windrows. The course itself is very
unsightly, even in summertime uninviting; but
when winter comes it is a travesty of earth, its
fairway tufty, like an unshaven tramp, its rough,
coarse and lumpy; its putting greens bilious; its
pits and traps and bunkers like sores of the king's

338

evil. And here and there are great puddles of water or boards of uncomely ice. And stunted trees like human dwarfs. And over it in the cold months the winds howl like a witches' Sabbath.

The village below is sordid and deserted, too. The tradespeople drowse off until the summer comes and the colony from New York arrive. And then the village hums with pretentious motor-cars of the cheaper make, and women whose dresses are bought on Division Street, "where Fifth Avenue models are sold at cost price," call to each other, from sidewalk to sidewalk, with strident voices and easy endearments. Their men-folk arrive on the five-fifteen train, for they are the smaller kind of manufacturers, and unimportant brokers, who can sometimes take a whole afternoon off to play what they call golf, and on Sunday and Saturday the links are filled. But through the winter the place is unoccupied. The tradespeople fish in October and November, going out in dories after flounders and black and frost fish, smelts and scallops. But what they do for the remainder of the winter, God only knows.

But up on the golf links there were two people who saw the winter through. They were Jock Sanderson, the professional, and Kaufman, the steward. Sanderson never came down to the village. By a dispensation of the house committee he was allowed a small room in the club-house, to eke out his preposterous salary of one hundred dollars a month. Occasionally he could be seen tramping around the links, a stocky, frost-faced man, with an old muffler about his neck, and egregious feet. Kaufman appeared at the village once every two days, to buy their scanty provisions. He was a thin, predatory-looking man, huddled up in ill-smelling furs and with the confounded arrogance of a waiter off duty. Once a month in the winter Jock would go off for a week. The station-master would mention it to his cronies.

"Old Jock took the train down this morning."

"Off to his party!" The hearers would laugh.

A week later the old Scot would return, his face twitching, every nerve shaking like a jangling piano wire, very pitiable to see. But the villagers only laughed.

Occasionally Kaufman went to New York, and came back that night or the next day, but there were no marks of dissipation on him. He would bring back the strangest things in bundles, a parcel of Chinese food, or some Jewish plum brandy, "slivovitz" he called it. Once he brought back an Angora kitten, and once a fox-terrier, a very valuable dog; but the kitten ran away, and the dog died. Where he got these things nobody knew.

But in the main, Sanderson and the steward were always together. In summer they were continually not apart—and speaking to each other—

unless when Jock was playing or giving lessons or superintending the Italians and Poles at work on the links or when Kaufman was keeping an eye on the Galician waiter he used to get from New York, and on Jubilo, the colored cook who came for the summer. You would find them talking, were you to look for one of them, and as you came up they would stop guiltily and Kaufman would come forward with an ingratiating leer, and Jock would nod, if you were a good player, and pull his forelock like an old groom.

The few people who saw them in winter said they played poker all the winter through, using a greasy pack with all the small cards out up to and including the sevens. Often they owed each other big sums, as much as two thousand dollars, but as they played steadily with no interchange of money they came out about even in spring. There was a legend in the country-side that they slept together in the same bed, so loath were they to part company for even a few hours. "David and Jonathan" some people called them with a laugh.

They were so inseparable one could hardly imagine them apart. Each was the complement of the other. One felt that they would grow old side by side, though both looked old already. Jock was forty-three and Kaufman only forty. Still one felt they were old.

So every one was shocked with surprise when

Kaufman, returning from New York one day, brought back the strangest thing yet. He took home a wife, the Persian girl.

II

Kaufman vouchsafed the old golf pro no information about her. He moved about the clubhouse in a hurried, pleasant way, like a woman who is preparing her home for visitors. On his face there was a smile, an offensive sort of smile, as though he had done something very smart and was tremendously pleased about it.

"Get out of the way," he would call to Sanderson, as he moved about with hammer and nails. "What the hell you hanging about here for? There wasn't anything for you." And he would leer at Jock.

"What you think of me as a married man, hey? Never thought I'd put one over on you, hey?" And then he would chuckle and leer and sing a little Yiddish song.

> "Veil shabes beim Yidele is die beste sach.
> Er sitzt sich bam sidele in ver is zu ihm gleich.
> Er vinkt zu sein veibele—"

"I got it what you ain't got?" He would interrupt his song. "I got it a little veibal. None of

your big thick Scotchwomen, with feet and hands
like an elephant. I have was fein is!" And he would
sing again:

> "Lom dom dom dom doi!
> Lom dom dom dom doi!
> Doi doi dom dom dom!
> Shulem a leichem freid zu a yeden!
> Shulem a leichem tam genei den!"

"Well," Jock cleared his throat, "why don't you
bring her out?"

"You'll see her time enough."

At supper that night Jock saw her. She came
into the deserted grill room like a ghost moving.
There was no sound and she flowed over the space,
it seemed. She was like a sail-boat going gently before the wind, so her motions suggested. Kaufman
called to her as he would to a favorite dog, making strange sounds to direct her.

"Here! here!" he called. "K-k-k-k!" And he
made an indescribable sound that was a compound
of whistling and hissing.

"This is Mrs. Kaufman," he introduced her.
She said nothing, but looked at Sanderson with her
face that seemed nothing but a strange whiteness
surrounding great black eyes.

"I am very pleased indeed to know you, ma'am,"
Jock said the speech he had rehearsed carefully,

"and I make bold to offer you my very best wishes indeed." And he sat down. But Kaufman laughed until he held his sides.

"She doesn't understand you," he gurgled. "She doesn't speak English."

"What does she speak?"

"Persian or something. I don't know!"

"You don't know," Jock was astounded. "How in hell do you talk to her, then?"

"For what we got to say to each other," the steward grinned, "there was no need of speech. Love," he leered, "talks with the eyes and the heart."

"Huh!" the pro grunted.

During the meal he examined her carefully. A slim lissom thing, she could hardly have been more than seventeen years old. She was not thin, though. Her frame and bones were small, but they were delicately rounded. Sanderson had never quite understood the implication of the slang and hackneyed term of peach, but she was so firmly soft, so rounded, so inviting as it were, that such was the only word to describe her. Her face was all but heart-shaped and had a brown tinge to it, very warm, and the little rounded nose "very pretty," he told himself. "Aye, very pretty, indeed." He had never seen lips the red of those two lips, and teeth so small and white and regular. Her eyes were like cavities into which some iridescent black liquid had been poured. He couldn't get over the wonder of her hair. It was like an infinity of strands of black oiled silk. She was marvelously beautiful. The restrained lines of the cheap smart frock which Kaufman had bought for her could not hide that.

"There's not much to her," he told Kaufman, "but she's dainty. Och aye! She's very dainty. And where did you say you got her?"

"I don't remember saying anything," Kaufman smiled warily, and Jock knew no information was forthcoming. But he guessed and was all but sure that the steward had come by her in that strange world south and east of Fourteenth Street. Jock had gone down with him there once or twice and Kaufman had shown him that motley quarter with the pride of one born there. They had eaten in a strange restaurant where tea was drunk out of glasses with a rind of lemon—a strange way. And then Kaufman had brought him here and there. All the races of the world were in that place, the golf pro thought with simplicity—Greeks and Turks and Poles and Arabs and Chinamen. Strange traffic went on there and there were immense vices, too. Down there Kaufman had undoubtedly found the Persian girl. He might have won her at cards, or paid money for her, or he might even have stolen her. Nothing Kaufman would do could surprise the golfer, unless it were to take part in an honest transaction.

"If she could only speak English, she would be good company for us," he said.

She impressed him in an uncanny, seditious way. She was like a flower he had once seen, a velvety barbaric thing called an orchid, that had a strange beauty and a great monetary value. It had looked out of place in a man's buttonhole, but very likely it was all right in the jungle where it belonged.

They rose from the table.

"She doesn't seem to fit in, somehow. Out o' place, as it were! Aye, out o' place!"

The steward broke into his strange song again:

"Lom dom dom dom doi!
Lom dom dom dom doi!"

Then he did a few steps of a very peculiar dance he called the gasatski. He hunkered to the floor, and moved across the room shooting out his legs with incredible swiftness. He seemed like a grotesque mechanical toy, such as is in a nursery. And the Persian girl laughed. It surprised Sanderson, that laugh. It was so low and soft and very musical, like a stringed instrument.

Kaufman stood up and took her by the arm. He led her toward the stairs.

"Good night," he called to Sanderson.

"Huh!" the pro grunted.

"I said good night!" the steward grinned.

"I say: go to hell!"

III

The Persian girl did not so much worry the golf pro as disorient him. For four years now he and Kaufman had been together at the club, and while they had the utmost contempt for each other, they suited each other. Until the Persian girl came, each had been satisfied to operate in the small groove of the Sunnybrae. And they could have gotten along with none else.

The truth was they were both broken men. Twenty years ago Jock had been one of the world's greatest golfers, if not the greatest. Three championships had been his portion. But drink had gotten him by the throat and would not let go, no matter how hard he fought against it. He was still a great golfer, when the spirit descended on him. Even in America he held seven records on courses, like the record on the new championship course in Massachusetts, where he went out in thirty and came home in thirty-two—sixty-two—unbelievable figures. But then he would celebrate that, and a week afterward it would hardly be possible for him to go around under a hundred, so much did his hands shake. Little by little officials discouraged his appearance at tournaments, for they didn't care to have the game discredited by the appearance of an extremely drunken player, no matter what a marvelous game his was. And the good clubs let him go for the same reason. So here he lay, at a hundred dollars a month, on a course whose membership was limited to, as the phrase went, "the cheapest skates in America."

He was a morose drinker, very ugly in his cups, so when he was on a bout he was alone, save for casual acquaintances. And when he was alone and drinking he brooded all the time. In the good clubs there were a new tribe of professionals, smart upstanding men, clean, well-dressed, polite. "They have no' the gowff!" he told himself. "There's none of them I couldn't beat if I were off the stuff." This was probably true, but it didn't help him any. There were pros who played marvelous golf when they were drunk, but he couldn't do it. What was the use?

So all he saw himself was as an outcast, very alone in the world until Kaufman came.

Kaufman's history was very vague. From things he let fall he had been in many lines of business that were not at all reputable. He had been actor-manager of a Yiddish stock company in Brownsville, and his performances in "The Bells" had been quite a success. Then he dabbled in vaudeville.

Then he had managed the saloon in a railroad terminal. Then he had had a saloon of his own, which had been more of a surreptitious hotel than a saloon. Sanderson knew that he had been waiter in a great country club and had been discharged under suspicion of theft. All his activities, it was certain, had ended in a misunderstanding as to money, if not actual theft, at any rate such sharp practice as to render his associates or employers unwilling to have anything more to do with him.

In fine, the steward was as broken a man as the professional. He was all right as long as he stayed in this little country club, whose members demanded nothing, or knew nothing to demand. He had acquired a fulsome, flattering manner which charmed the members and their wives. He could not go into any other calling now, nor move to another region, for the community of his co-religionists would spot him as an improper person, and they were very powerful.

So to the two of them the world was a prison, and they were the two prisoners. Each had a great contempt for the other. The golfer despised the steward for his dishonesty, the steward the pro because of his constitutional weakness; but the twain united in a common contempt for the members of the club. They would stand apart and discuss them a few yards away from their very ears, Jock comparing them very disfavorably to the men in the important golf club where he had once been pro, and to the great amateurs he had met in the tournaments of his youth. He would tell of disgraceful little cheating incidents on the golf-course, of cheap meannesses that were more damning than big crime just because they were so small. And Kaufman would discuss the women with a knowledge of the sex he had picked up nowhere reputable, commenting on their faces, their figures, their dress, their improbable chastity. This in summer and poker in winter was their daily discussion.

And so they would go on, all things pointed that way, until the end of their days. Their lives had abutted suddenly into a cul-de-sac and the alley closed. They couldn't go out, though possibly others might come in later. But they were in a way satisfied. And now the Persian girl had arrived, and somehow in the air Sanderson felt that Kaufman had a chance, and later he felt a certainty, of escaping. The Persian girl was the secret. And at the thought of the steward's escape the golfer became panic-stricken. How Kaufman would escape, or when, he didn't know, for the steward was very secretive. But he would—of that he was assured.

Sanderson had a contempt for the steward. He didn't like him. Indeed, if he had examined deeply enough he might have found he hated Kaufman. Even a rat in a prison cell is company for a condemned man. . . . And Kaufman was escaping—

on the frail, beautiful, olive shoulders of the
Persian girl.

IV

Then Sanderson found himself steadily, pro-
foundly, inevitably falling in love with her.

When she moved through the room he was affected by her presence. Though his back were to
her, he would know she was standing there.
Though she were in a room above him, he would
know. To see her for a minute was an event to
color the whole day.

At night he would unconsciously think: "When
I get up in the morning I will see her." The thought
was a great delight to him, as the thought of a
circus or a show or something of the kind fills the
lives of children with pleasantness when it arrives
in their town.

This was all the queerer because her beauty was
not the beauty that appealed to him. His ideal was
that of the peasant or lower-class laborer, a flashy,
buxom type of woman with an accentuated figure.
Her movements that flowed like a precious wine;
her oval olive face; her eyes filled with spirit so
near the surface as to make one fearful of the
spirit escaping—all transcendental beauties that
would make an artist or a woman rave—of these
he was immensely ignorant. He only knew that
since she came to the sinister house, in the rough

bark of him sap had begun to circulate, and the withered tree he had become was likely to shoot forth into twig and branch and spray of queer volcanic foliage. He had become strangely young.

Once an errand of some kind called him to the neighboring town, and when he was there he thought he would like to give her something. But flowers were a dreadful price, and jewelry not to be thought of. The only thing that occurred to him was a large box of chocolates, so he brought those home.

"I thought you might like to have a few sweeties." He presented it to her. She looked at him inquiringly a moment, and took it, thanking him in some strange liquid tongue.

"Not at all. You're welcome, I'm sure."

"It's very nice of you, Jock." Kaufman seemed to take the little compliment entirely to himself. He was a little touched at the gift.

They all sat around the card table. Kaufman put the chocolates beside him.

"Lom dom dom dom doi," he sang, looking at his hand.
"Lom dom dom dom doi!
 Shulem a leichem freid zu a yeden!
 Shulem a leichem tam genei den!"

He helped himself to two of the chocolates, and chewing them voraciously was dipping his hand in the box for more.

"Hey!" Sanderson called out. "Ca' canny there! Those are no' for you."

"What's mine's hers," Kaufman grinned and patted his wife's slim hand, "and what's hers is mine. That's what love is, Jock. Ain't it, cutie?"

For that Sanderson could have broken his face.

The Persian girl began to smile at him now all the time, and the golfer showed a surprising readiness—very surprising to Kaufman—for doing things that required exertion, moving tables and such matters. He would take his coat off and roll up his shirtsleeves, showing his forearm packed with prodigious muscle that slipped under the skin like oiled machinery. Once by a stratagem he made the steward take his coat off and compare forearms, and he laughed and she with him, at the comparison—Sanderson's like the forepaw of some great hunting animal, Kaufman's fat and white and flabby, like some disagreeable meat exposed for sale.

The sun broke one morning and a fine day arrived. He persuaded the steward and his wife to come out to the first tee.

"Come on out and I'll teach you to drive," he told him.

"For nothing?"

"To be sure, for nothing."

"What's wrong with you? Gone crazy?" Kaufman laughed his high, disagreeable laugh.

Sanderson drove six balls from the tee, hurling himself forward with every ounce of his weight behind the club. The balls shot through the air like bullets, clean and straight, whistling loudly. Down the course two hundred and fifty yards they poised for an instant motionless, then dropped to run along the hard ground like white-scutted rabbits. At the third ball the girl understood and followed their flight with eager eyes, giving strange little sounds of pleasure at the distance of them, and clapping her hands just as a Western woman might.

"You try it now," the pro told Kaufman.

The steward gave a mighty lunge and all but fell on his face, the ball untouched. He tried again with like result.

"Gee, that's funny!" He laughed. Then he topped it a couple of yards forward. After Sanderson he was worse than ridiculous; he was pitiable. The girl looked at him in wonder.

"I'll show you again," and Sanderson drove, a clean two hundred and eighty yards carry. Hardly ever before had he driven such a ball. The girl's laugh of pleasure was sustained and ringing, like a note on a flute.

"It's only a trick," Kaufman decided and tried again, and as he banged and foozled Jock caught the girl's eye, and he gave a great look of contempt at the steward. And the steward's futile efforts made her look contemptuous, too. Kaufman caught the expression on their faces and was aware on the instant. He turned to the golfer fiercely.

"What the hell you trying to do?" He threw the club down. "Trying to make a monkey out of me? Why, you couldn't make a monkey out of me, not even if you tried, you poor souse." He was very excited. "You may be able to hit at a golf-ball, but I got it up here," he tapped his head. "I got it where it counts, you poor rummy!" He was foaming at the mouth. "Come away, you, come away!" He caught his wife's hand and dragged her toward the club-house. "You drunken bum, you try to make a monkey out of me——"

From that moment on a sort of war was declared.

Winter had tightened its grip all of a sudden, a very bleak, melancholy winter this year, with the trees dripping either with sleet or water, and a great yellow fog out, and the horns on the reef in the Sound emitting warning growls like some angry savage animal. One might have thought themselves in some forgotten and melancholy country where the sun never shone, nor did Spring come; some plan imagined by a religious writer as an abode of lost souls. And through the club-house there went a sense of danger keen as the edge of a knife.

Kaufman no longer sang his "Lom dom doi"

song, but was nervous and irritable, and he kept the Persian girl out of sight, hardly permitting her to come to meals even, and addressing her in short, brusque accents, no longer playful. And into her eyes there had come a sense of fear, the look of a doe when it sniffs the hounds, or a marmoset who hears a snake rustle in the grass; nothing definite, just a sense of trepidation without certainty, an intuition of ununderstood things in the air. She no longer smiled at Jock Sanderson that little ripple of delight that affected him, "like a fine putting green" was his own technical phrase. And Kaufman seemed waiting, waiting.

Then one night the old thirst gripped Sanderson as in a vice.

Usually he could tell when it was coming on. For days before he would brood and brood, and it would advance on him like a thug on an unarmed man, steadily, warily, inevitably. And then he would take the train to New York.

But this time his mind had been occupied with the Persian girl, and it had come along unawares, catching him murderously of an instant. It was nine o'clock at night when it became unbearable, and he could have caught a train to New York then, and begun. But instead of that he huddled himself up and walked out into the zero weather. For miles and miles and miles he walked, and through his mind there ran the chorus: "Don't be a fool! Take the train! You've got to have a drink. That's all there's to it. You've got to have it. You can't do without it. So stop fooling yourself, good man. Take the train. There's a sensible fellow." But back of that there lay another idea: "If I take a drink Kaufman's got me." If he were to turn up after a week, broken, bloodshot, shaking, Kaufman would point him out and mercilessly laugh at him, draw the girl's attention to him every minute. Kaufman was the one to make every ounce of a point in his favor.

Then the thirst left him suddenly, miraculously; one moment his throat was gasping for a drink and the next he didn't want it. Peace broke out in him like a great perspiration. He was very awed.

"It's a miracle," he said. "It's a bloody miracle."

He could have sung for joy there in the dark arctic morning. For a while he couldn't believe it was true, but the thought remained in his head; he didn't want a drink. He had found he was all of twelve miles away from the club-house, but he didn't care, so joyful was he, and he walked home in the cold mist in a sort of daze. Now he understood Kaufman's certainty of escape. If he had the Persian girl he could escape, too. And vague places ran through his head for a future he could make, if she were his. He could go to Australia, for instance, changing his name, and it wouldn't be long before he got a job, playing the golf he could when he was off the booze. It would be a new life, so it would, none to say: "He's a fine golfer, Jock is, but you can't do anything with him. He's too far gone with the drink. Have nothing to do with him." No, he would be fine there, he and the girl. And letting thoughts like this run through his head he came home with the dawn and slept like a tired child.

A few days later Kaufman tackled him straight.

"When are you going down to the city, Jock?"

"I'll let the city by for a while, I think."

The steward looked at him and laughed.

"You'll be going off on your little party one of these days."

"I'm no sure o' that. I wouldn't be either, if I were you."

The steward was puzzled at the calm confidence in the pro's voice.

"You can't do without your booze, you know. You never could."

"Damned well I can do without it, if you want to know." Sanderson's voice had a peculiarly new strength, and his eye was direct, and meaning. "I'm giving it up, Morris," he smiled. "I've found out there's nothing to it."

He was elated at the gray dismay in the steward's face.

V

Now that he was protected, his job was to find where Kaufman was vulnerable. Kaufman could not destroy his credit before the Persian girl. For he couldn't speak her language, and so couldn't tell her that Sanderson was notorious as a drinker, and that he was down and out so far as his reputation went. Now the business in hand was to get her, if he could. Married to Kaufman or not married, he'd get her, if he could. And his conscience didn't worry him at all. He would be good to her, as Kaufman could not be, hadn't it in him to be. Could he get her? He didn't know. He could try.

He went to the near-by town and took his savings from the bank. Drinking man though he was, he had money. Old matches won with heavy side bets, the sales of clubs and giving of lessons had made him comfortable enough. In the bank he had about two thousand dollars. He drew it all out in bills, and said nothing. But he kept away from the cards.

"Ain't you going to play any more?" the steward asked him finally. "What is it? You got cold feet all at once?"

"Well, I'll tell you, Morris," the pro shrugged his shoulders. "I'm no' keen for playing for paper money. There's no sting to the game. If we're playing for money, let's put the money right on the table and be damned to the first man that goes broke."

"That's funny from you." Kaufman remembered that to carry the debts from day to day was the pro's own economical plan. "Still if you're game, I am."

"Oh, I'm game, all right." And Sanderson lugged out his immense roll, and thumbed it. The steward said nothing, but he gulped a little in his throat, and his eyes glittered, and he moistened his lips with his tongue.

For days then, except for meals, they played poker, sitting opposite each other and watching each other with wary eyes. There would be just a few things for Kaufman to do in the morning, such as running down to the village for provisions, or putting chairs in their place, or going down to the cellar to tend the furnace. And when that was done, he would turn to Sanderson and rub his hands.

"Well, what do you say?"

"All right," the Scot would nod laconically.

Then they would sit down, shuffle, cut and deal, and the game would be on. After a hand the steward would be very talkative, though he hardly spoke while playing. If he had won he would lean back and sing his song of peace to all men:

". . . lom dom doi!
Shulem a leichem fried zu a yeden
Shulem a leichem. . . ."

"I'll open for a dollar," he would smile.

"I'll stick." All through the game Sanderson was cold and imperturbable, sinister even. One might have the impression of him waiting, ready to pounce.

When Kaufman ran into a losing streak, he growled continuously, talking to himself in strange foreign gutturals.

For three days this went on. A gray wet spell had settled around the club-house. Outside there was only drip, drip, drip, and a mist of rain that turned everything hideously drab and cold. At meals and other times occasionally the Persian girl would come into the grill-room. And when the steward was losing he would speak viciously to her:

"Get out of here! Get up to your room," and his little black reptilian eyes would be beady as a snake's. And then a panic would come over her, and she would stop, gulp, and shiver like a nervous dog.

But when he was winning he would coo at her, and strangely enough she seemed more scared of this than of his whiplike snapping.

"Come here, Fatima," he would sing-song. "Come here, Mecca. Come here, Camel!" And he would laugh at his own joke. "Come here 'till I love you." And he would draw her to him, and pat her and kiss her. She would look up and catch a sight of Sanderson's face, set like granite. And then she would begin to shiver and shiver and shiver, like a dog.

She came into the room when the game was finished, ignorant of the result. Kaufman was leaning back in his chair, his face white, and streaked with perspiration. His eyes glassy. Sanderson, cool and sinister, was packing up the bank notes into a mammoth roll.

"You won't lend some? Hey? Lend me a hundred?" Kaufman was whining piteously. "You got two thousand out of me. Gi' me a chance, Jock. I been a good friend to you. I been nice, I been fine to you. Gi' me a chance to get it back."

"Not a red copper!"

Kaufman was about to grow hysterical when his eye turned to the girl. He gave a manner of gulp. He looked meaningly at the golfer. He rallied jauntily.

"A last flutter, hey?"

Sanderson said nothing.

"It's good. I tell you. It's good."

Sanderson turned to look at her too, and some intuition must have told her what was going on, or their eyes must have terrified her, for she turned and went up the stairs whimpering. They could hear her feet upstairs pattering like a dog's, and another faint whimper came down to them.

"Well, what about it? Hey, Jock, what do you say?"

"I'll go you," Sanderson nodded.

"Against the roll?"

"Against the roll, one hand."

"Against the whole roll. You won't hold out?"

"I won't hold out." Sanderson chucked the bills in the center of the table. "Shuffle those cards."

He shuffled them uncertainly. Sanderson noticed his hand shaking as he laid down the pack to be cut.

"How many?"

"I'll take three cards." The golfer noticed a sudden exultation in the steward's voice.

"Dealer takes two."

Sanderson looked up to see Kaufman grinning across at him.

"Well, you ain't got the luck, Jock. I guess I got you this time. Maybe when you got a little more money I play you again."

"What have you got?"

"I got four kings."

"No good! I've got four aces." And Sanderson put his cards on the table.

VI

It was probably only an instant, but to each of them it seemed an interminable time that they looked at each other across the table. At length the golfer got up and put the roll in his pocket. Kaufman was like a man turned to stone. Sanderson took out his watch.

"Well, we've got a half an hour to make the train to New York. I've got to get the clubs, and a bag packed. So—so long, Morris."

The steward was silent.

At the foot of the stairs he turned to look at Kaufman again. The steward hadn't moved.

Sanderson said nothing but went up the stairs and as he turned into the corridor where her room was, the heavy scent of peaches was in the air, and it occurred to him that she must like peaches. He would buy her all the peaches in the world. . . .

He opened the door to her room. He all but fell.

She seemed very small on the bed, very much smaller than she had been in life. The passing of her spirit had deflated her body extraordinarily. The little phial that had fallen from her fingers produced a large stain on the counterpane that was, he noticed, widening every instant.

"Kaufman!" he shouted terribly. Then he turned and ran down the stairs.

"Kaufman . . . she's dead!"

"The hell you say!"

"She's killed herself."

"The hell you say!"

Then Sanderson fell forward on the table and began to cry suddenly in great, startling, harsh sobs. He was for a long time that way, and toward the end it became certain to him that he was not crying for the death of her, but because the prison was closed forever now. . . .

"Don't cry, Jock. Don't cry," Kaufman was patting his shoulders. "What does it matter? We'll be together always, same as before. We'll call all bets off, just as before we played, and go fifty-fifty on expenses, hey? I won't leave you, Jock. We'll be together."

Jock knew they'd always be together, always, now, always. Fate had evidently willed it. That was the important thing, that they should be together. The girl was only an incident. They hadn't even known her name. . . .

THE END